ROY REES

A SEARCH
FOR ALL
SEASONS

The search for a former officer who was reported
missing after the Gothic Line Battle

ROY REES

A SEARCH
FOR ALL
SEASONS

The search for a former officer who was reported
missing after the Gothic Line Battle

MEREO
Cirencester

Published by Mereo

Mereo is an imprint of Memoirs Publishing

1A The Wool Market, Cirencester, Gloucestershire, GL7 2PR
info@memoirsbooks.co.uk www.memoirspublishing.com

A Search for All Seasons

ISBN: 978-1-909874-42-8

A SEARCH
FOR ALL
SEASONS

I had no foreboding that Fate would play a particular hand that summer evening, that my life would take a certain path simply because I happened to read a certain newspaper at the end of a day's work. Was it Fate or Destiny, or the outcome of an obsessive deliberation? Perhaps it is difficult to say in retrospect.

The year is easy to identify when it all started. London was gay—in the 1953 sense of gay. The Coronation and the conquest of Everest were causes for rejoicing in a capital which had been at the heart of a World War now some years distant. The World War may have ended, but the country was still forced to endure the crippling economic restraints and the legacy of rationing. A further war, in Korea this time, had not long ended.

It had been a muggy, oppressive day at the office, and as I walked through the Embankment gardens towards the Underground, I looked forward to a cool, refreshing bath in my Kensington flat. I managed to find a seat on the rush hour train, and then I opened my morning newspaper, having failed to read it in the crush of people on my way to work in the morning.

Suddenly my eye caught a small photo in the newspaper, a photo of a face, familiar in uniform but bareheaded. At once I recognised the fair hair, the Roman nose, the imperious chin and wide brow. The caption read "Artist seeks Major", and the article went on to describe how an Italian painter named Arturo Manzoni had kept one of his own paintings for nine years, hoping that one day the young Major who had sat for him would call at his home again. Apparently Arturo Manzoni wanted to make a present of the portrait to the officer or his family. It seemed that the Major had paid for the sittings. Maria Manzoni, the artist's daughter, had indicated that the officer was a Doctor, and she remembered his musicality at the piano.

Stephen was no more a Doctor than I was, I thought to myself. However, I did remember his talent at the piano.

I left the stifling heat of the Underground and walked from Earls Court Road towards Old Brompton Road.

Stephen Hardinge with an "e" as he always used to say.

It wasn't difficult for me to turn back the clock for nine years; the War years would always be embedded in my mind, but surely Stephen had been killed in action, or wounded and reported missing or taken prisoner. I remembered with a vague uneasiness that there had been an air of mystery surrounding the circumstances of his demise or disappearance.

I turned off the Old Brompton Road into the quiet of the Little Boltons. A hint of Autumn already tinged the plane tree leaves. The air was cooler as I entered my second floor flat in the substantial grey brick house.

My briefcase included a couple of case files which I intended to peruse with my gin and tonic before Lydia was due to call.

What had really happened to Stephen, I wondered? I tried

to tell myself that it was nothing to do with me, but we had been friends, at least for a time, and fleetingly I recalled some happy days together when we were rested from the fighting.

I had a cool bath and then scanned the two legal case files in the sitting-room. It did not take me long to peruse the files, both of them dealing with intestacy matters, and I had just finished reading the papers and annotating some points when the front doorbell rang somewhat shrilly.

I hastened down the two floors to the entrance hall, and opened the heavily-framed black front door.

"Lydia, how nice to see you," I said

"That's what you always say," she smiled whimsically as I ushered her up to my flat.

She sat down on my antiquated settee, a recent second-hand local purchase. The springs of the settee jangled their objection, an admittance of age and hard wear.

I suppose that I had known Lydia Maidment for a year now. She had come over from South Africa to see England, and she had been given an introduction to our senior partner in the office, Tom Preston. Apparently, a Durban friend of Tom's had been responsible for the introduction. It was not surprising that Lydia had already been taken around the sights of London, and when opportunity occurred she had been touring the West Country, Scotland and Wales.

Tom had taken Lydia onto the staff on a short-term basis. Normally, I did not enjoy mixing business with pleasure, but Lydia was not only an efficient secretary and a pleasant companion—she was strikingly attractive. I suppose she was in her early twenties, and that evening she was wearing a cool white cotton blouse which set off the pink of her skirt. Her long titian hair stretched down the back of her slender, snowy neck; her sapphire blue eyes with long eyelashes contrasted well with her hair. Her complexion was fresh, the cheekbones high, and the sensual thick lips were set in an almond-shaped face.

She reminded me, in some ways, of African tribal femininity. Perhaps it was the way she walked, her bone structure, her figure. Pleasantly I recognised the aura of her musky perfume.

It had come as no surprise to me when a short time ago I learnt that there had been a shipboard romance on her way to England and that she had become engaged to the ship's purser.

"David, why are you looking at me like that?" she asked smilingly.

"A cat can look at a King, or Queen in your case," I smiled at her over the top of my long glass of gin and tonic.

"Don't underestimate yourself, David. I can be quite catty myself."

"Anyway, no cat food this evening. I've heard there's a pleasant little restaurant just off the Old Brompton Road towards South Kensington. Shall we give it a try?"

"Yes, if you like, David. I'm famished after all the typing I've done for you today." She smiled again with those wide, full lips of hers.

Soon we were sitting opposite one another in a small dimly-lit restaurant. The restaurant was well patronised, and after some difficulty we had found a table just as a couple were leaving.

Lydia seemed to be enjoying her steak and side salad. She looked up at me quizzically.

"Is something worrying you, David?" she asked. "There usually is when your brow is so furrowed."

"Not really worrying me," I replied. After a pause I asked, "When will you be leaving to get married, Lydia?"

"Now you're changing the subject. I expect I shall go back to Durban soon. Richard seems keen for us to get married before the end of the year, but I think it will be best to wait until next Spring, especially as I want to have a further look around the old country before going back home and settling down."

"Perhaps you're right," I ventured. "Anyway, you've only known Richard Prentice for such a short time. You need a breathing space to take stock generally."

Her enigmatic smile was non-committal, so I introduced the subject of the photo which I had seen in the newspaper, and the mystique surrounding it all.

Lydia stirred her sweetened coffee as though distilling her thoughts. Presently she suggested that as I was thinking of taking a holiday in Italy in the Autumn, why didn't I take the opportunity of visiting this Italian artist and his daughter?

"I'd need to carry out some research first. Besides, if Stephen or any of his family have seen the newspaper article and photo, they will probably claim the painting for themselves."

"Your legal mind would consider that the research is a fair challenge." She continued to stir her coffee thoughtfully.

I looked into the deep-set blue of her eyes. In the following days I was to wonder why I put the following question to her. Was it the need for her company or for her feminine attractiveness or was it merely my innate romanticism?

"If I find that there is a mystery surrounding this matter after my investigations in this country, would you come to Italy with me—to help, I mean?" I tried to speak casually as the waiter cleared the empty wine glasses.

There was a slight pause before she answered: "Unlike you, I'm only entitled to a fortnight's holiday."

"That doesn't really answer my question. Would you like to visit Italy—if you have someone like me with you? Someone who knows the country a little," I hastened to add.

Smilingly she threw back her long mane of hair. "It all sounds very enticing. Certainly I'd like to visit Italy."

"Then you'll come with me—if I go to Italy in the Autumn?"

"Yes. On a strictly business basis," she added.

That was how we came to order another carafe of wine, and as our glasses chinked together

we drank a toast to our future travels together.

★ ★ ★

It was only a short walk from my office to the Public Records Office in Chancery Lane. Many years were to pass before part of the Public Records Office was moved to Kew.

Having completed the usual vetting forms in the reception area, I was directed to the office of an employee, a young man of spare frame, bespectacled and owl-like.

"Your name, Sir?" he asked.

"I've put my name on the forms which I completed in the reception area—it's David Thompson, with a 'p'."

"Why do you wish to read the War Diary of your Battalion?" The question was asked in a challenging tone of voice.

It took me some time to explain my presence there, and the reasons why I was trying to obtain further information regarding the Battalion during the war years. The young man then peered over his spectacles and emphasised in a whispery manner the confidentiality of such records and the need for security even in peacetime.

It was with reluctance that he passed to me a further form for me to sign; this particular form related to the importance of non-dissemination to the public. Finally I was guided to a small enclosed space and given a brown leathery volume to read.

Already the pages of the War Diary were beginning to look as though they themselves had been through a war. Without much difficulty I found the diary entries for 1944.

Searching my memory back to those times I remembered that Stephen had survived the battles in the mountains around Monte Cassino. Subsequently we had been moved to a so-called quiet sector of the front.

In the Diary, I came across the name of a small town— Lanciano—that was it, that was the place we had returned to in the Eastern Sector. Was it here that Stephen had somehow found the time to have his portrait painted? I didn't think so. He had spent most of his spare time in a medium-sized villa where the Italian owners lived cheek-by-jowl with some of our big guns; Stephen had discovered the Italian family to be musical, and they had allowed him full use of their piano.

The main entries in the War Diary concerned the periodic battle casualty numbers, and the paper also listed those officers serving at the time.

I traced through the list of officers on the thin parchment paper, particularly the name of Hardinge. His name was still in the list in June, 1944. I saw references to the Ortona Sector. Then I remembered. Stephen and I at one time had been sent on a three weeks tactical course at the Central Mediterranean

Training Centre in Benevento. It was the time of the start of the Second Front in France, and the taking of Rome in the battles in Italy.

Perhaps it had been in the pleasant and peaceful oasis of Benevento that Stephen had found an opportunity to have his portrait painted.

The War Diary indicated that in August, 1944 we had been engaged in mountain operations. Then there had been the fall of Arezzo, and the advance and severe engagements in the Gothic Line Battles. By this time, in the Italian campaign, both Stephen and I had become Company Commanders.

There was a dryness in my mouth as I recalled those hazardous days—momentarily I remembered one of the first Gothic Line battles which involved capturing Urbino. After Urbino we had moved forward—but the Germans had been waiting for us on the next ridge. That was it—Stephen's Company had gone forward with the Bren Gun Carriers. They had been fired on by a couple of Tiger Tanks. The Carrier Platoon and the Infantry Company had suffered severe casualties, and Stephen had been posted missing, believed killed. But where was the page of the War Diary showing this battle or Stephen's demise? It seemed to be missing—the War Diary continued by describing later grim battles and lists of casualties. Certainly, Stephen's name no longer appeared in any active list of officers in the War Diary. Had someone deliberately taken out a vital page of the War Diary, or was it simply a case of Fate playing its part? After all, the war had been fairly mobile at the time of Stephen's disappearance, and it would have been difficult to have maintained continuing progress reports for the War Diary— or the necessary details may have been lost at the time.

Unconsciously, in those quiet precincts of the Public Records Office, I had been sweating profusely—just being reminded of those hazardous days still caused an inner fearful dread.

Eventually I emerged from the portals of the Public Records Office into Chancery Lane. I felt better in the fresh air. A light rain started to fall as inwardly I decided to pursue the matter further by visiting Justin Townsend in the Cotswolds even if it meant more delay before going to Italy. After all, he had been Battalion Commander in those grim days of 1944.

★ ★ ★

"Why bother with any search at all in Italy?" asked Lydia. "If you speak to Stephen Hardinge's family they will surely give you all the information you need, and they can claim the painting themselves. We can then go to Italy just for a holiday for ourselves."

"It was you who suggested that I combine a holiday in Italy with the research on Stephen," I reminded her.

We were walking through Temple Gardens on the way to the Tube. I was feeling tired after an exhausting day with clients.

"I didn't think that it would be anything too complicated, but now I'm not so sure." Lydia spoke tentatively. "In any event if we don't go soon the Autumn will be over and I don't fancy Winter in Italy any more than I do here, David."

I laughed at her yearning for the South African sun. There was no doubt about it. Lydia was good company, and I was glad she had agreed to come back to the flat after work that evening.

"You only want someone to cook your meal," she smiled as we stood pressed together in the crowded tube.

The twilight shadows from the lamplight showed the first Autumn leaves to fall on the pavement in the Little Boltons as we entered the flat, but the weather was still mild.

It was later in the evening when I took Lydia in my arms and felt a surge of enjoyment as I kissed her sensuous lips. My fingers around her waist entwined with her long hair as I looked into the pellucid eyes.

"What about the purser chap?" I asked.

She looked away towards the window and the huddled grey tall buildings. "I thought I only wanted my old life back in South Africa, and Richard coming home from cruises."

There was that enigmatic smile again.

"And now?"

"Now I'm not so sure. Although why anyone should want to live amongst the crowds and smog of London I don't know."

I suppose this was the evening that our friendship became more intimate. Later on the moon lifted clear in the sky and shone into the bedroom where Lydia lay in bed with me.

We made love and then lay close together. She seemed so innocent and yet to me so wonderful. She lay asleep beside me as the dawn crept in, and as I longed for her again. Gently I fondled her firm, upstanding breasts. This time I hoped that true love would run its course.

The weekend was much taken up with our lovemaking, with occasional walks to the Round Pond in Kensington Gardens. Just for a moment life seemed to stand still as we gazed into the water; I would always remember this place, I thought.

A few days later I drove my small Ford out of London onto the A40, and headed for the Cotswolds.

Colonel Justin Townsend lived in a somewhat isolated village a few miles from Burford. He had given me firm directions on the telephone as to how to locate his residence set in the Cotswold countryside, and sounded genuinely pleased that he would have a chance to relive old battles again with lengthy conversations. However, he had sounded decidedly cool when I mentioned on the telephone that I was seeking information about Stephen Hardinge, and he seemed to think that my search was of no importance.

There was a fiery red sunset on the horizon as I drove into Burford and headed for my village destination.

As in London, the partial burnishing of the trees and landscape forewarned of the imminence of Autumn.

The house had a pleasant façade of yellowing stone. It was a typical Cotswold house lying in its own grounds with a short drive to the front door.

I pressed the bell tentatively, and this brought forth excited barking from the Colonel's dogs. The stout wooden door was opened by a middle-aged prematurely grey-haired lady of medium height and build.

"You must be David Thompson," she smiled. "I'm Justin's wife, Daphne. I hope you had a good journey. The Colonel will be back soon. He had to go to Burford for a check-up. He hasn't been too well since he retired from the Army."

"The Army was his life I imagine." Immediately I felt my remark had been tactless, especially knowing that they had no children, but it went unnoticed. The two labradors were making a great fuss of me.

"The dogs seem to have taken to you. I expect you'd like to freshen up before dinner. I'll show you to your room, and we can meet for a drink in the lounge at seven."

★ ★ ★

The house was probably run on military lines, I suspected, as I soaked myself in a large old-fashioned enamel bath. The bedroom was pleasant enough, and had a peaceful outlook over fields of grazing sheep, the fields being divided by the low stone walls of the Cotswolds. The room had a country decor of chintz, but a hard bed would ensure that I would not outstay my welcome.

Later that evening after we had dined on plain but adequate food, the Colonel sat with his dogs at his feet, as Daphne knitted patiently beside him. Their two large armchairs were side by side, and faced my smaller armchair. For a moment I thought of it as a scenario for an inquisition.

However, Justin Townsend soon mellowed after his third whisky. He was a tall man, and his bulky frame filled the large armchair. His hair was now almost white.

It wasn't long before he was talking of the Battalion's exploits in the not too distant war. I tried to bring the conversation round to the Gothic Line Battles, but as soon as I mentioned these operations he cut me short:

"You want me to talk about Stephen Hardinge, I know. Let's leave that until tomorrow morning. You and I can exercise the dogs whilst Daphne is getting lunch."

"You ought not to be too late going to bed anyway, Justin.

You know you have been told today to take it easy." Daphne looked palely anxious at her husband.

"I shall never 'take things easy', my dear, but I expect David is tired after his journey anyway." The Colonel spoke in his usual crisp manner as he rose from the depths of his armchair.

Presently upstairs I strove to get comfortable in my hard bed. A slight breeze moved the lightweight curtains. Perhaps I should soon learn what really happened to Stephen. Anyway, I fell asleep thinking of Lydia, and realised that she was now beginning to become a significant part of my life.

* * *

"And Autumn leaves like blood and gold
　　That strew a Gloucester lane."

Justin loudly proclaimed these apt words as we strode along a lane hedged by stone walls. The labradors went bounding on ahead.

"You know who wrote that, David?"

"No," I replied miserably.

"I shan't tell you. Look it up when you are back at home."

Typical, I thought. As though we were still on some Army exercise and needed to learn the hard way. I wondered how soon I could raise the matter of Stephen, but I need not have worried. We were moving up a narrow bridle path at the side of a field which fringed a wood when Justin called back to me:

"About Stephen. You probably remember that in the Gothic Line operations he was posted missing, believed killed."

"I remember that all right," I countered. "But was it actually confirmed later that he was killed? I never knew the final outcome."

"There was never any confirmation of his death. My own opinion is that he was taken prisoner." Justin cleared a stile with more ease than I expected.

"He had gone to make contact with a Bren gun carrier crew who were all killed, weren't they?" I asked.

"Yes, that's right," the Colonel answered.

"Then why do you think that Stephen was taken prisoner?"

Justin paused for a moment. "Just regaining my breath. The Doc. told me to take it easy you know."

I waited. A pheasant shot out of the wood and lumbered overhead.

"Not much sport, shooting pheasants, David."

I couldn't let the matter go at that. Justin sensed my frustration:

"You remember we went to Greece from Italy, and had our struggles with the Greek Communists, the E.L.A.S.?" he asked.

"Yes," I replied. "The Communists made life unpleasant for us there for a while."

"That's right."

"But what has that to do with Stephen?"

"There were unconfirmed reports that Stephen was taken prisoner by the E.L.A.S. in northern Greece." Justin called his dogs to heel.

"How could that be so? And even if it was so, after the cessation of hostilities with E.L.A.S., all prisoners were released and rejoined their units. In such circumstances Stephen would have rejoined us."

"Quite. He didn't rejoin us, did he?" He paused. "And they never found his body in Italy you know. Now, I think we have earned a beer," he remarked, changing the subject, and heading for an attractive Cotswold inn.

I still tried to keep him on the subject of Stephen:

"I had a look at the War Diaries at the Public Records Office, but there seemed to be a vital part missing," I called out as he turned into the inn.

"I know nothing about that," he commented sharply. But he didn't say he would look into it or get someone else from the Regiment to correct matters. Perhaps Justin was losing interest if his health was not good, or was there something to conceal, something about Stephen in particular?

"Good health," he smiled, as he lifted the tankard to his whiskered lips.

"Cheers," I called back across the midday hubbub of the village inn saloon bar.

The question of whether there had been a cover up or not continued to occupy my mind on the return journey to London. The traffic was light, and I made good time by-passing Oxford and then going through High Wycombe at a favourable time of day. Lydia had been right, of course. The visit to Justin Townsend had only served to complicate matters, and I needed to contact Stephen's family direct before going to Italy, or Greece for that matter.

The lights of the Western Avenue beckoned welcomingly as I drove towards the East and the flat in South Kensington. If Lydia hadn't been kept late at the office, she would already be at the flat preparing one of her delicious meals. Forget about the food; Lydia seemed to be all I had ever wanted, and each time we met I felt our relationship was deepening further. Poor Richard, I thought, but perhaps pursers in general had a different relationship on each cruise with members of the opposite sex.

★ ★ ★

The hall lights were on as I unlocked the main door of the flat. Lydia came to greet me. Her wide voluptuous lips creased into a smile.

"How did you get on?" she asked.

"I didn't make much progress I'm afraid; in fact, apart from Italy, there is also a possibility that Stephen ended up in Greece," I answered.

"You would do well—"

"I know. You were going to say that I could save myself some bother if I spoke to Stephen's relatives," I cut in anticipating her remarks.

"This mystique could surely be clarified by his family," she smiled. "Now you must be starving. Go and wash quickly and I will serve up the meal."

Dutifully I obeyed. Of course Lydia would have no idea of the difficulties presenting themselves as regards contacting Stephen's family. I left those thoughts for the morrow. Tonight we made love soon after our repast. Our bodies mingled in harmony as I caressed her long strands of autumnal golden hair. I loved the way she smiled with the corners of her mouth slightly turned upwards; her blue eyes smilingly danced as well.

Fortunately Tom Preston at the office was amenable to my taking time off, and indeed having a holiday on the continent; he was appreciative of the hard work I had undertaken since my return from the forces. Even so I had been putting off my visit to Stephen's family as long as possible. I remembered when Stephen and I were on the tactical course together at Benevento in Italy. One evening we had decided to explore Benevento, and we had ended up in a small taverna down a cobbled alley.

The wine had been rough, the atmosphere smoky, but it was civilization of a sort. I was a good listener. As the wine loosened our tongues, the fair headed, good looking and tall Stephen suddenly showed tears of sadness.

"My parents were killed in an air raid," he choked on the words. "Our house in Chelsea suffered a direct hit one night during an air raid. There is really nothing to go back to."

"Have you no relatives, brothers or sisters?" I asked.

He hesitated a moment. "I've only a sister, but she is older than me, and we never hit it off."

I decided that there was no point in my inquiring further. Besides, at that time, the life expectancy for Stephen and myself was very much in doubt.

Looking back now to our wartime conversation in Benevento it was possible to conjecture that the sadness and the tragedy of Stephen's life in general lent credence to the continuation of his misfortunes ending up with his disappearance and possible death on the Italian battlefield.

I was able to daydream—it was for once, a comparatively quiet morning in the office. The faint clattering noise of typewriters came through the walls of the building, but it was a muted reminder of the work going on around me. My own room was lined with bookshelves containing the vast tomes on Law of Succession, Contract Law, Tort and Criminal Law, and other special aspects of my chosen profession. The sash window had a pleasant outlook towards the square and the small central garden. The leaves of the plane trees were already tinted with Autumn gold, yet another reminder of Summer's wane.

I picked up the telephone directory in order to ascertain how many Hardinges there were in London. If Stephen's sister was his only living relative it was possible that she lived in London. If she lived outside London a search could be of indefinite duration.

I made a series of phone calls; it seemed to be possible that if the parents had lived in the Chelsea area the daughter might still be living in the same area or in Kensington.

I had worked my way through half of the Hardinges in the telephone directory. Lydia had put a hot cup of coffee on my desk.

"Margaret Hardinge here." She spoke firmly with a hard, military style voice.

"Would you by any chance be related to Stephen Hardinge? He was an infantry officer in the last war," I added.

"My brother Stephen was lost in Italy during the war. He was killed out there." She sounded definite on the point. "Why do you ask?"

I hesitated only fractionally. It seemed that I had located Stephen's sister at last, and that she was based in London.

"May I come and see you please? I am trying to clear up some matters concerning Stephen, and you might be able to help. We served together in Italy," I explained. "My name is David Thompson."

There was a pause from the other end of the line.

"Do you really think I can help?" she asked. "Stephen and

I didn't keep in touch all that much, and his son Eric will be coming to stay here next weekend from boarding school. I don't want him disturbed in this way."

"His son?" I queried. "I didn't know he was married. At least I don't think he ever mentioned it."

There was an audible sigh from Margaret Hardinge. "Perhaps you had better come round. I will then try and explain. Can you come round tomorrow evening, say about six thirty p.m. for drinks? Clearly you have the address from the telephone directory."

The voice had ceased to be diffident, and it had that militant air about it.

"All right. I'll look forward to seeing you then," I agreed.

"You said your name was Thompson?"

"Yes, Thompson with a p," I quipped. "Like Hardinge with an 'e'."

She had hung up, and I was left with a feeling that Margaret Hardinge was only going to see me on sufferance and that I was causing an unnecessary intrusion into her life.

★ ★ ★

Lydia had proposed a candlelit supper, but she could sense that I was preoccupied.

"What is it, David?" she asked. "Have you gone off my cooking already?" She smiled appealingly at me.

"No, the food's fine," I replied as I toyed with the crisp pastry of the steak and kidney pie. "I tracked down Stephen's sister today."

"Good. Presumably she lives in London then?" Lydia asked.

"Yes, not far from the Chelsea embankment. I'm going round to see her tomorrow evening, but only for a drink."

"It sounds as though you might make some progress at last," said Lydia encouragingly. "Though I can see that something is bothering you."

There was a pause in our conversation as Lydia cleared away the dishes. When she returned from the kitchen with the cheese and biscuits, she sat down opposite me at the small oval table in the recess of our living room. At this time of the day the last rays of the sun highlighted the golden strands of her long hair.

"Well?" she waited patiently.

"It seems from what Margaret Hardinge said on the phone that Stephen had a son, Eric by name, who was currently away at school." I spoke in a perplexed manner.

"I thought that his sister was his only living relative?" Lydia questioned me.

"I was certainly under that impression," I replied. I tried to think back to our conversation those years ago in Benevento. Certainly Stephen had spoken of his parents and sister, and I had assumed that because he had intimated that he had nothing to go back to other than a none too friendly sister that there were no other near relatives.

"Anyway, perhaps I shall learn a little more tomorrow when I visit her ladyship." I smiled.

"Her ladyship. You mean—"

"No, I only mean that she sounded haughty and somewhat dismissive when I mentioned my connection with Stephen."

* * *

Later that evening the moon pierced the thin bedroom curtains and patterned Lydia's silken body. As she slept peacefully in my arms my mind hovered back to the conversations I had had with Stephen all that time ago on that course in Benevento. Stephen had certainly not given any indication that he was married, nor indeed that he had any offspring. In fact, I remembered all too clearly his many dalliances with the opposite sex when time and circumstances allowed behind the front in Italy. Somewhat wild in his behaviour, and yet he always managed to get away with it. There had been those occasions in Alexandria and Rome for instance.

Lydia stirred slightly as the moonbeams faded. My last waking thoughts were of Stephen smiling sardonically as he recounted tales of his female conquests in the Middle East and Italy. No doubt I had been envious of his qualities that attracted females to him, but I had no cause for jealousy now.

★ ★ ★

I left the embankment and turned down a quiet Chelsea road. I found the number of the house I was looking for and then pressed the bell tentatively, scraping off the damp leaves that clung to the wet soles of my shoes.

The house was more modern than its neighbours, and contented itself with two floors as opposed to the three floors of all the other properties in the street. Clearly it was a well maintained house, and the brown red brickwork was pleasing to the eye.

The door opened, and Margaret Hardinge invited me inside, but not with any outward enthusiasm.

I was directed into a sitting room at the side of the hall, but at the back of the house. It was a room filled with antique furniture and several bookcases and valuable paintings. There was an aura of opulence with the heavy drapes suitably swagged, and with the large-lapped armchairs and cretonne covered settee.

I looked at Stephen's sister as she set down a tray of drinks and two glasses on a substantial sideboard. I could see the likeness with Stephen; the high forehead, the grey-green eyes with prominent nose, the same height and fair hair. She must be attractive to men, just as her brother was to women, I mused. Although there was an impression of a tightening around a narrow mouth which gave her a severe expression.

"Sherry or Whisky?" she asked.

"Whisky with water please," I replied.

"You are making inquiries about Stephen. He was a friend of yours?" Quickly she honed in on the subject of my visit.

"Yes, we were in Africa and Italy together. It was a great loss when Stephen was killed." I looked steadily at her for any reaction.

"It was all very unsatisfactory. His death I mean," she countered. "They never found his body, you know." She gulped down a strong measure of whisky.

"You are convinced that he died in Italy?" I asked tentatively.

"Yes. I feel sure of it. Oh! I know Justin Townsend had some theory that Stephen had turned up later in Greece, but these unsubstantiated rumours don't hold water. Certainly the last time I heard from Stephen he was writing from Italy. I'll never forget that letter."

I raised my eyebrows encouraging her to continue. There

was a pause as Margaret refilled my glass. She lit a cigarette and started pacing the room.

"Why was the letter so important?" I asked.

She hesitated before replying, her eyes on the river traffic. "It was a novelty to get a letter from Stephen. You see, we never had much in common."

"Except your looks, perhaps," I smiled.

She ignored this remark, and retraced her steps to sit in the armchair facing me.

"It seemed that Stephen had been involved with a Canadian nurse in Rome. I don't need to go into all the sordid details—"

"Sordid? Why sordid?" I interrupted. "Was the girl's name Joy? Joy Mitchell?"

"Yes, that's right. Anyway, this Joy became pregnant. Eventually a baby boy was born, but the mother died in childbirth."

"This boy is the Eric you mentioned on the telephone?"

"Yes. I know that he's young to be at boarding school. You see, our parents died during the Blitz; all our home and possessions went. Eric is only nine years old now, but as he is without parents the least I can do is to have him here for his breaks from school."

It all sounded very plausible, and yet if Stephen and Margaret had not been the best of friends she seemed remarkably equable on having to bring up Stephen's son. And how did she manage to live in an expensive property in Chelsea, I wondered?

She interrupted my thoughts. "Why are you so interested? You said on the telephone that you were trying to clear up some matters?"

"Yes. I don't know if you saw this in the London paper a short while ago." I produced the newspaper cutting from my wallet.

Margaret read the details, and looked at the newspaper photograph.

"Well, that's Stephen all right. It would have been typical of his conceit to have a portrait painted of himself." She lit another cigarette. "I certainly hadn't seen this in the newspaper."

"Tell me," I leaned across to her from my angled chair. "I know that Stephen was an adequate pianist, but what is all this about a Doctor?"

"Stephen had qualified as a Doctor, but only just before the outbreak of war," Margaret explained. "For some reason best known to himself—perhaps he wanted to see more of the action—he didn't go into the R.A.M.C."

"Do you mind if I go to Italy to see the artist? I can collect the painting for you."

"I don't mind. Perhaps one day Eric will be pleased to have the painting, but we don't want any more scandal in the family. Now, if you'll excuse me, I have a lesson shortly."

I moved towards the hall and front door. "Lesson?" I queried.

"Yes. When I am not playing at concerts, I give piano lessons. So you see, Stephen and I did have something in common apart from facial features." It seemed to me that she smiled for the first time, but perhaps that was because she was seeing me off the premises. She had opened the front door.

"By the way, I went to the public records office, but there seemed to be a page or two missing regarding the Battalion at about the time Stephen disappeared." I decided on this parting shot.

"I don't know anything about that," she said sharply, reminding me of Justin Townsend's response.

★ ★ ★

The evening rush hour was over, and I sat back reasonably comfortably on the armed seat of the tube. Certainly Margaret Hardinge had been less than warm regarding my inquiries over Stephen, but then they had never really liked one another. Apart from this coldness I sense a lack of candour. There was nothing specific I could challenge in her statement, and yet my legal training had ingrained into me a sense of unease when the total truth seemed absent.

I soon stopped thinking of Margaret Hardinge, however. The mention of Joy Mitchell's name brought back memories of Stephen and I in Rome some considerable time before the push in the Gothic Line. We had been given a week's leave, presumably to fortify our morale for the battle ahead. Sometimes, fate plays cruel tricks, but the cruelty hurts some more than others.

I climbed up the steps of Earls Court Station and then walked down Earls Court Road to the Little Boltons. The flat was empty. Lydia had already told me that she wouldn't be round that evening.

"It's time I sorted out my own quarters and a few other things as well," she laughed. Lydia had furnished rooms in Earls Court, not far really from my own flat, but she needed to become detached for a short time. I knew she still thought of Richard Prentice, and knowing her disposition, any breaking off of relations with him would have to be done in the least hurtful way.

I felt tired for some reason. After a full day's work in the office, and then the strained discussion with Margaret Hardinge, I sat in my favourite armchair, a whisky by my side. My eyes became heavy-lidded, and then closed as my memory of that leave during the war in Rome with Stephen returned to disturb my evening.

The first few days in Rome had been uneventful really. We were billeted in a small hotel halfway down a side street off the Piazza Del Popolo. The military authorities had arranged daytime sightseeing visits for us.

"To keep us out of trouble," quipped Stephen.

Rome in early August was very hot. The heat shimmered over the city under the Mediterranean sky as we visited the Castel S. Angelo, Saint Peter's Square, the Victor Emmanuel monument and the Colosseum.

We usually finished up on the Via Veneto drinking coffee on the outside pavement of cafes, resting our exhausted limbs, too warm for comfort. The famous landmarks were all very impressive, untouched by the bombs of war. In the evening there had been one organised visit to an officers' club, but this turned into a disaster. We had been challenged by two staff officers to drink each drink on the list of alcoholic refreshments, one after the other. I cannot remember the result as to who won, but the general outcome had been that Stephen and I were in a more than delicate state at breakfast the next morning.

At the next table in the hotel dining room we had noticed the arrival of a group of Canadian nurses. They were presumably in transit in the same way that Stephen and I were really, except our stay was officially a leave.

I left Stephen finishing off his breakfast. He seemed to be

able to face breakfast better than I could. The hotel only had four floors, which was just as well as the lift was permanently out of order. I was slowly climbing the stairs towards the bedroom on the third floor which Stephen and I were sharing.

One of the Canadian nurses overtook me on the stairs but in her haste she dropped her handkerchief. Unlike the few others in her party she was blonde and tall. Now she had disappeared into one of the bedrooms on the second floor before I could gather my wits. I noticed the initials 'J.M.' on the handkerchief. Shrugging my shoulders, I placed the handkerchief in my pocket. I was intent on reaching the lavatory as soon as possible after the previous evening's misadventure.

Clearly I would have to take things quietly that morning, although Stephen had decided to take a long walk as a recipe for our misdemeanours. Just before lunch, however, I thought that perhaps a cognac would help my morale, and I strolled down to the small bar on the ground floor. I ordered my drink, and then noticed the fair-headed Canadian nurse sitting at a table on her own. She already had a drink in front of her, a glass of white wine I think it was.

I then recalled the alien handkerchief in my pocket, and lifting it out I called out: "Is this yours?"

She looked up from the Italian language text book she was studying.

"It has 'J.M.' on it," I explained.

"Then it's certainly mine." Her laugh revealed such perfect teeth.

"What does 'J.M.' stand for?" I asked.

"Joy Mitchell," she answered.

"Joy. I like that name. Have a drink?" I smiled.

"I already have one as you see. What is your name?" Now she was doing the questioning.

"David. David Thompson with a 'p'. Will you be here long?"

"I don't know how long we shall be here. We are really only in transit for some field hospital."

"I realise that. Stephen and I are only here until the end of the week. A spot of leave."

"Stephen? Your tall fair-headed friend with the Roman nose. The ladies find him quite attractive I imagine."

I should have taken more notice of this seemingly innocent remark, but in truth I was smitten by her own stature and appealing looks and fresh complexion.

"You also are tall and fair and attractive, but no Roman nose," I laughed brazenly. "Look here, I've only a few days left. Could you cheer up my evening, and come out with me after dinner?"

She hesitated only fractionally: "All right, David, but where will we go in this big city?" she asked.

"Well, there is an Officers' Club not far from here. It's reasonably quiet."

"I'll look forward to it." The soft Canadian drawl was very appealing.

★ ★ ★

The air was still warm as Joy and I made our way along the scorched pavements, avoiding the evening walkers as best as we could. Soon we were ensconced in the somewhat primitive lounge of the Officers' Club sipping our glasses of white wine. Joy was telling me about her family in Vancouver, but I have to confess that although I still found her very captivating, the previous evening's mixture of deadly concoctions had left me still alcoholically remorseful. To aggravate the matter I seemed to have developed a mild dysentery necessitating several absences to the cloakroom. Damn! I thought. Just my luck when in fact I had experienced no further dysentery since we had left Egypt.

There is no point in belabouring it. The evening was a disaster, entirely due to my state of health.

"Can I see you tomorrow evening?" I enquired back at the hotel.

"Are you sure you want to?" She raised her fair eyebrows over her deep grey eyes.

"Of course." I kissed her soft inviting lips as I left her on her bedroom landing.

Then, feeling weak with the dysentery, I turned into my own bed. Stephen was already sound asleep, a slight nasal snore emitting from him from time to time.

I must have been in and out of bed half a dozen times that night in order to go to the toilet, and by breakfast time I told Stephen he would have to eat by himself.

The morning continued to follow the same pattern as my night-time upheaval. Lunch was also going to be out of the question.

"Bad luck your feeling poorly on your leave, old man. Anything I can get you?" Stephen was getting ready to go downstairs for lunch.

"No thanks, Stephen." I hesitated. "However, if you see that blonde Canadian nurse perhaps you will tell her of my circumstances, and send her my apologies as I won't be able to take her out again this evening. Her name is Joy Mitchell."

"Again, did you say?" Stephen had that knowing smile on his face. "You are a dark horse, David. You'll have to enlighten me as to how you go about your conquests sometime." Needless to say his voice had a sarcastic tone to it.

★ ★ ★

That day was hot as usual. The curtains at the open window remained still. I was sweating profusely, and felt inward relief when the first signs of dusk appeared. A flock of birds seemed to hang in the sky as I gazed out of the window. The blue sky had now turned to pewter. Perhaps a storm was on its way at last.

Stephen came in. "I'm going out this evening, David, but I've run out of clean shirts. Can you lend me one?"

I threw him a clean shirt. It wasn't the usual khaki drill shirt. It was an open-necked white shirt, I remember. Something I had bought and kept for special occasions when there would be no strict discipline over dress.

"Thanks, chum. Hope you're feeling better. You're always better when you're back in the action."

"Don't remind me," I groaned. "Have a good evening."

★ ★ ★

There is little I remember about the next few evenings, except that Stephen seemed to be out all night, every night until our departure.

As Stephen had predicted, I felt decidedly better as we headed back to our battalion on the Sunday morning. Just my luck, I thought. Always fit when the unpleasant part starts, and always some snag when everything should be so amenable, especially when contrasted to the shelling, mortaring and being shot to pieces perhaps.

The sun was warm on my back as the fifteen CWT truck ferried Stephen and I back towards the battle lines. The road was badly rutted, but I felt I might soon be closing my eyes and nodding off. Anyway, by keeping my eyes closed the dust from the road had to find other repositories.

Stephen seemed cheerful. He usually was when further battle actions were imminent. I cannot say I shared his bonhomie. We had lost too many friends now, and the whole Division was sadly depleted and tired.

"Bad luck you had that dysentery, David. Joy Mitchell was a cracker, excusing the Army parlance," he called out from the other side of the truck.

I didn't open my eyes: "So that's where you were all night and every night?" I asked.

"Right first time, old man. After all, we couldn't let the little lady down could we?"

"There wasn't any 'we' about it, was there? Anyway, she wasn't little. Quite tall in fact, like you."

"Not jealous are we? Sorry, I mean are you?" He seemed to bark above the noise of the engine.

"Why should I be? I hardly knew her." I could scarcely keep the disappointment out of my voice.

It wasn't just this one incident. After all, there had already been numerous occasions in Africa and Italy when it seemed that he had succeeded with the local girls, where other officers including myself, had failed. To be honest I suppose I was jealous of his exploits, but I had to admit to myself that my dark looks, my medium height with its slight rotundity, and dark brown eyes could not compare with his physical attributes for women to be attracted by. I was an 'also ran', but did it really matter? We both might be dead before Christmas.

★ ★ ★

Before putting out my reading lamp at my bedside in the Little Boltons, there was one feature I had overlooked. Perhaps I hadn't wanted to recall it. I started to break out in a sweat just as I had done in the Public Records Office. That white shirt, the one I had lent Stephen in Rome. A member of the Bren Gun Carrier Platoon had brought it up to me in that battle when Stephen was lost. The white of that shirt was soaked in blood.

"We found this, Sir," he said in his country burr. He was scarcely more than a boy. "But there's no sign of Major Hardinge."

It had been that white shirt. The one he had been wearing before he went to have his sexual intercourse with Joy Mitchell.

A blooded white shirt that had belonged to me, but where was Stephen? Where was his body?

I put the light out, and tried to sleep. It seemed that I had come full circle. There could not have been many nights that Stephen had been with Joy Mitchell because of the fluidity of the War—but she was dead and now they had a son. A son called Eric. Who had given him that name I wondered, and why was Margaret Hardinge seemingly so wealthy now? The night seemed cool. Without Lydia there was an emptiness within me, and I had a restless night. Sleep only came when the first signs of London's awakening were at hand. Before losing consciousness I decided that Lydia and I would go to Italy to obtain the painting of Stephen, and endeavour to resolve the mysteries that surrounded him.

★ ★ ★

In those years not long after the War there was no easy air or road route to the part of Italy that was our destination.

First of all, we had to obtain of course the address of the Italian artist who painted the portrait of Stephen. This necessitated a visit to Fleet Street, and fortunately an old army colleague of mine (from my service days before I had left England for the Middle East) had become a journalist on the newspaper that had published the photograph and article concerning Stephen.

Robert Chester was, I suppose, of medium height with black wavy hair swept back. His black myopic eyes and sensuous mouth no doubt gave him a mystical appeal to the opposite sex. He had always given the impression of an oily pastiness, but I had put this down to his Latin ancestry to which he periodically referred.

It had been some time since I had met Bob; I had heard indirectly that his war had not been too hazardous. With his command of languages he had transferred from the Infantry to Intelligence at an early stage. In some ways he reminded me of Stephen with his tales of female involvements, but whereas I could understand the physical attractions of Stephen which appealed to the opposite sex, I took Bob Chester's stories and descriptions to be largely lacking in foundation and embellished to impress his male colleagues.

In a well-known Fleet Street watering-hole I introduced Bob to Lydia, and struggled through the lunchtime throng to make an order at the bar. The beer was inevitably slopped by the elbowing crowd as I returned to Lydia and Bob who were standing near the entrance.

I explained to Bob at some length the information that I needed and why I needed it.

"Tell me," he asked, "are you simply trying to obtain the painting for his family (or what's left of his family), or are you hoping that your journey will shed light on the disappearance of your friend Stephen?"

"Both," I said. "Obviously to get the painting for his family would be very pleasing."

"But you're also still curious to know what really happened to Stephen, aren't you?"

"I suppose I am. After all, we had been together for a long time, and as Company Commanders there was a friendly rivalry between us," I added.

"Perhaps you had other rivalries when off duty," Bob Chester smirked. I had forgotten that smirk of his.

"Can you or can you not help us?" My anger was slowly surfacing.

"Of course," he answered. "I'll telephone you the information in a day or so."

★ ★ ★

To be fair, Bob kept his word, and I wrote the address of the Italian artist on my office desk scribbling pad.

"Urbino?" I queried down the phone.

"Yes, Urbino," Bob confirmed on the line. "You sound surprised?"

"No, not really I suppose. It's just that Stephen never had a leave there."

"Why not?" asked Bob.

"Because we captured Urbino before the battle when he was lost. The city had only just been liberated. There was no fighting in the city itself. For reasons which I can explain."

"Don't bother," said Bob. "I have to dash now. Tell me about it some other time. Good luck on your mission, and give my love to Lydia."

"Thanks. Take care." I put the phone down.

Somehow the mystery was deepening, but I knew I had to go on with my search. What exactly was I searching for? Was it a body or the reliving of the past? Was the past something contradictory and unpleasant which I was steeling myself to face up to? A Pandora's box which would only disclose evil?

* * *

That evening Lydia was able to come back to my flat, but she seemed upset and somewhat tearful.

"What is it?" I asked. "Has Tom Preston been working you too hard today?" I laughed.

"No, it's not that." Her blue eyes moistened attractively.

"Tell me," I whispered in her ear. They were such dainty ears, I thought.

"I heard from Richard today. A letter from Cape Town. His ship was in port there."

"And?"

"He was upset that I had broken off our engagement. It wasn't a very pleasant letter, but I had to tell him how matters stood."

"You had to be honest with yourself," I held her close. A stray tear rolled down to her nose. I wrapped it away in my handkerchief.

★ ★ ★

Late that evening we were lying in bed together. Our lovemaking seemed to have brought Lydia to a more peaceful and sleepy state.

"You say that you heard from Bob Chester today, and that this Italian artist and his daughter live in Urbino." Lydia turned over to face me.

"That's right, so you and I will head for Urbino as soon as we can make travel arrangements. I have told Tom Preston that we will be off shortly."

"What is all this about there being no fighting in Urbino?"

"Urbino was in the Gothic Line, but the Germans had decided to respect this university city where Raphael was born, and its historical palace and churches. The city wasn't shelled, and the Germans had moved out just before our attack went in. That's what I find mystifying."

"Why?"

"Because after a brief pause at Urbino, it was on the next ridges to the north that Stephen went missing, believed killed. So he could never have had a leave in Urbino. We only had two nights—"

I looked up at Lydia; she was now asleep. Her body was warm against the coolness of the night.

I was looking forward to our holiday together. At least it would be different from my time in Rome with Joy Mitchell; there was no Stephen to come between us this time.

★ ★ ★

In those days of the early nineteen fifties our planned route was to take us by rail for the most part. Looking back on that journey now I can remember the thrill of excitement coursing through my body. I suppose there were three reasons for this; there was the anticipation of revisiting certain battle areas, and the possible clarification about Stephen and what had happened to him. Most important it seemed to me, however, was the expectancy of happiness with Lydia in an Italian setting.

The weather was still mild. The sun had warmth as Lydia slept with her head against my shoulder; the train was taking us southward towards the Marche.

We were quite tired, I remember, as we searched out a modest hotel in Urbino. The small town, which did not boast a first class hotel, was at peace, but very much under Communist influence. The peacetime welcome did not seem as genuine as on the day in nineteen forty-four when we had entered the city. Then the welcome had been tumultuous and the best hotels had been open to us. Now there was a muted acceptance that, with the coming of peace, foreign tourists would spoil their placid existence.

The small hotel was clean, but our bedroom was sparsely furnished. Lydia had gone down the corridor in search of a bath as I opened the shuttered window.

I was able to look across the landscape of the marche to the ridges to the north of the city, to the outskirts of a village where we had met German opposition with their Tiger Tanks all those years ago. Somewhere around that region Stephen had disappeared before we advanced further into the Gothic Line defences.

The late afternoon sun was playing on the campanile of that village church. I could hear the distant chime of bells. It seemed so very tranquil now.

We had a quiet meal in the hotel that evening. The Chianti wine was pleasant if slightly rough. Lydia suggested a short walk through the city before we retired for the night, and after coffee we strolled through the main Piazza to look over the stout walls towards the vineyards to the south.

I suppose that I would always remember that hot summer's day during the War when we had approached Urbino climbing up through those vineyards, not knowing whether there would be hand to hand fighting in the streets of the city. It could have been a bloody business for us, with a full daylight view of the landscape controlled from the high vantage point of the buildings of the city.

Lady luck had been kind to me that day. I turned to Lydia and smiled.

"Do you think you will enjoy it here?" I asked

"Oh yes! It's very peaceful after London. No fogs either," she laughed.

Darkness was suddenly descending on the hills and valleys.

"Come on. Let's get some sleep. You must be tired." I took her arm, and led her back to the hotel.

I would like to think that I slept well after the long train journeys, but I had a restless night, and wondered if I'd been prudent to return here. After all, was it really any of my business? Sometimes stones should not be overturned; there might be a scorpion underneath.

The next morning Lydia was up before me, and my erratic hours of sleep made me reluctant to get up. We seemed to have the dining room to ourselves as we ate our continental breakfast. The hot strong coffee was a welcome antidote to my furry mouth. Lydia was dressed sensibly in a white shirt and black slacks, and we left the hotel after our breakfast.

The sun was already warm as we made our way down the narrow hilly alleys towards Arturo Manzoni's apartment. I had already sent a telegram from London to forewarn Signor Manzoni of our impending visit, and after seeking directions once or twice we arrived at a substantial stone building with a yellow façade. There was a pleasant adjoining courtyard with the waters of a fountain glistening in the sun. We found the correct number of the apartment we required. It was on the first floor overlooking the ridges to the north.

It was Signor Marzoni's daughter who came to the front door of the apartment to let us in.

At first I thought she looked the typical north Italian woman still in her late twenties, but as I looked more closely I could see the delicate porcelain nature of her skin; it was like a Fragonard shepherdess. She had deep brown eyes and a dark black mass of hair. Her round clefted chin led off from sensuous lips.

"Buon Giorno," she greeted us. "I expect you would prefer that I speak English."

"That would be helpful," I grinned sheepishly. The few sentences of Italian which I knew from being in Italy during the war would not have been helpful to our conversation. "You speak English well," I spoke encouragingly. Lydia surreptitiously slid the pocket dictionary she was carrying into her shoulder bag.

"I studied languages in Verona as a young girl, but sometimes I forget the words and pronunciation. My name is Maria," she called over her shoulder as she led us into a large room stacked with paintings, a working easel and the general clutter of an artist's tools of trade. The rays of the sun shone through the partially glazed roof.

Maria found a chair for Lydia to sit on and then went off to fetch her father.

Lydia and I walked over to the full length studio window and gazed across the countryside. The sun was burnishing her long auburn hair; it seemed to be aflame. I put my hand out to touch its imaginary heat, but I was interrupted:

"Bon Giorno, Signor Thompson," a pleasantly deep voice called out.

"Bon Giorno, Signor Manzoni."

We exchanged greetings, with Maria acting as interpreter. Arturo Manzoni was aged about fifty with crinkly grey hair. He was of small stature with a darkish grey beard. His eyes were deep brown like his daughter's and they twinkled with friendliness.

"So you knew Major Stefano—unfortunately I never knew or remembered his other name," Arturo explained.

"Yes, we were in the army together. You mean you never knew his surname? It was Hardinge."

I volunteered this information as we sat down on an old settee in the corner of the room; Maria served us all with coffee.

"For some reason he never seemed to want us to know his surname. It did not matter; there were so many soldiers around at that time—but he seemed different," Maria smiled wistfully.

"Why different?" I asked.

"Usually they were all only too willing to give their full names, especially if my father had completed a portrait of one of them, but not Stefano." Maria looked sadly away for a second.

"How did you meet Stephen?" I asked Maria.

"It was shortly after the troops had moved northwards through our lovely city. We were so pleased that our buildings, palaces and churches had been spared. I was in the main piazza with my friend Teresa. There were so many people rejoicing even though a few days had passed since the liberation. We could still hear the rumble of gunfire in the distance. In the throng I fell and twisted my ankle."

"And what happened then, Maria?" I encouraged her to continue, as her father nodded agreement.

"He was tall and fair and his eyes reminded me of the, how do you say—grass?" She laughed at me.

"Yes, a greyish green actually, I suppose, but—"

"He spoke a little Italian," she interrupted my impatience, "and he had seen me being pushed by the crowd, and then falling over. He asked if he could help, he said he was a doctor."

Her father then interrupted her, and through Maria's translation I understood him to say that there had been an Army Casualty Clearing Station just outside the city. They had not been surprised that Stephen was in the medical arm of the Army. It seemed that Stephen had screened off any reference to his having been in a fighting unit. Did it really matter? I seemed to be constantly clutching at red herrings, and his sister Margaret had confirmed that he was a qualified doctor at that time.

The main discovery seemed to be that Stephen had lived through those battles beyond the city; he hadn't been killed then, probably not even wounded, and only missing as far as the Services and his family were concerned.

Maria interrupted my thoughts: "Stefano was very helpful when I fell over in the piazza; with his aid I hobbled back here to our apartment. He treated my ankle, and after that he called several times to see how I was."

Arturo again spoke volubly, waving his hands in a Latin manner.

"Yes," Maria continued. "It was during these visits to check on my ankle that Papa painted his portrait."

"It is a good likeness," I remarked.

Lydia had been quiet all this time, but she seemed to be absorbing the main gist of what was being said.

"We must not keep you too long," I said apologetically.

"It is all right," smiled Maria. "My father would like you both to come and have your evening meal with us today, if that is possible."

I turned to Lydia who seemed amused at something. She nodded agreement.

"That is very kind of you." I accepted the invitation and ascertained the time they would expect us.

★ ★ ★

"We'll find a tavern for lunch." I was leading Lydia gently down the steep alley. I turned to her: "What was amusing you when they invited us for a meal? I thought it was very kind of them."

"It was kind of them, but it seemed to me that Maria could scarcely take her eyes off you."

"Don't be silly. Anyway, what's so funny about that, if it was true?"

Lydia shook back her long hair: "Many a romance under an Italian sun becomes jaded later on. Italian women age quickly you know." She laughingly took my arm.

Little did I realise then that laughter can turn to sadness so easily.

All right, I agreed to myself, there was a depth of beauty, an aura of wistfulness surrounding Maria, but turning to Lydia to steady her movement down the slope of the cobbled way, I realised how young and fresh and appealing she was. I was grateful that she had chosen me instead of Richard Prentice. The future seemed settled at last.

The sun was still warm enough for us to lunch alfresco, and I felt contented as we lunched on an agreeable local cheese and wine. My mind focused back on our earlier conversation with the Manzonis. Why had Stephen been reluctant to give them his surname, and why was he anxious to use his guise as a doctor?

One thing was now clear. Stephen hadn't been killed in those battles north of Urbino, but what had actually happened? If he was still alive, where was he and why had he seemingly decided to go missing indefinitely?

Several motor scooters roared into the square where we were sitting and finishing our lunch; their noise drowned the question on Lydia's lips. Eventually the noise subsided.

"Shall we walk through to the vine and olive groves this afternoon?" she asked. "It should give you an appetite for your meal with the Manzonis this evening."

"Yes, all right," I answered. It seemed far more sensible than to linger around the hotel. "I can show you the original city walls on our way. You will be able to see the woods. They say that the oaks provided timber for the ships of Sir Francis Drake."

The weather was still benign as we worked our way down the steep slopes beyond the city walls and through the young vines. Once or twice Lydia nearly fell, but each time I managed to catch her; each time I held her in my arms, and kissed her wide sensuous lips. Yet somehow I felt that her gaiety and laughter was more forced, that I was just being humoured.

"We'd better turn round and get back to the city," she called out. "The nights are drawing in and we don't want to lose our way in the dark."

It was instinctive to call Urbino a city even though in size it was only a small township.

★ ★ ★

We felt quite tired when we arrived back at the hotel, but there was still an hour or so before we were due at the Manzonis. We climbed the stairs to our bedroom on the first floor. As Lydia closed and shuttered the bedroom window I started to embrace her.

"Let's make love now," I whispered in her tiny ear.

"No, not now," she freed herself, and called out from the bathroom: "How much longer do you expect to have to stay here? If you see to the despatch of the painting to Stephen's sister, Margaret, won't that be sufficient?"

"It still wouldn't solve the problem about Stephen and what actually happened to him," I countered.

"I think we ought to go back to London soon," she spoke wistfully as she came back into the bedroom.

"Darling, after only a couple of days we still have plenty of time, and we are together; don't you like it here?" I asked as I used the clothes brush on my jacket. I was facing the mirror, and could see Lydia's face reflected in the background.

She paused: "Somehow I feel that our relationship is on firmer ground in London."

I was watching her mirrored face. Was I imagining it, or was there a look of sorrowful accusation in her eyes?

★ ★ ★

Later that evening as we sat eating lasagna al forno with the usual Chianti Classico, the candlelit mellowness of the evening was pervasive. I looked across at the darkling glimmering shadows playing on the jet black of Maria's hair; her brown eyes were very deep-set and piercing. Her lips played on the top of her wine glass as she looked up at me. Was Lydia right? Perhaps I reminded Maria of someone in her past, or was there a direct physical magnetism developing between us? Arturo Manzoni was talking to Lydia, so Maria's attention was now being diverted with her efforts at translation: "You must stay long enough to see the art treasures of Urbino. The chapels and frescos and sculptures, and the palace. Maria will be pleased to show you both around, and then we can see to packing Stephen's portrait."

The sweet was a delicious almond concoction, and Maria had obviously taken much trouble in preparing the meal. Presently we moved from the small dining area to the living room which was comfortable without being over-furnished.

Maria handed us our coffee as we arranged the time the following morning for her to be at our hotel to take us on a conducted tour of the artistic and historical sites of the Renaissance Period.

We were not late leaving the Manzoni's, but back at the hotel Lydia was soon asleep. I realised as I lay awake between the coarse sheets that she had not wanted to make love anyway. There was some invisible barrier building up between us, but it was intangible and to me there seemed no reason for it.

I hoped that I would be able to galvanise her interest the following morning when we were to visit the palace with twin towers and the churches and frescos of the university city where Raphael was born.

★ ★ ★

Maria arrived promptly at our hotel the next morning, and enthusiastically guided us around the Palazzo Ducale.

The weather had turned cool and the sun was fitful. Grey clouds were skimming across a pale sky.

It was natural that Maria should first of all take us to see the Renaissance architecture of the Ducal palace with its impressive towers. I listened to her soft voice describing the Montefeltro family, the historical overlords of Urbino, and in particular Federico Montefeltro who had been not only a soldier of fortune but had also engaged a foreign architect to design this Renaissance masterpiece of the Ducal palace.

There was something odd about the portrait of Federico Montefeltro; it was the nose—part of it was missing. Maria saw my puzzled look, and quietly she explained that the duke

Federico had lost part of his sight in combat. Federico had then had part of his nose removed so that as a soldier he would still have good views with his one sound eye. Suddenly I thought of Stephen with his Roman nose—I felt quite sure that he would never have parted with any piece of his nose for the sake of his observation powers. He would have been too mindful of people observing him, being all too aware of his own good looks. But was I really being fair to him?

Listening to Maria again, it was not difficult to conjure up a vision of painters and sculptors working here in the Ducal palace. Alas, there had been a subsequent period of decline, although happily this had been followed by restoration work, and eventually much of the palace became devoted to a national gallery of the Marche Region.

There were no crowds; it was so much more pleasant just to be with Lydia and Maria. There were no guided tours, no throng to hem us in as I marvelled at the architecture, the interior design and the paintings.

Maria quietly explained how Pasquale Rotondi had saved some of the world's greatest paintings from the Nazis during the war. Rotondi had been director of the national gallery of the Marche Region, and had been asked to hide the art treasures of the Urbino Ducal palace and of the Venetian Academia gallery and of the St Mark's Basilica and Milan's Brera gallery for the duration of the war.

Some of these paintings had been hidden in the cellars of the Urbino Ducal palace; others had been hidden in castles.

When the allies eventually signed the armistice with Italy, Mussolini set up his last stand in the republic of Salo. Signor Rotondi had been ordered to take the paintings there, with the exception of those of St Mark's which were to be sent to the Vatican.

Maria reminded us that these valuable paintings included Piero Della Franscesca's The Duke of Urbino and Raphael's The Betrothal of the Virgins.

Signor Rotondi had been loath to allow the Nazis to have these priceless paintings, and so he had arranged for the Vatican to take all these art treasures, not only those of St Mark's. This meant that he had to make many trips from the Marches Region to the Vatican through Nazi-occupied territory and roadblocks, even sleeping directly over the paintings. At the same time he had had to use delaying tactics with Mussolini's Salo republic.

"No painting was actually lost," whispered Maria finally.

Meanwhile I had been reasoning whether these valuable paintings had been in the cellars of the Ducal palace at the time when our battalion—including Stephen and I—had occupied the city during our advance. Of course, we had not been there long enough to find out for ourselves.

Presently, Lydia, Maria and I wandered through the cool, arcaded courtyard and then up the broad staircase and into the tapestried throne room. From here we walked slowly to the study with its three-dimensional scenes in wood along the walls.

Raphael was born in Urbino, and yet the palace contained only one of his paintings: "La Muta," explained Maria, as I gazed in awe at the portrait of a young woman with bare shoulders. Quietly, Maria then guided as to Piero Della Francesca's 'La Flagellazione' with its figures of character.

The more Maria told us about the history of the city the more I felt glad that the war had not damaged these aesthetically pleasing monuments to the past.

Yet somehow Lydia seemed disinterested, and she tended

to wander off when we were looking at some church paintings.

"There's still much more to show you," remarked Maria as we retraced our steps to the piazza. I looked at my watch.

"Time for colazione," I hinted.

"Ah! You will soon learn Italian," Maria smiled.

"We'd like you to join us for some lunch. Then if we haven't had too much Chianti we can resume our guided tour this afternoon," I suggested.

"Va bene," Maria called out as she led us to a pleasant little cafe off the Piazza Duca Federico. There were several students in the cafe—Urbino was fast becoming a university city again. "Prosciutto." Maria was helping me with my pronunciation as we ate our ham and bread.

I was feeling quite hungry, and we had some melon as well. The Chianti was smoother this time and I thought we were a happy trio. I took a photograph of Lydia and Maria sitting together.

Lydia now seemed more relaxed as she listened to Maria explaining how her father had been a widower for some years. Apparently her Mother had died of leukaemia when Maria was but a child. However, I was wrong about Lydia. As I paid the bill she whispered to me:

"I think I'll lie down this afternoon, David. I have a headache."

Immediately I felt disappointed and deflated. It hardly seemed fair to Maria, to let her down when she was giving up her own time to make our stay more enjoyable.

Lydia, having made her excuses to Maria, turned to me laughingly and said: "I'll expect to see you back at the hotel for dinner."

So we went our own separate ways, and soon I was listening to the quiet voice of Maria explaining the historical significance of some frescos near a church altar. The baroque church was certainly impressive, with more paintings, illuminated manuscripts and reliquaries.

In the Via Barocci Maria showed me more frescos in the oratories, and finally she took me to the fifteenth century house where Raphael was born.

There were many paintings here, but again there was only one painting by Raphael, a Madonna and Child. How peacefully the Child slept.

Strangely, here in this house, I felt more at peace than I had done since the end of the war. This well-maintained house, and indeed the Ducal palace and the churches, possessed an aura that mocked and defied war.

Lydia was presumably now resting in our hotel bedroom, although the church bells may well have been keeping her awake.

At about tea time Maria and I had arrived back at the Manzoni's apartment. She asked me in and made some coffee for us.

"Where's your father?" I asked.

"He's gone to Siena today. There is some art exhibition there, and some of his paintings are being—how do you say it?"

"Displayed."

"Yes, that's right."

"Where do you keep that painting of Stephen? We shall have to think of getting it back to England. For his sister."

"Come and see it. It's hanging up in my bedroom." Maria led me along the passage to a cool shuttered room. The bedroom was larger than I imagined, and there was a typewriter set up on a table away from the area of the bed.

I looked at the painting of Stephen on the white splashed wall. Momentarily I was startled. To see him again as I remembered him in those youthful years when life hung by a thread.

And then I noticed that in the portrait he was wearing a white shirt; but surely it couldn't be the one that I had lent to him in Rome, when he went to meet Joy Mitchell.

I turned away from the portrait. "You use a typewriter a lot?" I enquired.

"Yes," replied Maria. "I write children's books when I'm not having to look after Papa," she smiled.

I walked over to the typewriter to see what words were typed on the paper in the machine.

I sensed her perfume near to me, and turned to meet those brown autumnal eyes.

I kissed her lightly on the lips, before moving to hold her firmly. Then I kissed her more fully and forcibly. As I looked into her eyes however, I followed their gaze to Stephen's portrait.

It was the look in those eyes, I suppose, which caused me to whisper:

"You and Stephen. You had an affair?"

"Affair?" she looked puzzled.

"Una relazione intima." The words and phrases from wartime Italy were returning to me. Her eyes seemed to well up with moist sadness:

"He was so kind, you see. He brought us some food and he looked after my ankle—"

"And?"

"And what?"

"You haven't mentioned his looks, his physical attributes," I goaded her on.

"Oh yes! He was affascinante, and we were young together."

"You are still young." I took her in my arms and kissed her again, but I saw that she was lost in the past.

"Strange—that white shirt in the painting," I remarked.

"Why? Papa found him a white shirt for his sittings."

"That explains it," I said. "I lent a white shirt to Stephen myself once," I added.

"So?"

I thought of that blood-splattered white shirt on the battlefield the day that Stephen disappeared.

"Never mind;" I looked away across the unshuttered windows to the Tuscan hills. Dusk was misting the landscape.

"I must go now—I'd like to see you again before we leave." I spoke with my usual slow words for her to understand.

"Yes," she whispered. "You have to make arrangements with Papa regarding the painting."

"I know; but I also want to see you," I murmured.

"Yes, that would be nice," she smiled.

"And you can tell me more about Stephen." I kissed her again as I left the apartment.

I crossed the Piazzale Roma with its monument to Raphael, making my way back to the hotel. A slight misty rain dampened my face. I thought again of Stephen. It was now clear at any rate that he hadn't been killed in the battle beyond Urbino; somehow he had survived. He had met Maria and then her father. There had been a relationship between him and Maria. But then there was a dark abyss.

Perhaps Maria could lead us further away from the abyss.

★ ★ ★

I was explaining matters as best I could to Lydia over dinner that evening in the hotel, but she did not seem to be listening too much, only now and then. She did, however, look across the table at me when I was telling her about the probable affair between Stephen and Maria.

"It seems that he beat you to it then," she smiled provocatively.

"What do you mean?" I asked.

"You know what I mean, David. She seems to have made a conquest with Stephen and you. I've seen the way you look at her."

"Lydia, please. It's not true; we're here to find out about Stephen and see to the portrait. Remember?"

"Oh! I remember all right but I've had enough, David."

"Enough of what?" I asked.

"This place, these people, your obsession over Stephen. What was all this rivalry between you two?"

We would have to pursue this later I thought. There was no point in having an argument in the dining room where everyone could hear. Lydia left the table, and I poured the last of the wine into my half-filled glass. Perhaps Lydia was right. Friendships can be soured by rivalry; the rivalry between Stephen and lover Joy Mitchell, for instance, and now with Maria Manzoni. At least Stephen hadn't met and seduced Lydia—his shadow lingered over us, however, and

Lydia obviously felt that the shadow was intrusive, upsetting to our relationship. At least that's how it appeared to me.

At breakfast the next morning I suggested to Lydia that we should have a day together out in the countryside, away from the history and architecture of Urbino.

However, she intimated that she was still not feeling well, and in any case she wanted to find a hairdresser near the hotel.

It seemed to me that the sooner I made arrangements with the Manzoni's for payment and despatch of the painting of Stephen then Lydia would feel more accommodating for the rest of the holiday or at least then we could go back to London, if that's what she wanted.

So I made my way once more to the Manzoni's apartment. This time Arturo Manzoni was at home, and he greeted me warmly.

Maria was out shopping for food, and it did not take Arturo and I long to make arrangements for the shipment of the painting. Arturo didn't want to accept anything for the painting, but I insisted on what I considered a reasonable price, bearing in mind the vagaries of artists' fortunes, and the seeming wealth of Margaret in London.

Maria came in just as we were shaking hands on the deal, breaking off her muted singing as she entered the studio.

The sunlight caught the jet of her flowing hair as her brown eyes searched around the room. "We must tidy the room Papa," she admonished Arturo.

"Yes, but not before lunch. Please stay to lunch, David," Arturo turned towards me. "At least I can put off the tidying of this room as long as possible."

I laughed and agreed to stay to lunch.

After drinking Vermouth we sat down to a pleasant lunch of roast veal, bollito misto and vegetables, followed by fresh fruit. My Italian was improving. However, I can't exactly recall how it came about, but both Arturo and Maria burst out laughing when I confused i calzoni with calzone.

We had been talking about food, so the mention of trousers was indeed not appropriate.

I helped Maria with the washing up, and then we had coffee. Arturo said that as Maria had cooked the lunch, he would clean up the studio. Maria and I were alone together at last.

"Where is Lydia today?" Maria looked somewhat apprehensive.

"She's still not feeling too well. Besides, she wanted to get her hair done," I replied.

"Somehow, I don't think that she likes it here," sighed Maria. I kissed Maria on her sensuous lips; she rested her head on my shoulders.

"Maria," I whispered.

"Yes, David."

"I realise that you and Stephen had, how shall I say it, an affair?"

"An affair? Yes, we were lovers for a short time. A short time was all he wanted." Maria's voice was sad.

"I'm sorry. But where did Stephen go after his supposed medical duties?" I asked.

"Supposed?" she looked up at me with curious surprise.

"Well, let's leave that part of it for the moment; I mean, where did he go when he left you, when he left Urbino?" I persisted.

Maria looked down into her coffee cup as though there were tea-leaves that would tell her the unknown future.

"Stephen came here one evening. It was late. Papa was away in Perugia; his brother there was very ill at the time."

"So you were alone?" I asked.

"Yes, but Stephen and I had been alone before, and Papa knew how things were."

"Go on." I persisted.

She looked at me, and it seemed through me. "We made love together. It all seemed so right; the war had moved some way up north. It was very peaceful without the noise of shelling and gunfire. I felt that we had a future together, until—" she hesitated.

"Until?" I urged her to go on.

"The dawn was seeping through the shutters as we lay in bed. I thought Stephen was asleep, until suddenly he looked at me and said that it was time for him to move on. I asked him what he meant. I knew that he had been visiting a farm near San Fratello not far from here. Signor Salvati owned the farm. He was a leading Communist in the area. You have probably noticed that the whole of Urbino is more Communist now, I'm sorry to say."

"What has this to do with Stephen?"

"I'm not sure of all the details, but I'm sure that because of Stephen's friendship with Signor Salvati, Stephen decided to go to Greece."

"To Greece?" This was certainly a surprise to me—until I remembered what Justin Townsend had said about the rumour of Stephen's captivity by the Greek Communists, E.L.A.S.

"Yes, David. I'm sure there was a connection between

Signor Salvati and the Communists, leading to Stephen going to Greece," she sighed again. "It did surprise me at the time, and I wondered how he could leave his medical post."

I didn't like to disillusion her about Stephen and the fact that I did not think it at all likely that Stephen had been helping in any medical work. But it did seem that once again Stephen had marked or injured a girl that I was also seemingly getting involved with.

I took Maria's hands in mine. "After he left, did you not hear from him again?" I asked.

"No; that was the worst thing about it all. I really didn't know whether he reached Greece; he may have died there, but Papa and I assumed he survived the War and went back home."

"So when you heard no more, after a few years, you tried to trace him?"

"Yes," she answered. "Papa thought that Stephen would want the painting, although I knew he didn't want me anymore."

"Poor Maria," I held her in my arms to comfort her. "So you tried to reach him through a London newspaper?"

"Yes." She looked at me with her deep-set eyes. "And you came instead, David."

"Did you not make inquiries with Signor Salvati? Surely he could have helped you?" I felt that I was clutching at straws again.

"I went to make inquiries at the farm. Stephen had told me that Signor Salvati would know how to forward a letter to him; but Signor Salvati did not help me; he persisted in talking about the War, and how he could not give away information useful to the enemy; although by this time I was not sure who was the enemy." Maria paused. It was the first time that I had seen her light a cigarette. She seemed strained. "When the War ended I went to the farm again, but Signor Salvati was no longer alive. His wife was now managing the farm with her young son; they could not help me."

I took out my handkerchief to wipe a tear from Maria's delicate porcelain cheek.

"Can you stay a while?" she asked.

"I'd better get back to the hotel." It was my turn to sigh. "I'll try and see you soon. Before I leave you today, let me have the address of that farm."

Maria wrote down the address. There was an air of sadness in her farewell kiss. Perhaps I reminded her of Stephen in some way, and yet her look seemed one of despair. Was Lydia right? Dredging up the past seemed to bring more sadness than fond memories.

★ ★ ★

I thought that Lydia seemed more cheerful at dinner that evening; she enjoyed the meal, and was not complaining of a headache. A plan had been formulating in my mind that we could possibly continue our mystery search for Stephen in Greece, but in view of Lydia's recent remarks I decided to leave matters until the morning. Besides, where in Greece would we start looking?

Later on we made love in the stillness of the night, but I think we both knew that our physical oneness was lacking in some way; our bodies seemed more like strangers again, striving to obtain the unison we desired. Somewhere in the distance an owl hooted, but the city was still. As I turned over to face the silvery moonlight through the shutters I tried to fathom the truth about Stephen; not only what happened to him, but why was it also that he seemed to leave a trail of sorrow behind with the women in his life; women with whom I also was involved. I thought I detected a slight tearfulness coming from Lydia, but I could not see her face.

I ought to have taken comfort from the fact that at least Stephen couldn't intermeddle in my relationship with Lydia, but then so often punishment is self-inflicted.

At breakfast the next morning I told Lydia what I had learnt the preceding day from Maria, and I described the association between Stephen and Signor Salvati's farm, Stephen's departure for Greece and then the years of silence.

"If I could trace where Stephen exactly went to in Greece, we could go there. After all, we've done all we can do here, and I've seen to the despatch of the painting," I suggested enthusiastically.

"No, David." It was an emphatic negative followed by the slamming down of her coffee cup into the saucer. "As I said before, you have arranged for this painting to be returned to Stephen's family. To take matters any further is merely obsessiveness about one particular man. I want to go back to London now." There was a visible appeal in her blue eyes.

"I'm sure Tom Preston won't mind if I take off another fortnight—as long as I let him know of course." I felt hopeful that I could get Lydia to agree to my ideas. "I'm owed quite a lot of time off."

"I'm not," Lydia cut in.

"I'm positive that Tom won't mind if you have a little more time on the Continent, Lydia." There was a pause. "Besides, how will you spend your evenings in London, if I'm not there?" I asked jokingly.

Lydia was getting up from the table. "Bob Chester seems keen to meet me again; I'll probably take him up on the offer."

"Offer of what, for God's sake? You can't seriously be thinking of fraternising with him, surely?" (How that word fraternising had crept into usage even after the War.)

"Why not?" she spoke over her shoulder as I hurried to catch up with her before she left the dining-room.

"Because, because he's a pasty-faced Italianate big-head, always boasting of his amorous tales. He must live a life of debauchery."

"Italianate? I thought you liked Italians," she smiled knowingly. We were now in the hotel foyer. "I've made up my mind, David; I'm returning to London tomorrow. I can make a suitable train connection."

I stormed over to the lift. "Perhaps you can get Bob Chester to meet you at Victoria," I called out.

"I've already wired him to do so." She seemed much calmer than I was.

★ ★ ★

That last remark of Lydia's was a body blow really. It meant that she had already taken matters into her own hands without consulting me. Why had it all happened like this? Surely she didn't need to go back to London yet. I walked out of the hotel towards the city walls. The weather was cooler; the grim metal clouds swept overhead blanketing a fitful sun. I needed to be alone for a while to think things through.

I walked down a side alley passing two small boys playing together outside a stepped archway entrance to a villa. It was all quiet and restful, and yet Lydia had never seemed settled here. It seemed that I had wrested her from her shipboard romance only to be threatened with her loss to Fleet Street glossiness.

All the signs were that I ought to rush back to the hotel and agree to take Lydia back to London tomorrow; yet somehow I couldn't bring myself to believe that this was right. After all the research I had done so far, to leave off now would perhaps be a sign of weakness that would haunt me all my life.

I couldn't really believe that Lydia was serious about Bob Chester. Possibly I would not be able to get any lead as to where to go in Greece anyway, in which event I would be in London myself within a few days.

So was it bloody-mindedness or pig-headedness or a quest for the truth on my part? Perhaps half-blindness, and an optimistic sense that all would come right in the end.

Anyway, later in the day I told Lydia that if I could make no further progress as to the whereabouts of Stephen, I would be back in London a few days after her.

And there the matter rested; the next morning a feeling of loss descended on me after Lydia's departure, a sense of unknown and uncharted future.

To cheer myself up, I decided to have lunch at the cafe where I had thought Lydia, Maria and I had been so happy together. I had little appetite for the pasta, however, and took solace with a flask of wine. I was fishing in my side pocket for a cigarette when I brought out a crumpled piece of paper on which was written the address of the Salvati farm.

Surely, I thought, there must be a lead at that farm, something that had been kept from Maria all these years. Perhaps I could hire a Lambretta and find my own way through the countryside to the Salvati home.

I drank another glass of wine as the proprietress of the cafe gave me details as to how I could hire a motor scooter and where to get a detailed map of the area.

I made suitable arrangements in the afternoon, having decided that I would ride out to the farm the following morning.

Needless to say, being alone in the hotel that evening, I found solace with the vino, and staggered up to bed quite late at night.

* * *

The next morning I felt somewhat subdued with a mild hangover and a very dry palate.

The weather seemed brighter with the sky tinted with pale blue; it would not be too long before the winter snows fell in the hills.

I had partly memorised my route to the farm, and set off firstly for the village of San Fratello. I passed the buildings being erected in a newer part of Urbino as I left the city walls and then I stopped at the side of the road before I came to the village.

It was a cool day, but I was already hot and sweating; I could see the outline of the village ahead, and the church and bell tower.

We had always considered that the Germans had sited an observation post in the tower. How else could their shelling and mortaring have been so devastatingly accurate? The Bren Gun carriers never had a chance against the Tiger tanks; I lit a cigarette as I leant against the Lambretta, looking at the landscape over the low stone wall. It had been as I was crouching in the shelter of such a wall that the blood-soaked white shirt had been brought to me; the one I had lent Stephen in Rome when he went and seduced Joy behind my back.

Perhaps I wasn't being fair to him. Strange how his portrait had been painted when he was wearing another white shirt. Had he been cleansed of war perhaps?

Soon I was astride the motor scooter, and beyond the village. The navigation was now more difficult, there being several unsigned tracks leading off the road. I had descended into the valley from the ridge and village; a small stream coursed through the low ground. This enabled me to locate from the map the turning towards the isolated farmstead where I hoped, perhaps in vain, that I could learn more about Stephen that would help me to continue my research.

I was reminded of the wartime slogan: "Is your journey really necessary?" And clearly for Lydia it had not been necessary. But then, Regimental ties of comradeship, particularly in wartime, were inviolate.

Whether you liked someone or not, in the Battalion you were all part of the same family. My concern for Stephen, and indeed for the Regiment, surely justified my search.

I eased the motor scooter over a small bridge astride the stream; the track was rough and dusty, but it led to a farmhouse of solid stone, and yet the impression was one of neglect giving an aura of rundown activity.

I parked the Lambretta in an untidy yard of rusting farm equipment; two mongrel type dogs barked and inspected my person, but they did not present any menace. Indeed, they looked sad and somewhat forlorn, like the building. The barking of the dogs had brought an elderly woman to the door at the front of the farmhouse; she was stocky, of medium height, her tanned face cracked and lined, her hair quite grey.

I smiled, but there was no returning smile, and I realised I should have brought Maria with me. My Italian was very limited, and Maria had been helpful in Urbino. Yet I had wanted to come here on my own.

It was easy enough to exchange pleasantries with this woman, but I had the impression that she did not want this intrusion, and there was a sullenness in her dark jet eyes and in her movement.

I tried to explain to her the purpose of my mission to the farm, and mentioned her husband and the War and Stephen's name.

It was clear that it was not just my faltering Italian that was obstructing any progress in our conversation; she evidently had no wish to discuss the War, nor any part her husband had played in it.

I was about to give up my quest when I heard an alien voice call out to me in stilted English: "Can I help you? My mother is not used to visitors." I turned around to face a well-built tall young man; I suppose he was in his early twenties, weather-beaten like his mother, but a broad grin stretched across his face. Black curly hair surmounted a forehead already lined. "I speak a little English, but I forget my school lessons," he laughed. "My father, when he was alive, also taught me." Again he repeated: "How can I help you? Are you interested in the farm and what we do here?"

"No," I answered quickly. "I am searching for an old friend from the War, but your mother…"

"My mother does not want to be reminded of the War." He spoke quickly to his mother in Italian. "You must share our meal with us, and some vino? My name is Giovanni Salvati."

There seemed no reason to stay in this isolated region any longer. As long as Signora Salvati was present I could not talk about the War, as she had closed the door on this.

However, I did not wish to give offence, and the fresh air had given me a rude appetite. And so it was that I told them my name, accepted their hospitality, and I entered the solid stone farmhouse. Mostly I remember the smell; the earthiness and the distinct animal odours, the sparse furniture and the silver-framed photographs over the fireplace.

The windows were small, and the stone flagged room was cool with a lack of sun. It was hardly surprising that I faced another pasta meal, but the mother looked on approvingly as I indulged in her food and the coarse red wine provided by Giovanni.

Slowly, with a pause to consume the pasta, I explained to Giovanni what had brought me firstly to Urbino and then to the Salvati farm.

At first Giovanni simply quaffed his wine, and seemed indifferent to my search. He talked about the weather and the crops and his labourers. I tried to bring the conversation back to the subject of Stephen and his departure to Greece at the time when Giovanni was presumably a young teenager, but he spoke of the lonely life on the farm, and of his mother now becoming too old to help much.

Signora Salvati cleared away the plates. Suddenly, to my surprise, when his mother had left the room, Giovanni whispered, "My mother will rest and sleep shortly. Then we can talk." He smiled confidentially as his mother returned with some thick, black, treacly coffee.

I realised that I must not raise my hopes too much; some young people today liked intrigue, and even if Giovanni proffered any information, how reliable would it be? Even if the information was reliable, would it shed any light as to where Stephen went, presumably in Greece? Why had he covered his tracks so thoroughly? Why had he not told at least his sister where he was going? Perhaps Stephen had died in Greece.

Just to confuse matters even more the vision of the blood-stained white shirt on the battlefield came back to me. Was there a rational explanation for all these matters? Eventually, Signora Salvati removed the coffee cups, and then I heard her slow tread on the staircase and in the room above; presently there was silence apart from the distant lowing of cattle. I offered Giovanni a cigarette which he accepted greedily. Speaking in a conspiratorial whisper he made it clear that when he was clearing out some of his father's possessions after the decease of Signor Salvati he came across a frayed sheet of paper on which there was some writing of his father's.

"I keep it in my wallet, so my mother does not see that I have it." He produced a well-worn faded leather wallet. "My mother never approved of Stefano; he was not a true Communist."

"Communist? I should think not," I interjected. What was Giovanni hinting at as regards Stephen?

He showed me the flimsy paper, but I found the ink-stained writing difficult to understand. Giovanni took back the paper exclaiming, "I will translate it for you."

The gist of the writing which appeared to be part of a letter written from some Communist guerrilla leader in Northern Greece was to the effect that Stephen Hardinge had safely arrived at last in the Northern Greek town of Trikkala, the Greek headquarters of E.L.A.S., and was now operating in the Mount Vitsi region and in Kozani to the Northwest. The letter went on to complain of the lack of military equipment which had been promised to be supplied, but the rest of the letter was clearly missing, and there were no further details.

Giovanni saw the puzzled expression on my face and tried to explain:

"My parents were both Communists; sometimes I think my mother was more, how do you say, Red than my father. There is much Communism around Urbino, but some of us young people prefer Western ideas and politics. Apart from the Partisan groups in Italy, there were groups of course in Yugoslavia and Greece. I think your friend Stephen wanted the adventure of working with Partisans behind the lines."

I interrupted: "He was not wounded when he came to this farm?"

"No; I remember he came one evening. He was not wounded. No blood, no, and he had no armaments with him. At first my mother thought he was a spy or Fifth Columnist but my father seemed to like Stefano."

"How did he get to Greece, do you think? Was it by air?" I asked.

"No. The port of Pesaro is not far from here; the smaller boats would hug the Yugoslav coast and then head Southward, but it took a long time. The only argument that my father had with Stefano was on account of his going to Urbino. My father thought that Stefano should stay here hidden until a pick-up was ready; Stefano seemed to think there was no real risk," laughed Giovanni. "I think he had interests in the town."

My thoughts turned to Maria, and once more I visualized her love for Stephen, and then her sorrow when he left—and yet it seemed that Stephen's feelings in return had had little depth—he had been marking time—just waiting to leave. Toying with people's emotions again, and having his portrait painted in the midst of battles and suffering.

Stephen hadn't been wounded at that stage, that was clear, at least not in Italy, and he had safely made contact with his overseers in Greece; but why had he taken this course? There seemed no logical reason why he had acted in this way. It had been desertion, and yet he had only deserted to engage in warfare elsewhere. Or so it seemed.

I was beginning to find the farmhouse oppressive with stale air, and I felt a strong desire to return to Urbino to see Maria again. The light would soon fade, and I took my leave of Giovanni. He was grateful for the cigarettes which I left with him.

As I mounted the motor scooter I sensed someone watching me from an upstairs half-shuttered window. I looked up to see Signora Salvati peering down at my presence in the farmyard.

There was no cheerful wave as I left, and the dried track soon dusted up with the wheels of the motor scooter, and the farm became obscured from view. Some cows scattered from the noise of the scooter engine, and the birds soared towards the clouds diffused by a gathering sunset.

I slept fitfully that night as my mind tried to assemble the details of the elaborate trail that Stephen had taken only to end up in Greece where his own Battalion subsequently had landed from Italy. Perhaps we had eventually been near him when we strove to disarm the Communist guerrillas after the departure of the Germans from Greece. It all seemed very confused, and then as I tossed and turned in an agitated sleep my thoughts turned to Lydia.

London would now be seeing the beginnings of winter and smog possibly. How would Lydia react to the hardness and vagaries of an English winter after the South African weather to which she was accustomed? Was she really infatuated with Bob Chester? Perhaps I had misjudged him. My hopes that Lydia and I would share an Italian idyllic interlude had been shattered.

* * *

The next morning I wired Tom Preston to tell him I was taking extra leave in order to make further inquiries in Greece. I doubted that he would be too pleased if I was away more than a month, but I was determined to try and find the further links leading to Stephen and what had become of him.

At that time there were restrictions on travel allowances, and I was pondering this matter deeply as I made my way instinctively to Arturo Manzoni's apartment.

Arturo welcomed me into his studio, and I sat looking out at the sunlight glinting on the silvery olive groves as he continued to concentrate on his painting; it seemed to be a painting of a village square with people loitering and greeting one another as a group of young choral boys filed into the church.

After a period of pleasant silence Arturo put down his paint brushes and turned to me:

"You seem to be worried, David. What is worrying you on such a pleasant day?"

"I found out some more information about Stephen yesterday. I went to the farm where he stayed."

"We knew he went to Greece, but that is all."

I told Arturo of what I had learnt from Giovanni Salvati, and how I intended to go to Greece to make a search for Stephen, hoping that he was still alive.

"Stephen is still alive?" Maria came in at that moment carrying her food shopping, her eyes alight.

"I don't know if he's still alive or not, Maria, but I will try and find out," I smiled meaningfully at her.

"Perhaps, it is best not to know anymore." Arturo spoke quietly, his back now to us as he returned to his painting.

Maria seemed to ignore this comment and turning to me she said:

"I know you will go , David—if only for me."

"How will you manage for money?" Arturo broke into the conversation, knowing how restricted British travellers in Europe were at the time over allowances.

"Perhaps I could get a cheap sea passage from Pesaro," I suggested. "But I would have liked to have gone to Athens first before going North; I still have one or two contacts in Athens from my army days, and they would probably be able to give me help and guidance."

"I think a sea voyage at this time of year is not advisable; besides it would probably take some time. No, you can make arrangements to fly from Rome to Athens." Arturo had now become brisk and enthusiastic.

"But—" I began.

"It is all right. I can lend you the money for the air fare," he smiled.

"That's very kind of you. I'll certainly pay you back when

I can." He had correctly read my thoughts and doubts.

"It is best if you travel by rail to Rome from here. Maria will explain your route, and then you can book your tickets." He went back to his painting. "Train time-tables frustrate and infuriate me."

Smilingly, Maria ushered me out of the studio, and we sat together in the smaller room where I had previously been dined and wined by the Manzoni's.

I held her hand. "Do you really want me to do this trip?" I asked earnestly.

"Yes, I think it is best, David. I need to know whether Stephen is alive or not and...," she hesitated.

"Go on," I encouraged her.

"And whether he is now perhaps married or ever thinks of me."

"He may not be in Greece any longer."

"I realise that, and I appreciate that if he's not in Greece then you will have to give up the search."

"Maria, does he still mean so much to you?" I had to ask her. A single tear floated down her cheek from her sorrowful deep-brown eyes:

"I was so happy with Stephen." She turned to me. "You are like him in many ways," she laughed through the tears.

"Ah! But he was the tall, fair-headed Adonis with grey-green eyes that they all fall for," I said bitterly.

"Who is all?" She looked up appealingly at me,

"Sorry, I don't mean that. I've no doubt he was very fond of you."

My words sounded hollow. I looked at Maria. She really was very attractive. I took her in my arms and kissed her on her full lips.

"In some ways you are much nicer than Stephen," she whispered. I thought of Lydia's remarks about Maria, when she hinted at Maria making conquests of Stephen and I.

Somehow Lydia would always be there, in my mind and thoughts. I released Maria from our embrace, and sadly she turned away.

Our conversation became more formal, and we talked about my forthcoming journey.

Two days later I was being trundled South West by the Italian railway system towards Rome and the airport.

Before I left Rome I had time to write to Lydia, explaining my plans. I asked her to be patient and understanding. I told her that I still loved her very much. In more practical terms I asked her to help Tom Preston as much as she could in the office, and to keep an eye on my flat, especially as she had a key to it. Finally, in a jocular fashion, I asked her to beware of journalists, especially one who was a mutual acquaintance.

★ ★ ★

But as the plane soared in a bright blue sky towards Athens I knew it wasn't as easy as that. When eventually I returned to London, the relationship between Lydia and myself would have to be put under a microscope; we would have to face up to any differences and hopefully overcome them. Or would it be too late?

There were not many passengers on the plane; winter was ahead, and my fellow travellers seemed to be businessmen and not holiday makers.

I thought of the two contacts in Athens who might be able to help me. I knew Bill Wyatt was still there. He had been a war correspondent who initially had been attached to me in the taking of Urbino. I had not thought that our paths would cross again, but during the difficult landings at Salonika after the German withdrawal—difficult because of the heavily-mined gulf—he joined our landing craft after we left Athens. Eventually Bill had landed back in Athens, and I had seen him there once or twice in the Grande Bretagne Hotel—the meeting place virtually taken over by cosmopolitan military personnel.

Then I heard that he had been a United Nations observer in the Greek civil war of 1946 to 1949. We had since kept in touch; I knew he was still in Athens and that he continued to be a correspondent, now for a London paper. Unlike that other journalist Bob Chester, Bill Wyatt was a strong character or so it seemed to me; he was tall with dark black wavy hair, and carried no surplus weight. Perhaps he had changed now.

Then there was the American Ken Dacre who had married Sofia Nestorides just after V.E. Day. Ken had been in UNRRA[1] and I had been instrumental in helping to distribute his medical and food supplies in and around Kavalla in Northeast Greece. Ken had been so grateful at the time that he had asked me to his wedding in Athens. I had 'borrowed' a jeep and had made the long mountainous journey through a country that had been ravaged by endless war. Sofia was dark and fairly short, as I remembered her, with a smallish head, yet somehow she engendered a sense of willowiness; her eyes had been autumnal brown and thoughtful. I remember that Ken had been in Athens to negotiate more supplies for the North East and that was how he had met Sofia who was a Greek Red Cross nurse.

After I had been demobilised, they had written to me to

tell me of the addition to their family, a baby girl named Athena, and they had proffered an open invitation to me. I understood that they were both working at a local hospital in the outskirts of Athens. I remembered that Ken was bespectacled with a small moustache and with copper blond hair; I supposed he was of medium height, and like Bill Wyatt and myself he was in his early twenties at that time in 1945.

The plane was dipping over Piraeus and I could make out the bay where the British cruiser had housed Churchill during his important 1944 Christmas meeting with Archbishop Damaskinos and the E.L.A.S. representatives. Sadly it was not the time of year for the orange blossom, and as we approached Athens the sun was setting over the myriad islands; we were now over the Acropolis which the Germans had forbidden the Greeks to visit during their occupation.

The landing was reasonably smooth, and I soon managed to seek out a taxi. I found myself instinctively asking the driver to make for the Grande Bretagne hotel, although clearly such a hotel would be too expensive for me in my present circumstances.

In any event the hotel was full; I decided it was best to phone Bill Wyatt; after all, he was a bachelor who would not be too inconvenienced if I shacked up with him temporarily, whereas Ken and Sofia had a marital establishment, and a very young daughter to maintain. My ingress would probably be inconvenient and a burden to them.

I could not get any reply on Bill's phone, although as I peered outside into the square the dusk was descending quickly, and I thought that he would be home from work unless he was away on an assignment.

Feeling frustrated, and thinking that I must make my way

to some small hotel further away from the centre of Athens, I picked up my luggage and struggled through the crowded lobby towards the front entrance hall of the hotel.

Then I saw him; it wasn't Bill Wyatt, but Ken Dacre. That copper blond hair and owl-like face peering through his spectacles; there he was saying goodbye to some important looking plain-clothed officials. Indeed, it seemed strange to see Ken no longer in his UNRRA uniform himself, but tidily dressed in a grey suit.

"Ken," I called out as he turned to make for the square outside.

He turned around, and a look of surprise, followed by a huge grin, lit up his face. He came striding towards me:

"David, what the hell are you doing here?"

I smiled back." It's a long story."

So Ken guided me out of the large hotel, along the crowded wide pavements, and towards Giannakis—it had to be Giannakis of course—the most popular Athenian cafe located in the square: the lights gave a burnished glow to his hair as he commandeered a table in the cafe, and the customary thick cups of black coffee appeared in front of us together with the glasses of cold water.

After Ken had quickly explained that he had been meeting some Swiss pharmaceutical officials at the Grande Bretagne hotel in connection with supplies to the hospital, I launched into a full explanation of my sudden appearance in Athens. It might of course seem very much a coincidence, our meeting like this, but in truth both during the War and the years after it the Grande Bretagne had become very much a meeting place for British and American military and civilian personnel, either stationed or passing through the capital.

I asked after Sofia and Athena, whereupon he persuaded me to return home with him to meet them, and to stay whilst I made my specific plans to travel North.

We finished our coffee, and Ken then led me to the pleasant residential area of Kolonaki. Ken and Sofia's home was in an apartment building, and he pointed out Mount Hymettus as we entered the main door. Their flat was on the first floor, and I imagined this was convenient when Athena was smaller; now apparently she was eight years old.

I was flattered by the welcome from Sofia and the excitement of Athena. Sofia was calm as I had remembered her, and listened with that thoughtful expression of hers as Ken went through the details of my quest in Greece.

Presently Sofia left us to prepare a meal, and I remember enjoying the food. It had been some time since I had eaten a solid meal, and the traditional moussaka was very appetizing. Sofia then produced some almond cakes followed by cheese pies. Ken ensured that my glass of retsina did not become empty.

Athena seemed intrigued at her new English friend; she was already bilingual, and I promised that I would take her to Giannakis the next day for some ice-cream. She had her father's fair hair, but her mother's expressive brown eyes.

It wasn't long before Sofia was seeing to the washing up, and ensuring that Athena was safely tucked in bed. Ken and I were left to ourselves as I gazed through the window at Mount Hymettus. Suddenly I thought of Lydia and how I missed her.

What was it about this place with all its sparse but comfortable furniture and furnishings? It was the people in it, the family scene completed now with Athena. It was something I had never had. Oh yes, I had travelled the world all right, mostly at the government's expense, but there had been no home life, only sometimes a shared pillow with some lady friend of the moment. I should not have let Lydia return to England, at least not without me. I would write to her tomorrow.

"From the top flats upstairs you can just see the outline of the sea," Ken explained, interrupting my thoughts.

In this built-up area it was difficult to imagine the sea being so near; there was a clear moon in the sky. I closed my eyes and conjured up the memory of my time in Greece during the War and the heady mountain air of North East Greece with its thyme, cistus and lavender.

Ken recharged my glass again, and then sat back in his armchair. He peered over his spectacles at me:

"Of course, David, you only remember the German withdrawal in Greece, and the British occupation when we had the E.L.A.S. troubles and then V.E. day—but before all that there was the Italian and German invasion when the Greeks so bravely resisted, and the British and Commonwealth help was so woefully light and then after that part you remember…"

"After?" I interrupted. "Didn't matters settle down after our departure?"

"No, it took a long time." Ken hadn't lost his American drawl. "There was a Greek civil war from 1946 to 1949."

"All that time? How did it end eventually?"

"After the British had moved out for economic reasons, the civil war was eventually concluded by the Greek national army; they were supported by U.S. arms and advisers. I think I should tell you something of these matters. It may help you to understand the problems and situations in which your friend Stephen found himself—if he survived V.E. Day that is." Ken lit his pipe as I followed his gaze through the window to the clear sky, now star-strewn.

I turned to him. "I suppose there were three stages really, weren't there? The wartime invasion of Greece by the Italians, and then the Germans; that was when the British and Commonwealth forces landed in Greece to help the Greeks, but our help was sadly too little; then the German withdrawal followed by the British occupation with all the E.L.A.S. communist troubles—that was when you and I met just before V.E. day; it seemed then that the troubles with the E.L.A.S. guerrillas were over."

"Yes, that's right," confirmed Ken, "and then your British formations left before the third stage—the three year civil war which seemed endless until the Greek national army, equipped by the British and then subsequently by the Americans, eventually became stronger than the communist forces. Can you imagine the grim reality of Greek fighting Greek in this way, truly a Greek tragedy."

Sofia came into the room quietly, and sat with us. Her voice was scarcely more than a whisper as she spoke: "It was our Greek peasants who suffered so much, so many of them innocent of anything except that they were Greek."

"You will of course remember the Olympic Games in London in 1948." There was tiredness but not bitterness in Ken's voice.

"Yes, of course," I replied. "I was lucky enough to see that Dutch woman. What an athlete she was."

"The ancient ceremony of the first Olympic torch to be lit and then relayed to London took place at Olympia near

Katakolon; but there was killing in that area even at that time—a time when the ceremony is meant to recall the eventual peace in the Peloponnesian Wars hundreds of years ago. A cruel turn of fate." Ken knocked out his pipe.

Suddenly I felt depressed with all this talk of strife and tragedy.

Sofia smiled at me. "You must be very tired, David. You have heard enough for one day; your bedroom is ready."

I expressed my thanks, bade goodnight to my kind host and hostess, and retired to bed.

It had been a long day, ending with firstly my self-pity because of Lydia not being with me, and then with sadness when I began to learn of the severity of the Greek civil war; but I had been so lucky to find Ken and Sofia again.

If I had similar good fortune I might also be able to trace Bill Wyatt in the next few days.

★ ★ ★

The next morning there was a cold wind blowing off the mountains, and I realised that Athens would soon be embraced by signs of winter.

At least it was dry as I accompanied Sofia and Athena on a bus to Constitution Square. Sofia showed me the shops and cafes and tavernas, and as promised I bought a large coloured confection of ice-cream for Athena whilst Sofia and I had the traditional black coffee at Gianakis. Alas, at this time of year it was too cold to sit on the pavement. A scud of wind was marshalling and scattering the last piles of dried leaves.

"You understand, I hope David, that Ken had to go to hospital as usual today." Sofia sounded apologetic.

"Of course," I hastened to reply. "Should you not also be there? Please do not stay away on my account."

"No, that's all right. I'm always home on Tuesdays. That is the day I do not have any help at home to look after Athena and so on." As Sofia spoke she waved to some friends of hers. The cafe was very much a meeting place for Athenians.

"Tuesdays—I remember that your countrymen were often loth to act in any significant way on a Tuesday," I laughed.

"Yes, ever since Constantinople fell on a Tuesday that has been so," Sofia smiled over her small thick coffee cup. The smile gradually left her face as she turned sadly to me and said, "You know we Greeks were proud to be Britain's only ally at one stage of the World War; we would not have had it any other way. There was a saying at the time: 'Greece has taught civilization how to live—now it will teach civilization how to die.' Then there were military misunderstandings between allies, and Britain could not spare more than a small expeditionary force as you remember."

"I remember how you routed the Italians," I continued.

"Yes, but when they had the help of the German Army the enemy was too strong for us with all their arms and air superiority. Can you imagine what it was like, for instance, having to send home our wounded peasants whilst the Germans commanded the military hospitals for their own cases?"

I placed my hand over hers to comfort her: "It's all over now; it is best to forget these things."

"I can never forget. There were such German atrocities—they requested the food, and there was only soup for the children. The Greek adults had nothing, and then there were the SS camps. Still, we did manage to help thousands of allied military personnel to escape from Greece; the peasants were so brave." She dabbed a tear from her eye with a linen handkerchief.

"And then in return we bombed Piraeus." My laughter was indeed hollow.

"We understood that. You had to do it. Then we thought that after the Liberation that all would be well again, but first there was the E.L.A.S. resistance to British occupation—when at last it seemed that this had been resolved, we then had the civil war."

"Poor Greece, poor Sofia," I muttered. Looking at Athena I said hopefully, "Her world should be better."

"Especially in the Spring." Sofia was smiling again. "With the orange blossom, cyclamen and anemones, the translucent blue sea and then the olive trees and hot sun."

Now that Sofia had closed her book of sadness, at least temporarily anyway, I told her that I wanted to contact Bill Wyatt, my war correspondent friend who was now a journalist.

"You can phone from our apartment. He probably stayed at the Grande Bretagne for some time but he may have moved out by now. If you have his address it should not be difficult to find him unless he's away on a job."

And so I phoned from Ken and Sofia's apartment, and I ascertained that Bill Wyatt was due back at his bachelor flat that evening at about six o'clock after visiting the docks at Piraeus to report on some visiting dignitaries.

The moon was already climbing over the Acropolis when I phoned Bill after another appetizing meal cooked by Sofia.

It seemed strange to hear Bill's deep voice after this gap of years. He sounded surprised and delighted to hear that I was in Athens, and suggested some drinks in a local bar that evening. However, I explained to him that I was staying with Ken and Sofia, and that I needed to speak to him and perhaps get his assistance.

Bill agreed to meet me the next evening—Yes, at the Grande Bretagne, but he indicated that we would then go to a taverna which he knew and which he thought that I would like.

I went to bed feeling that I was making some progress; I had even managed to send a postcard to Lydia.

★ ★ ★

The darkness was descending over Constitution Square as I made my way to the Grande Bretagne. There was the usual motley collection of a mixed cultured throng in the front entrance hall of the hotel. It was fascinating to try and determine the various languages that were being spoken. In any event I had always found it difficult learning more than the basic words of Greek.

I had only been waiting for a few minutes when the tall frame of Bill Wyatt peered over the mêlée, and we caught each other's eye. He seemed just the same, except perhaps his thick black hair was greying at the sides.

He gripped my hand vigorously until eventually I retrieved my limp fingers from his grasp.

"It's good to see you; you gave me quite a surprise when you phoned last night." He was already leading the way out of the hotel.

"It's good to see you too," I called out as Bill strode out to a parked jeep.

"You still have a jeep?" I asked with surprise.

"Let's just say that it's an old war souvenir," he grinned.

"The same old Bill," I laughed. "You always managed better than I at scrounging."

"This is all legitimate. I could have had a small car for my work, but this is better for all the rough roads I come across. Now I know just the place for our little chat." Soon he was engineering the jeep through the traffic and out of the city centre towards the suburbs of Athens.

I felt I was in safe hands and looked forward to our evening together. Before long we were travelling through the poorer suburbs and out towards the coast.

"Do you remember how we were cooped up in that landing craft almost stationary while the Navy cleared the gulf leading to Salonika?" he asked.

"Yes. I also remember you complaining of the hard rations," I chuckled.

"And then as soon as we landed at Salonika that old Greek lady came up to you and said 'thank God you've come'."

"Yes. It wasn't until I saw some surly-looking armed E.L.A.S. guerrillas that I realised what she was driving at," I added.

"Well, she had endured the German atrocities, and then the pillaging by the Greek Communists."

"And it was a bleak winter," I remarked.

Bill parked the jeep by the side of an unpretentious taverna; the coloured lights at this time of year had a pathetic appearance, and they wavered in the night breeze.

Soon we were drinking the retsina from small copper tankards and eating goat's cheese, and reminiscing over past history and the lighter moments of our experiences. It must have been after eight o'clock before I explained in detail what had now brought me back to Greece in the early Fifties. Bill pricked up his ears when I mentioned Urbino: After all, it was at Urbino that Bill and I had first met.

"We actually had a comfortable bed that night in Urbino," he mused.

"Only for one night," I reminded him. "Then we were on our way to join battle again against the Germans."

"Yes. I imagine it was always hell being in the infantry."

I pursued my story about Stephen and the various investigations I had made, and then asked Bill for his views.

"It's a tall order, old man. It's one thing to assume that your friend Stephen landed in Northern Greece, but at that time there were rival guerrilla groups. Apart from the E.L.A.S. Communist group, there was for instance the non-Communist Republican band called EDES—but they were mainly in the North-West of Greece. The E.L.A.S. became the more powerful group, and they had always planned to seize power when the Germans left. Even when it was all over there was a civil war."

"Yes, I know that." As I sipped the retsina I was beginning to get a defeatist feeling about the whole enterprise.

"Cheer up," grinned Bill. "At least you don't have to undergo another Dunkirk at Kavalla this time."

"You mean that time when we were so thin on the ground, and before Churchill came to Athens to mediate. Still, we went back there eventually," I countered.

"Kavalla, that place has happy memories for me," sighed Bill.

"Yes, I thought at the time that you might get hitched to that ENSA girl."

"My work is rather disruptive to contemplate marriage— at least that's what I always say." He finished his wine and we settled the bill.

The fresh air and sea breezes seemed to instil new life into me as Bill drove back to the city. The Acropolis was shrouded in clouds that night. The streets were much quieter now. Bill took me back to Ken and Sofia's apartment.

I thanked him for the evening, but before he left he said, "I think perhaps Salonika or Kavalla would be a sound place to make for first of all, and then we can think about Kozani and the mountains."

"We?" I questioned.

"Let's sleep on it, David. We're both tired now anyway. I'll phone you tomorrow. Cheers."

With that farewell, the jeep roared into life and it was soon out of sight. I settled back in the apartment and told Ken and Sofia of the entertaining evening in the taverna, but when eventually I went to bed the way forward seemed an endless labyrinth.

★ ★ ★

The next morning Ken and Sofia went off to the hospital, and as was their custom apparently they took Athena to her school en route.

The thought of waiting for Bill to telephone and being cooped up in the flat was not very appealing. The weather was still dry, and I decided to go for a walk. There was still some warmth in the sun.

My steps took me to the Royal Gardens; I remembered the palm trees and judas trees from visits long ago. I sat for a few minutes on one of the park benches near some pepper trees. I could hear the trickle of a fountain near at hand.

I thought of the chapter after chapter of Greek tragedy.

Perhaps it was understandable that my mind turned to the British landings after the Germans withdrew. The Communist red slogans had been daubed around all the famous landmarks in Athens, even below the Acropolis, and lit up at night.

We had been supplying the left-wing guerrillas with arms and equipment so that they could engage the occupying German forces, but instead these guerrillas used the arms and equipment to fight the right-wing guerrilla groups—and then they had caused terror to the supporters of the right-wing guerrillas in the mountains.

After the Germans left, many of these E.L.A.S. guerrillas moved down from the mountains and converged on Athens. There were demonstrations, food shortages and spiralling inflation.

This had been followed by a General Strike—and then the shooting began. Bloodied bodies coated the pavements as British troops had to engage in action against their Greek allies.

We had been originally earmarked for Greece as a rest from the severe and long fighting in Italy—only to be attacked by our own Allies. Shells and mortar bombs rained on the small British enclave around the Grande Bretagne hotel—the Communist E.L.A.S. forces occupied most of the city, and their armed civilians sympathizers silently passed into the British occupied buildings to take shots at innocent British soldiers. Even some of the British and American press seemed hostile at the time.

In the early days of this uprising the E.L.A.S. superiority in arms was very worrying; fortunately for me our brigade was sent to Salonika.

There were very many young girls in the E.L.A.S. ranks, but even so the E.L.A.S. atrocities against prisoners and mothers and children became well known.

Then Churchill came to Athens at Christmas, 1944, and there was an attempt by the guerrillas to destroy the Grande Bretagne hotel. This was not successful, but in any event Churchill was based on *HMS Ajax*, a cruiser in Piraeus port. He did, however, travel to the British Embassy for conferences, and one wonders what crisis would have developed if he had been hit by a sniper's bullet. As a result of these conferences, Archbishop Damaskinos was appointed Regent, and gradually we were reinforced by further troops and gained the ascendancy.

By Mid-January peace came back to Athens, but it was not until February that an uneasy Agreement was signed.

Originally our brigade, having landed at Salonika, had pushed out to Drama and Kavalla, but our tenure of Kavalla airfield was impossible with E.L.A.S. guerrillas on the surrounding mountains. A cruiser had enabled us to evacuate, Dunkirk style, at Kavalla. However, after the so-called peace agreement we returned to Kavalla—that was when I met Ken. My thoughts returned to the present as an elderly Jewish citizen came to sit alongside me on the park bench:

"You're English?" he asked.

"Is it so obvious?" I laughed.

"I have been to London. I speak a little English. You are here on holiday perhaps?"

I hesitated. "Not exactly. I have some old wartime friends in Athens that I am visiting."

"Ah! The War. It was terrible here, was it not? The Germans took about eighty thousand Jews to their concentration camps. They would be interrogated at the SS headquarters in Merlin Street and then taken to the camp Haidari. There were few who came out of Haidari alive. My son died there."

I looked at his lined brown leathery face, his quiet clothes and black hat. I followed his gaze towards a line of cypress trees, but his gaze was blurred with tears.

It was still too soon after the end of the War for the world to realise the full extent of the horrors of the Holocaust. I bade farewell to this stranger who had disturbed my own thoughts, and entered a small cafe just outside the park.

Slowly I sipped the black coffee and listened to a heated conversation on the next table. It was difficult for me to make out all the words as the two middle-aged men spoke so rapidly with their arms waving expressively—but I knew what they were arguing about. It was politics as usual. In Greece you were either Right or Left, the chasm was never bridged.

I should have felt hungry by now, but I decided to return to the apartment. I wanted a rest from all the complicated trials of Greek history and politics. It was just as well that I returned before lunch; the phone was ringing as I entered the flat.

It was Bill on the phone. "David, is that you?" he barked out excitedly.

"Yes, there's no one else here," I chuckled.

"Look, I've managed to convince my newspaper boss that it's time that I reported on the progress of revival of the tobacco industry in the Kavalla area and also on how the mountain peasants are coping with peace at last. I know that Kavalla is further East than perhaps you need to go, but this way I can combine business with pleasure."

"You mean that you can come that far with me?" I asked enthusiastically.

"Yes. You can relive old times in Kavalla before you move on," he laughed. "Although we could fly up to Salonika, I think we'll drive up there in the old jeep. We're bound to need the jeep up there. Can you be ready the day after tomorrow?"

"Of course. I'll explain the position to Ken and Sofia," I answered.

"That's settled then. By the way, David, I can only be with you for a fortnight. I shall have to return to Athens then for other assignments. In any case I want to return South before the winter snows set in. The good news is that I can provide you with sufficient funds for your enterprise."

"I understand! Thanks a million-Drachma." I added laughingly—"I'll see that I repay you in due course."

The remainder of the telephone conversation was taken up with the finer details of our preparations, and Bill told me that he would call for me after breakfast on the day of departure .

I put the phone down with a sigh of relief. It wasn't just that I was taking another step forward in my search for Stephen and in my quest to learn what had become of him; there were too many tragic memories in the history of Athens overshadowing all one did or thought here, particularly it seemed in winter time. I needed to leave the Athenian winter.

I looked forward to the crispness of the mountains and the humanity of the peasants and the waters around Kavalla.

★ ★ ★

I remember having a convivial last evening with Ken and Sofia and Athena which resulted in a slight hangover the following morning as I helped Bill to load up the jeep.

Once we had left the environs of Athens, however, my head soon cleared, and Bill drove expertly on the narrow roads through the mountain passes.

I noticed that there were still Bailey bridges in position over some of the rivers and gullies; it would take a long time before proper communications were restored in Greece.

Occasionally we passed a bus or lorry with an icon swinging against the driver's windscreen. Later on we stopped near Larissa to eat our bread and goat's cheese; there was a quiet at the mountain side, a peaceful solitude. Wintry clouds gusted across the pale sun. The hills were a rugged brown; the valleys looked dried out, but the air was wonderful.

By the afternoon we were heading towards the coast roads, leaving Mount Olympus to the West. The Greek summer was lingering on, and the fiery beech and plane trees were still clothed with leaves.

The jeep had behaved well and Bill showed no sign of tiredness as we neared Salonika. As night fell I could make out the silhouette of the White Tower overlooking the waterfront and promenade.

Bill turned to me and smiled. "That's where you and I came ashore," he said.

"For the Liberation," I added.

"The Liberation?" He spoke mockingly. "For the Greeks it certainly didn't mean the end of trouble. Perhaps at long last they have found peace now."

We had been driving along Vasileos Konstantinou, and I had thought that Bill would drive to the Mediterranean Hotel where he and I could reacquaint ourselves with its food and bar. However, I soon found that we were in the old part of the city, and the streets were flanked by two-storey houses long established. Their ochre brown and white colours were now dulled by the grime and weathering of time. It was quite dark when Bill stopped the jeep at one of these houses, and led me through the stone-pillared entrance to the front door.

"I thought I would surprise you; some old friends of mine live here," Bill smiled. "They are expecting us."

Later that evening Bill and I were lying in a state of pleasant tiredness in beds of a sparsely furnished room.

I found it difficult to keep my eyes open as Bill explained that Constantine and Marina Sophoulis and their daughter, Zoe, were a family he had met when he and I first visited Salonika in 1944. Before we finally went to sleep I remember him joking about the fact he had first met their daughter Zoe at the bar of the Mediterranean Hotel; that she had invited him to come to her parents' home to learn Greek; and that she had been chaperoned by her father as Bill had been pressed to wrestle with the Greek alphabet and language rather than being allowed to make amorous advances.

His last words before unconscious sleep were:

"So you see, my relationship with *Zoe* has always been platonic, although she's older now and not so much under the wing of her parents."

* * *

The next morning I awoke duly refreshed, and watched Marina Sophoulis as she waved goodbye to her husband, Constantine; he set off for his daily work as a pharmacist, a farmakio in a shop in Salonika. Both of Zoe's parents were now middle-aged with greying hair, but with athletically slim figures; they had given Bill and I a friendly reception with courteous and old-fashioned formality. I had noticed that Constantine continually passed his fingers over his traditional amber beads, the Eastern Mediterranean custom I was to see so much of. Marina set about the task of maintaining the stove in what I took to be the sitting room.

Bill explained to me that he was going into the shopping area with Zoe to get some maps, and I've no doubt that I expressed surprise when Bill added that Zoe would come at least as far as Kavalla with us. I looked at Zoe for a moment; she was tall with her mother's aquiline features, and with her father's grey eyes; her eyelashes were long and striking; her hair was as long as Lydia's but darker and she possessed the athletic build of her parents. I would say that she was attractive without being pretty. She had a certain Levantine beauty.

I was wondering how the three of us would get on together in proximity to one another over a period of weeks. Perhaps she read my thoughts:

"I will be able to help you as an interpreter," she smiled at me.

"I've no doubt," I replied. "Your English is very good." I was prepared to leave matters there, but she added:

"I lost a brother in the mountains. Perhaps it will be possible to visit his grave. We shall see."

"Zoe works at the archaeological museum in Salonika, but she is able to come with us. At any rate for a time," added Bill.

I waved them off in the jeep, and then decided to make the most of a sunny late October morning before the traditional Greek siesta.

I did not want to interrupt the morning's activities of Bill and Zoe, so I decided to explore the western side of the city, away from the archaeological museum.

I strolled down the main thoroughfares, now being modernised with fashionable shops, thinking that I would look at some of the Byzantine churches with their wall paintings and mosaics. As I moved through the market displays of sausages, cheese, olives and grilled octopus I thought of the long history of these people here; there had been five hundred years of Turkish rule, and there had been four major fires the last of which in 1917 had destroyed most of the city.

As I passed a local citizen at work painting icons, it seemed comforting to muse that this authentic tradition had continued since the Byzantine era.

During my previous visit and when I had been involved in the difficult times with E.L.A.S. it had been a very cold winter; there had been no power, little fuel and there had been a drinking water scarcity. I had sometimes wondered if we would ever leave Salonika alive. The guerrilla forces ranged against us seemed well armed, and certainly they had outnumbered us.

Eventually my walk took me to the remains of the old city wall, and I entered the church, Agii Apostoli. The Byzantine art within the church was remarkable; there was a charming mosaic there showing the bathing of the infant Jesus whilst the midwife tests the heat of the water; the baby seemed apprehensive in the nurse's arms.

It was not far to walk to the market, the Bezesteni, and I soaked up the oriental atmosphere of the bazaar shops of clothes and jewellery.

Presently I sat in a cafe and ordered iced coffee; I felt like a tourist as I wrote my postcards to Lydia and Maria and Tom Preston. There was much that I wanted to say to them all, but it would have to wait. I thought of Lydia receiving my card, and then reading it in a crowded tube train as she travelled to Tom's office; they would perhaps compare notes. There would soon be smog in London, and I conjured up a vision of Bob Chester taking Lydia into El Vinos—but perhaps it had gone further than that between them.

And what about Maria, who after all these years still thought and dreamt so much of Stephen, willing him to be alive?

The words on the postcards seemed trite and formal, and with Tom Preston I asked for his patience and forbearance with my extended tour of Italy and Greece.

I watched the people scurrying to and fro outside the cafe; they seemed fairly cosmopolitan, but this veneer had a Byzantine core I felt sure. It had been one of Alexander's generals who had founded Salonika a few hundred years BC. The general's name had been Cassander. What a sensible fellow Cassander had been, I smiled to myself; he had not only married a half-sister of Alexander, but had also given the town her name.

It was a mystical city, lacking uniformity, a city where history meets modernity. The visitor to the city was pulled back into history and then suddenly impelled again to the present time.

Yet it was a haunted city as well, haunted by the liquidation of most of the Jewish population, the many Thessalonians transported to Auschwitz in 1943.

In spite of all this the City had a cultural and literary prominence with its hundreds of Kafenias or coffee shops used as public meeting places, and obscured from view the hashish dens to which the authorities turned a blind eye.

It was the sea and weather that determined and moulded the city; the sea where St. Paul disembarked from Philippi to found an apostolic see, and the weather with its dense fogs in winter and the oppressive Vardar wind in summer. The gunmetal sea would change through the spectrum to cobalt, indigo and azure. Then I started thinking of Kavalla. In fact I began to fret over going to Kavalla as it seemed that it would take us further away from the area I wished to search, and I scarcely wished to play the odd man out if Bill and Zoe had some sort of personal relationship.

However, as I walked back to the Sophoulis home I realised that my thoughts were ungrateful ones. They were doing so much for me already that a few days further delay seemed immaterial.

After the long siesta there was much activity in the kitchen quarters where Marina Sophoulis and her daughter Zoe were preparing the evening meal.

That evening I drank ouzo for the first time since being in Greece during the War, and it was a convivial evening I remember. The main part of our meal was a doner kebab, the lamb having been roasted on a revolving spit; it was a change from the fish and sea food so predominant around the Aegean sea front.

In the mixed conversation of Greek, English and French I suddenly felt very tired, and I have a recollection of Constantine Sophoulis declaiming some of the Greek tragedy of the fire and history of Salonika and of the mass deportation by the Germans of sixty thousands Jews to Poland during the War. The earthquakes in the region came later.

I went to bed feeling pleased that Zoe spoke English and French apart from Greek, and if she wanted to visit her brother's grave in the mountains this might help us in our inquiries—although my inquiries for Stephen logically would start with the villages in the Grammos mountains where at least it was known he had first operated in Greece. We were to leave for Kavalla the next day to search for a whisper of history.

★ ★ ★

I sat in the back of the jeep, somewhat uncomfortably, watching the kilometres drift by; Bill Wyatt's curly black hair frizzed up in the breeze. Clearly, Zoe was enjoying the journey—and Bill's company of course; she seemed to have a genuine rapport with him, and I felt that they were perhaps retracing old journeys made together.

I was glad that Bill was driving along the coast as much as possible; I had no wish to return to Drama; I remembered it as oppressively hot and Communistic when I had been stationed there around VE day. In fact it did not take us long to reach Kavalla, a port that depended on the fishing industry and tobacco export. Even though it was now early November the buildings and boats seemed to shine with the blue, yellow and red—the cheerful colours of paint used locally. There was a busy purpose to the fishermen piling their nets on the harbour front, and the blue ceiling of sky gave an aura of cheerful anticipation. I could trace the outline of the island of Thasos with the silvery olive trees and beaches. In Kavalla itself, the aqueduct continued to dominate the scene.

My own wartime sojourn in Kavalla and Thasos had been short-lived, and Bill had not been with me at the time. Clearly, however, he and Zoe knew the port well, and they parked the jeep at a quiet hotel half way up the hill which formed a backcloth to the harbour and boats and caiques.

They soon took themselves off together whilst I was content to freshen up and sit on the balcony of my hotel bedroom. It would be no use champing at delays during the siesta.

That evening we ate some delicious red mullet whilst Bill and Zoe described to me their spring and summer outings to the sandy beaches between Kavalla and Alexandroupolis; it seemed to me that Zoe would probably like to give permanence to their relationship, to become the 'woman of the house' as they say in Greece. Perhaps Bill would come to this way of thinking. Clearly he was very fond of Zoe, but I could understand the innate restlessness of a correspondent.

The distant harbour lights and Greek music, and the intake of some local wine induced me to consider abandoning my search for Stephen, but my reverie was interrupted.

It was Zoe, her grey eyes alive with enthusiasm, who whispered across the table at me:

"We're going to Philippi tomorrow. I have to go there on behalf of the archaeological museum of Salonika, and meet a curator."

"That should be interesting. Can I come too?" I asked.

"Yes, of course. Particularly as the curator comes from Florina," she smiled conspiratorially.

"Florina?" My eyebrows showed surprise.

"Yes, Florina is not far from Mount Vitsi. You never know, perhaps this curator has heard of your friend Stephen, but, David, it is like, how do you say in English...?"

"A needle in a haystack. I know," I smiled.

"Let's drink to tomorrow." Bill sounded cheerful as we clinked our glasses.

★ ★ ★

I suppose any optimistic thoughts would have been misplaced; after all, Stephen might well have left Greece altogether, or he might not even be alive; and if he was still alive and in Greece it might not be possible to find him, particularly if he had decided to blanket out the past and remain incognito.

These thoughts moved through my mind as the sharp morning air cut across my face; the jeep was moving quickly towards the archaeological site of Philippi which was only about nine miles from Kavalla.

Presently, whilst Zoe was engaged in research work, Bill and I wandered around the excavations and ruins. I tried to visualize the Roman battles when Caesar's assassins, Brutus and Cassius, were defeated. Wherever you went in Greece, history always intruded.

Later in the morning Zoe introduced us to the curator from Florina, who was older than us. I would say that Nikos Solomos was now in his fifties; he had a square, squat build, with a dapper appearance; and his large forehead seemed to highlight his prematurely white hair. I could, with difficulty, understand his English.

Enthusiastically Zoe and Nikos showed Bill and I the prison where the Apostle Paul and Silas were incarcerated; Nikos then quoted the Bible and described how Paul and Silas had prayed and sang, and then an earthquake had caused the cell doors to open and this had led to their release. Later I remembered how Nikos at the beginning had quoted from The Acts—about when a vision appeared to Paul at night saying 'come over into Macedonia'. Was this a sign or omen for me, I wondered?

Zoe persuaded Nikos to join us for lunch on the Kavalla

waterfront, and we drove away from the tobacco fields towards the sea. The cafe was certainly not overcrowded. The moussaka was covered with a white sauce and grated cheese, and was well received by all of us; the fresh cold November air had sharpened all our appetites. The retsina seemed overlaid with the taste of resin, but Nikos assured me that it was good for the digestion. He seemed to be able to converse fluently with Zoe in French which I could mostly understand also. As clearly as she could Zoe explained to Nikos the reason for my visit to Northern Greece, and for some time we listened patiently to the description that Nikos gave of life in Florina during the various stages of warfare over the last decade, ending up with the most recent civil war when Florina had been attacked by guerrillas. The Greek national army had used Florina hospital for many casualties of both sides.

I had no doubt that Nikos could tell us of many tragedies in the towns and villages surrounding Mount Vitsi where Stephen had originally been known to join the guerrillas.

It seemed to me that Nikos was vividly describing episodes from the latest civil war, and yet he had not said much about the German occupation prior to the main uprisings. This was no doubt because it was further back in history and memory, so I taxed him about the time of the German occupation. He told us about the competing guerrilla groups, particularly the main E.L.A.S. Communist group. Bitterly Nikos recounted how some of the parachute drops from the Allies were not used to fight the Germans; some of the arms and gold had been secreted away as the E.L.A.S. intended to take over the country when the Germans eventually withdrew.

I interjected to point out that at least E.L.A.S. had cooperated with the British officers in blowing up the

Gorgopotamos Bridge which effectively cut the German supply line through Greece to Rommel's forces in North Africa. Nikos, however, was quick to point out that E.L.A.S. only cooperated because the British had brought in the rival anti-communist E.D.E.S. guerrillas; E.L.A.S. had to maintain their reputation as heroes, so this action became a joint venture.

Nikos kept repeating stories of E.L.A.S. fighting other guerrilla groups instead of harassing the German forces; they would hack their victims to death. Not unnaturally his face had a look of horror as he recalled these gruesome details.

Again, I felt that Nikos was moving away from my main enquiry, and I kept mentioning the name of Hardinge to him, hoping that it would strike a chord.

We had finished eating and we were rounding off the meal with black coffee,

Perhaps because the tale was horrific Nikos had kept this episode to the end, I don't really know. He was describing some Greek village called Kalahori. Apparently the resistance groups had been particularly effective in the surrounding area, and the Germans in retribution had assembled the whole village, and then separated the women and children from the men. The women and children had been forced into the school-house and locked in. The men, about seven hundred of them, had been taken to the cemetery and shot in cold blood. The Germans then set fire to the school-house; they all perished except for two or three women who were saved by some Englishman. His name, Nikos believed, was Stephanos. Then Kalahori suffered again in the civil war when it was attacked by guerrillas; they looted the bank, then destroyed buildings and plundered the homes. Kalahori has never been allowed to recover, Nikos ended sadly.

It had been a terrible series of tragedies in Kalahori. It was no doubt because of the devastating tale that there was a pause of silence before Bill and I simultaneously asked Nikos to repeat the name of the Englishman who had apparently saved a few of the villagers.

"He was called Stephanos," replied Nikos. "But I never knew his full name."

"It could be the Hardinge we are looking for," I spoke excitedly. "His full name was Stephen Hardinge."

"Stephen—Stephanos. It could be," added Bill.

"Where exactly is Kalahori?" I asked.

"It's not far from the Albanian border, Kyrios, David, high up in the Grammos Mountains," answered Nikos. "If you would like to stay with me in Florina I will try and help you."

"As long as I don't impose on your kindness for too long." My acceptance was received with delight by Nikos, and he explained that it would be best for me to come to Florina in a week's time when his work as curator could be delegated temporarily to his deputy. In the meantime he volunteered to try and make some transport arrangements.

Then, I waved goodbye to Nikos for the time being as Bill and Zoe drove him back to Philippi for his transport to Florina.

That evening, in our peaceful hillside hotel overlooking the harbour lights, it was clear to Bill and Zoe that I had become animated with the thought that possibly I was making more progress at last.

We had finished our meal, and were relaxing in the easy chairs in the sitting-room.

"Don't get too excited," warned Bill. "It may be a red herring for all we know."

As if to dampen my enthusiasm, Zoe added, "You must remember, David, that it is winter now. It may not be easy to travel in the mountains. I hear that the snow is early this year."

"We'll take you as far as Florina to meet Nikos," explained Bill. "Then Zoe and I must return to our work, I'm afraid; I shan't be able to leave the jeep, David, you do understand, don't you?"

"Yes, of course I understand," I assured him. "You have both been very helpful, and I mustn't encroach on your time anymore."

"I'm going up to Drama tomorrow so that I can make a report on the tobacco industry. What will you get up to?" Bill asked.

Without thinking I replied, "Perhaps I'll take a boat trip to the island of Thasos. I haven't been there since I was stationed in Kavalla during the War. There's probably a caique going across I imagine."

"I'll come with you," smiled Zoe. "There's now an archaeological museum near the harbour of Limin on the island and there is much to visit there."

★ ★ ★

I was restless that night in bed. I wanted so much to believe that I would find Stephen up in the mountains; I wanted to think of him as a heroic figure saving life whether in a fire or in other circumstances; I wanted to draw a veil over his defection in Italy.

If Stephen was still alive, did he know about Joy Mitchell and his son Eric?

So many questions were unanswered, and sleep did not

come easily. Perhaps a restful visit to the Greek island of Thasos on the morrow would be an antidote to all this agitation.

The following morning I regretted that it was not a blossoming spring day as a cold wind cut across the bows of the caique.

The Aegean waters looked uninviting as we neared the circle of the island of Thasos with its groves of olives and sandy beaches.

It seemed to me that it would not take many years before Thasos became an island invaded by tourists on holiday in the spring and summer; they would emerge into the sun like the locusts themselves (this proved an accurate prognostication). Just now, however, it seemed very peaceful as Zoe and I landed at Limin and made our way to the amphitheatre. I remembered the site from my Army days. It was just as the European war was ending. The theatre, which would be lizard-strewn in the spring, had such wonderful acoustics, and with a backdrop of the blue sea and the pine trees, it would become famous for classical performances in the post-war world.

I looked out across the alpine meadows and pine forests, the olive trees, beaches and smoky mountains. The pine trees acted as a break against the sharp wind, and Zoe and I relaxed on the stone seats. I looked at her silvery grey lively eyes.

"You and Bill…" I started to say, but she interrupted me.

"Bill and I are more than just good friends. That is what you want to know I expect, David. He has asked me to marry him."

"And will you?" I asked.

"If I do, it will be in the spring. I'm not too happy about

leaving my parents in Salonika as they have always had me there." She stood up preparatory to taking me to see the archaeological museum near the old harbour.

"I expect your parents will be pleased for you. You and Bill would live in Athens, I imagine," I spoke encouragingly.

"Yes, I suppose we would have a base in Athens, but Bill might get assigned to another country. Who knows? I'm not sure if I'm cut out to be, how do you say it?" she asked in her pigeon English.

"A 'camp-follower' is what you are inferring," I added.

She laughed. "The acoustics here mean that everyone will know about my love life, except fortunately we are the only ones around at present."

In the museum Zoe quietly explained to me the history of the god Dionysus, and it seemed that the Dionysian cult embraced far more than Bacchanalian rivalries. After admiring the statues and sculpted heads, Zoe guided me to the Silene Gate where smilingly she touched the statue of the Satyr.

"Why did you do that?" I asked.

"Legend has it that it gives hope for having children; you can see where the statue is worn away where women have touched it."

We walked a short way and found a quiet cafe. It was near the long sandy shore of Makriammos Beach I remember. We were made welcome in the cafe, and the soup gave warmth in the chilly November air. I could taste the fish, onions, carrots and potatoes, augmented of course by the olive oil.

"Kakavia—it is called. You see, your speaking of Greek will improve all the time," she laughed.

"Yes, thanks to you."

We drank some ouzo, and I recall that we had some Thasos honey, and finished up with figs. It seemed to me that Bill had found an admirable mate in Zoe. I looked beyond her to the water curling in on the beach.

"What could be nicer than a wedding in orange blossom time?" I smiled at her.

"I take it you approve of the match?" she chuckled.

"Oh! Yes. Sometimes life is like a tree, an evergreen. If a tree is green and healthy, keep it that way. Some of us, myself included, don't always practice what we preach. I think I may have allowed my tree to lose some of its leaves, but I hope not." It was then that I told Zoe of my love for Lydia.

If only Lydia was with me now, my sadness would disappear, I thought. At least it helped to talk about her, and Zoe was a patient listener. As the caique headed back towards Kavalla, Zoe and I were both silent; I was still thinking of Lydia, and my approaching trip to Florina, and perhaps Kalahori in the Grammos Mountains. Zoe was probably thinking of her future with Bill.

We smiled at each other, her long hair flowing in the sea breeze; there was no need to speak; there was a trust and intimacy in our silence.

★ ★ ★

For a large part of the journey to Florina, Bill drove the jeep back towards Salonika, and then eventually we moved North West towards the Yugoslav border.

It was another cold day and sleet powdered the road. I felt sure that Bill and Zoe would now be glad to be back in Salonika. After all, they had gone out of their way to be more than helpful to me, and their bases of Salonika and Athens were no doubt beckoning to them before the snows of winter.

The reliable Nikos Solomos was waiting for us in his apartment in Florina, and considering that he was a bachelor he produced a welcome hot meal of Keftedes, lamb I think it was with onion and other seasonings. We washed it all down with retsina whilst Nikos explained to me the preparations he had made. He proposed that he would come with me in my search, which was comforting; it appeared again that his work in the museum was not heavy at this time of year.

Nikos went on to explain that it was possible for the two of us to travel in his small black car as far as the village of Trikousa in the foothills of the mountains, but from then on he had arranged mules to take us up the goat tracks to Kalahori—he hesitated— "If you still want to go that far, kyrie." He looked at me, somewhat sadly I thought, out of his dark, black, deep-set eyes.

"Having come as far as this, I'd like to reach Kalahori," I spoke enthusiastically.

"It will sadden you, kyrie, but I will come with you." Nikos seemed determined to accompany me, and I felt very grateful to him.

We spent the day poring over maps, and loading the small Beetle car with equipment and clothing; also a supply of tinned food and a medical first aid kit.

That evening there was an enforced liveliness amongst us that could not hide the sadness of our approaching departure; Nikos and I to the mountains, and Bill and Zoe back to Salonika and Athens. Zoe would not be visiting her brother's grave this time after all.

Fortunately Nikos had cut some wood for the stove and

we kept warm. As so often since my return to Greece, my mind drifted back to the days of liberation following the German withdrawal. The Germans had cut down the telegraph poles to disrupt communications, and then in the bleak cold of wintry despair, the peasants had used the cut down poles as fuel.

Before we left Florina I had found time to write to Lydia. Urbino seemed a long way off now, and I hoped she hadn't despaired either of the London winter or of me. Hopefully she had seen through the wiles of Bob Chester by now, but even if she had, perhaps she had gone back to that bursar, Richard, instead. Optimistically I thought that perhaps Tom Preston was keeping her so occupied with legal work in my absence that her time for amoral relationships was limited. Someone as attractive and appealing as Lydia, however, was always bound to have a strong male following, like bees round honey.

I suppose that in seeing Bill and Zoe so at one with each other, and prior to that seeing Ken and Sofia so happy in their domestic life with Athena, I had become envious, and longed for a similar stable relationship. The old bachelor adventures in which Stephen and I had engaged with the opposite sex no longer appealed. Was I growing mature or simply dull?

I carried to bed with me a visual imaginary picture of Lydia stepping briskly up the wide steps of Earls Court station, and out into the Earls Court Road with that swing of her hips, the late sun turning her long strands of hair to gold; her purposeful and strong feminine walk and musky aura of perfume drawing appreciative eyes from the male commuters.

Perhaps London had become rather sad after the dismantling of the skyloned Festival of Britain.

I tried hard to see sadness in her blue eyes, sadness at our separation, but her long eyelashes discreetly covered all, and eventually I went to sleep not knowing of course, whether she was happy in the metropolis or not.

★ ★ ★

The next morning Bill and Zoe set off early as they knew that Nikos and I wanted to be on our way to the village of Trikousa and to reach there in daylight.

We waved farewell to the departing jeep which had brought me so far, and I looked more dubiously at the little black machine that would take us to Trikousa.

"It's all right," chuckled Nikos, "it has a reliable engine, and the smaller the better in the mountains."

I nodded in agreement at the latter remark and climbed into the passenger seat. At the third attempt the engine burst into life, and it seemed that we were enveloped in a cloud of smoke. However, I'm glad to say that this grey cloud was only temporary, and with confidence Nikos drove out of Florina, waving to some old friends he observed standing on a street corner.

The calendar had move on, and we were now in the early days of December. It would be cold from the time we left Trikousa and climbed to Kalahori, I mused unenthusiastically.

I did not anticipate that our journey to Trikousa would take very long. It was a dusty road that twisted and turned in the foothills of the mountains. We passed through several villages where the peasants seemed burnished into the landscape.

In each village there was the usual odour, unmistakably

Greek. It was a compilation of the scents of dried dusty spaces, dung and excreta, and dregs of wine. Sometimes church bells rang out, as if in our honour.

It wasn't actually snowing, but the sun was pale and fitful as it shimmered over the olive groves.

As we passed through each village we were greeted with the sight of emaciated children, black skirted peasant women, the barking of dogs and the squawking of hens.

Nikos drove at a slower pace than the speed of the jeep which had been driven by Bill. It was as though he was reluctant to journey towards the mountains, and yet the civil war had been over for some years. It may well bring back unpleasant memories, I thought, of the time when Greek fought Greek.

As we neared the borders of Yugoslavia and Albania it was as though Nikos was telepathic. He was talking above the noisy engine about the decisive part played by the mountain peasant women during the civil war. With a deep sigh he pointed towards the border villages and explained how the guerrillas had snatched the children of these villages and then took them across the border into Albania and Yugoslavia.

"What happened then?" I asked, willing Nikos not to take his eyes off the road as he had been doing with his gesturing arms.

"These children were indoctrinated in Albania or Yugoslavia, and given rifles; they then came back to join the guerrillas and they were told they would be fighting for Macedonia against the so-called fascists in the Grammos mountains."

We arrived in Trikousa as the light was fading, and a blackness was descending on the massifs beyond the village.

Already here the air was crisp and fresh, and I stretched my legs whilst Nikos went to the front porch of a house just off the main square. I noticed the bread oven outside the house which I had seen so often in Greece. A peasant woman came to the solid front door, and first of all looked suspiciously at Nikos. Then, recognising him, her weather-beaten face creased into a smile, and we were both embraced and taken into her modest clean home.

I only knew her as Chrysoula and, as if for a special occasion, her middle-age stolid frame had been enveloped in the peasants' national costume; proudly she stood with her embroidered tunic coat over the customary long dark skirt, ready to greet us.

I remember Chrysoula had two children of about five or six years old running around the house, but I was not surprised that her husband was not there. A legacy of the guerrilla and civil wars had been an exodus of the males to the West or America in an endeavour to earn money for their homes and families; some of course had lost their lives in the wars, and a terrible burden had fallen upon these uncomplaining mountain women.

As Chrysoula fed us with freshly baked bread and eggs and cheese and olives, she told Nikos that the mules were ready for us for the morrow.

Our plan was to start off early the next morning for Kalahori. A guide had been arranged, and there would be four mules for ourselves and supplies.

Chrysoula, of course, tried to coerce Nikos and me to use her spotless bedroom, but it was her only bedroom where she slept with her children. We were certainly not going to allow this, and by the dying embers of the open wood fire we dozed off to sleep.

Loud snores seemed to emanate from my companion as soon as he closed his eyes, but as so often when one is over-tired, it took some time before I felt myself slipping into oblivion.

Soon we should reach Kalahori. Frankly I had little hope of seeing Stephen there; I had played these long shots too often, but maybe Kalahori would give a clue to what had happened to Stephen. Pessimistically I realised also that Kalahori would not only show the sores from its history of horror, but it might shed light on a Stephanos who was in no way identifiable with Stephen Hardinge.

* * *

We set off at dawn the next morning, that is to say, Nikos, myself and the guide who was called Paul. It seemed to me an appropriate name with the country's biblical connotations; Paul was a strong looking youth, no more than seventeen years old I should say. He had a typically weather-beaten tanned mountain skin, and seemed cheerful enough. It was not often one came across a healthy looking young man in these parts since the wars; his command of the English language was not bad, and I soon realised that his linguistic skills were directed towards plans to go to the United States.

Riding on one of the mules through the pine and cypress trees as the sun came up, I felt exhilarated in the mountain air, and at peace with the world in the dappled light.

After a while we left the trees behind and followed a dried-up water-course before we came to a rocky, dusty goat track.

It had been some time since I had last been associated with mules; I suppose my initiation into mules had been during the grim mountain battles in and around Monte Cassino and Monastery Hill during the last war, when I had developed a healthy respect for these uncomplaining animals, particularly when they came within the range of shell-fire.

Now the mules were taking us higher through the rock-strewn terrain and the snow covered mountains. I suppose we were never far from the Albanian and Yugoslavian borders, but we seemed isolated in a landscape becoming more stark.

Clouds had now rapidly changed the sunlit early morning to a day forbidding in its melancholy weather. Even the mules seemed to sense the change to a colder climate as they slowly ascended the mountain track, now covered with snow.

We came round a bend in the track and ascended a ridge; it was then for the first time that I could see the village of Kalahori. It was, like so many Greek villages, perched astride a mountain peak, as though at any moment it would topple into the dried-up valley below.

We stopped a moment as Paul came back to speak to me. Nikos also seemed glad of a break; he produced some mountain-fresh water for us to drink. Paul was dressed for the mountains with a thick homespun goatskin top and black kilt; he wore the Greek mountain shoes which turned up at the front and curled back, the soles being very thick.

"Kyrios, David, I will take you to Andreas who is now the village patriarch in Kalahori. He will tell you the whole history," Paul called out as he set off again. Paul was a young man of few words, and his cheerful disposition was now displaced by a look of sadness as he gazed at the crags embracing the village homes of Kalahari.

This mood of despondency spread to Nikos and myself, as we recalled the terrible tragedies which had enfolded this village. I had never liked steep heights and often suffered from vertigo, but eventually our mules stumbled into the village which was precariously held on a cliff-side. The houses clustered around the main square, dominated by the church. Even further up the rocky terrain was a cemetery, but nearer to the church I could see the gutted remains of the school-house. It was still there.

The mules were tethered in the yard of a small two-storey stone building. As was customary in these villages, the ground floor storey housed the animals, which seemed to consist of two of everything—two goats, two donkeys, and two hens. An outside stone stairway led to the upper floor where Andreas resided.

There was the usual distinctive village smell, augmented by the smell of food cooking, but there was little time to consider this as Andreas came down the stairs to greet us. He was an old man, with a thick greyish white beard, and dressed in the customary peasant clothes, but apparently he still tended his sheep on the mountainside. He gazed at us with his sad, brown eyes. He welcomed us into his home, but there was no joy in his speech.

We ascended the stairs to the living quarters which consisted of one room for living and sleeping in. It was a clean room, and the thump of our boots on the bare boards echoed through the house in solemn noise. The walls were whitewashed and held icons and religious pictures.

We sat around the fire eating some cheese and black bread. The coffee seemed to give us new vigour after our journeying. I watched the smoke from our tobacco curl up towards the ceiling.

First of all, Andreas remained silent as Nikos and Paul

explained to me the early history of Kalahori; it had been destroyed by the Romans, and then by the Turks. Kalahori had then suffered in the Greek War of Independence.

Against this background Paul then interpreted the slow, soft words of Andreas. Apparently during the last war, the resistance groups had been active in this area and had been successfully attacking German troops with raiding parties. As punishment and retaliation the German Commander for the region had chosen Kalahori to suffer the dire consequences. Just as Nikos had explained and described it to me in Kavalla, the men of Kalahori were separated from the women and children. The men were taken to the cemetery—and shot out of hand. Apparently, the operation took but a short number of hours.

The women and children of the village had been herded into the school building and locked in. The Germans then set fire to this building.

Andreas hesitated as he stared into the flames of his own house fire.

"Did anyone escape from the school building?" I asked tentatively.

"There had been an English doctor with a resistance group, Kyrios, David. His name was Stephanos. At the time he had been with a few guerrillas in the mountains near here. He had seen the flames in the village, and ran down into the village. He heard the screams from the school hall. Desperately he tried to unlock the heavy doors. Eventually he managed to pull two women to safety. They were sisters. The doctor and the sisters were all badly burnt, but they survived. No one else did. I was away on the mountain with my sheep at the time."

Before Andreas could continue I had to ask him, "Can you describe this so-called doctor?"

Andreas paused a moment. Slowly Paul interpreted. "He was tall and fair; I think his eyes were grey or green."

Then as I saw Andreas pointing to his nose, I knew what Paul would say about the doctor's nose. "Outstanding" was the word I think he used for Stephen's aquiline Roman feature. Anyway the words were not important. "He could play the piano," smiled Andreas.

It seemed that, for his own reasons, when Stephen had landed in Greece during the war, he had turned from being a fighting combatant to become a medico. In the sense that he had gone through medical training before joining the infantry, it was not entirely illogical.

These thoughts were going through my mind when Andreas again launched into a long speech. When Paul translated these words it became clear that the poor Greeks had not yet, even at that horrific time, had their final suffering. When news of the tragedy of Kalahori had reached the West apparently there had been material help given in the form of gifts and financial payments. Reconstruction had commenced, and men, women and children had moved into Kalahori from the surrounding hillsides and villages.

Then, during the civil war, the Communist guerrillas attacked Kalahori after they heard of the material help that had been given, looking for spoils and loot. The guerrillas killed some of the peasant villagers; others fled. Women guerrillas looted the homes. The peasant women were too frightened to return to the village.

"There are still only a few of us villagers here," said Andreas quietly as he finished his account.

Presently he lit his pipe. Twilight had descended, and the mountain cold air invaded the house.

"Andreas, what became of Stephanos and the two sisters?" I asked. Again, there was a pause as his heavy-lidded eyes sought the light of the window.

"When I came back into the village from my mountain shepherd hut they were not here, kyrie. The only person left here was the village priest. He had been visiting the next village. On his return he met the two sisters and Stephanos. In spite of their bad burns they headed away from Kalahori after they described to the priest what had happened."

I became quite animated as I asked Andreas if he could take me to this village priest.

Slowly he replied that it would not be possible. A tear fought its way down Andreas's cheek to hide in his beard like a bird in a nest. Paul translated quietly: "In the civil war, the Communist guerrillas hanged the priest and the female guerrillas shot and killed Andreas's wife."

"Why?" I called out. "Good God, Why?"

At last Nikos spoke. "If a priest did not agree politically with them, then this was the fate of a priest."

"But why also your wife?" I persisted.

It was Nikos who again answered my question: "When the Communist guerrillas came here in the civil war, as you have been told, the girl guerrillas looted the homes. Andreas's wife resisted and tried to keep her possessions and animals, so these female guerrillas shot her."

★ ★ ★

It was now quite dark except for the flames from the fire which cast shadows across the weather-beaten faces of my companions. There was no noise save the tinkling of goat bells. Andreas's sheepdog lay stretched out by our feet.

Some hot milk was heated on the open fire, and we ate some dark appetizing bread.

As nightfall came, Andreas fetched a jug of wine, and we all participated. As much as anything I think we all needed to be cheered up after learning of all the tragedies of Kalahori.

Perhaps Andreas realised this. Friend as he was in all this sadness, he quietly took an old wooden flute from a shelf, and his mountain music floated into the night.

Our conversation cheered a little when Andreas asked me what tobacco I smoked. I remember answering him literally, and then Paul chuckling. He explained that the question what tobacco I smoked was a Greek expression asking what sort of person I was, whose side I was on in any political movement or revolution. I had found this everywhere in Greece, of course. Ardent discussions on politics, and in Greek eyes you were either of Right or Left political persuasion.

However, I realised that on this occasion it was only a joke. No doubt Andreas had suffered enough politics for his whole life. Perhaps he ought to become a nomadic shepherd, a Sarakatsan, I thought to myself.

I must have fallen asleep shortly after I had cloaked my body against the cold. My last thoughts before sleep had been of Stephen, and a fantasy entered my dreams wherein he shouted to me for help in the licking flames of that school building.

★ ★ ★

I think that we all arose fairly early the next morning, and over the coffee and home-baked bread I asked Andreas if even now he knew, or whether there was any way of knowing what had happened to Stephanos and the two sisters.

"Kyrie, I remember asking the village priest these same questions, but I learnt nothing, although I always thought that perhaps the village priest had urged them to go somewhere else but he would not say. Anyway, alas, the village priest is no longer with us, and some years have passed since these tragedies—and the presence of the good doctor Stephanos. The names of the sisters were Anna and Elena Katsimbalis."

"Nothing at all has been heard of him, or where he might be?" I persisted with my questions.

"No. I believe his injuries and burns were very bad, but here in these mountain villages, not only in Kalahori but in other villages near here as well, I have heard nothing." He paused. "Perhaps it was meant to be that way."

"Yes. Perhaps so," I added, trying to hide my disappointment.

★ ★ ★

A little later that morning Nikos and I visited the cemetery where all the carnage had taken place, and then we gazed sadly at the ruins of the school building which had been left there, perhaps as a symbol and solemn reminder of the horrors of war, and in memory of the villagers' loved ones.

The paths were covered with freezing snow and there was a cutting wind. My first thoughts were that perhaps we might

118

glean information about Stephen from one of the neighbouring villages, but at the same time I felt sure that if there had been any further news in this area of Stephen's whereabouts, Andreas would have been sure to have heard of it. Not only did he graze his sheep in the mountains, but apparently also he bought and sold livestock in the villages round-about, even though these villages were far apart on neighbouring cliff-hanging mountain tops.

I shivered in the cold air and Nikos seemed to read my thoughts.

"Maybe, David, we should return to Trikousa and Chrysoula with the mules now. I expect Paul wishes to return home also." He spoke in a practical way.

"Of course. I seem to have reached a dead end again," I remarked with a heavy sigh.

"What will you do now?" Nikos asked.

"I'm not sure. Maybe I should return to Kavalla before long," I replied. "After all, the weather is now very wintry in the mountains."

★ ★ ★

So we collected Paul and the mules, and as Andreas waved to us from his home in tragic Kalahori, we set off on the difficult slippery descent towards Trikousa. The snow on the path was two feet deep, I should think.

The lonely figure of the bearded Andreas was to remain pictured in my mind permanently; the horrors and tragedies he had endured, and yet in spite of his brave endurance he had also lost the 'woman of the house' as they say in Greece.

The mules seemed sensitive of the icy goat track but they

instinctively knew where to place their hooves, and this was just as well as I looked over the precipitous sides of the pathway; it was a balletic movement of these uncomplaining animals as Paul confidently led the way down the slopes.

Paul seemed more subdued now, as though Kalahori was still looking over his shoulder. It was only when we reached the tree-line, and the smell of pine trees wafted through the milder air that he looked round cheerily at me: "Soon we shall be back in Trikousa Kyrios David," he called out.

In spite of my despondency and frustration over the progress in my search for Stephen, I looked forward to seeing Chrysoula again, and her warming fire and the waiting food and refreshment.

Clearly also Nikos was anticipating the pleasure of once more driving a car rather than being carried by a friendly mule.

As for the wine, that would hardly be necessary when the air was so intoxicating.

We stopped amongst the pine trees to eat our bread and goat's cheese, and then we drank the clear, cold water of a mountain stream.

The sun was beginning to sink in the West as we followed the track curling round a spur of a ridge, and there below us was the village of Trikousa. Already a wintry mist was creeping up the valleys towards us.

As if knowing that they were near their journey's end and their home grazing, the mules seemed to increase their pace, and the villagers in the main square of Trikousa gazed curiously at our ill-assorted group. Still, they could hardly think of us as tourists at this time of year.

Chrysoula and her two children were warm in their

greeting, and after cleaning ourselves up, Nikos, Paul and I enjoyed the zucchini and rice and minced meat. The warming food restored our conviviality; I added some water to my ouzo which had the usual aniseed flavour. The traditional Greek coffee was served in small cups.

Paul was interpreting Chrysoula's words:

"After tonight, will you come back to Trikousa?" she asked.

Nikos looked at me. My thoughts and future plans seemed blurred and undecided.

"You have been very kind," I replied, "but unless anything more is heard about Stephanos in these Grammos Mountains I cannot foresee that we could continue our search in this area with any advantage."

I looked at Chrysoula and wondered when, if ever, she would see her husband again. He was probably sending her money from time to time from his job, whatever it was, in the States.

Yet she did not seem sad or hangdog; I had read somewhere that a Greek had two souls, the Romios and the Hellene that blended to form the whole. Chrysoula had the fatalism of the Romios, and the reliance on the long view of the Hellene.

Once again she begged us to use her bedroom for sleep but we insisted that we would sleep around the dying fire. We bade farewell to Paul who had now regained all of his former cheerfulness, and Nikos and I settled down somewhat uncomfortably on the hard floor with a dusty blanket thrown over us to combat the cold as the fire ebbed away.

I was very tired, but my body stiffened against the hard floor; I could tell that Nikos was soon asleep with his deep breathing and occasional protesting snore.

I felt a long way from my way of life and my friends in England. Perhaps I should go back to England soon; I did not seem to have achieved success in my mission, although having made such progress it would be a melancholy outcome not to have completed it finitely.

My mind and heart strayed to Lydia; perhaps there would be a letter from her awaiting me in Kavalla. I had sent her the address of the small hotel where I had stayed with Bill and Zoe. I wondered if perhaps she was yearning for the South African climate in the midst of a smoggy, cold London in December.

Again and again I thought and dreamt of her perhaps being with Bob Chester, or I imagined her going up the gangplank of a liner bound for Durban when the purser, who was Richard Prentice of course, took her in his arms and they were re-united.

Reality and imagination play tricks with us all, but where does one begin and the other end? Sometimes they merge in a self-constructed blurred picture.

"Love is not love if it does not fear the loss of itself." I could not remember who wrote that line, but I truly feared the possible loss of love from Lydia.

I tucked the blanket more closely around me as the wind increased and whined around the house.

★ ★ ★

It seemed strange to be travelling again in a car; the black Beetle, as usual, was reluctant to start, and we left Trikousa enveloped in cloudy smoke.

Soon, however, the little vehicle settled down to return

through the foothills of the mountain ranges, and along the curvaceous road towards Florina.

This time the weather was not so benevolent, and the large snowflakes began to fall across the road and car. The windscreen wipers battled against the odds to give clear vision ahead. The squat figure of Nikos seemed entrenched in his driver's seat, as though the car had been made around him. Already he seemed to be regaining his town dapper appearance as we quietly drove through the villages towards Florina.

I gazed at the whitened countryside. My thoughts were of the general and immediate future.

The general future seemed to be obscured by an impenetrable morass in the search for Stephen. Admittedly it had seemed that I had traced a region where he had operated, with particular bravery, in the interests of the local people. But where had he gone from Kalahori? And had he taken with him the two sisters who were rescued by him? The answers seemed to be blanked out, just as the snow presently falling was blanking out the landscape. The tragedy of Kalahori was played out some years ago. If there was to be no further general advancement in my searches, then I must turn my mind to the immediate plans for going home to London, and the hopeful prospect of seeing Lydia again.

As regards the immediate future, however, Christmas would be upon us in a week's time, and whilst in most circumstances I would be happy enough in Kavalla, the thought of Christmas on one's own in the small hotel there was not exciting.

We had reached the outskirts of Florina; I took one final look at the distant mountains as the last of the daylight tarried on the peaks; and in a cursed fashion, the snow flurries had now ceased. Before long Nikos had the little black car under cover—it had not let us down—and as darkness began to win the battle over daylight he had contrived to light the stove fire.

Needless to say it took some time before the apartment warmed to our mutual satisfaction, but with some hot soup we soon regained our spirits. Nikos found some honey-covered cake in the kitchen, and some fruit, so it was in a state of some contentment, which vied with my frustration over the search, that we settled around the stove that pre-Christmas winter evening.

Like a magician forever producing a different article from his top hat, Nikos then came out of the kitchen with some beer. I was surprised at this, but in fact the beer was quite palatable and refreshing, and made a change from the wines and ouzo.

I was smoking my occasional cigarette; I noticed the addiction of Nikos to the komboloi—as he clicked his amber beads. In a way it was like my smoking, although the playing with the beads seemed more of an antidote to anxiety than my cigarette smoking.

"I will be working tomorrow at our museum, but I know we have an establishment vehicle going to Kavalla within a couple of days if you wish to return there." Nikos paused. His bead clinking stopped temporarily. "Would you like to have Christmas here at Florina? You are very welcome Kyrie." He smiled.

"No, thank you, Nikos," I answered. "You have already done enough for me, but I hope we can meet again before I leave Greece." Alas, so often hope does not become reality.

We drank to our next meeting—if there should ever be

one—and I suppose if the night had not been so cold I would have slept reasonably well.

In fact, the museum truck left for Kavalla the next morning, and once I was across the River Struma I soon sensed the wintry sea breezes beating in off the Aegean Sea.

I left the truck by the main harbour, and carrying my kit I made my way up the cobbled alley to the small hotel where I had stayed with Bill and Zoe. My small room was awaiting me. There would be no more sitting out on the balcony, however, until the spring.

It was pleasant that evening to re-acquaint myself with the well-cooked local fish dishes. It was not red mullet this time, but grilled swordfish with oregano flavouring. I remember also the retsina-soaked apples, and the cheerfulness and courtesy of the few hotel staff.

Perhaps Christmas here would not be so bad after all, even if a lonesome one.

That evening I wrote a long letter to Lydia giving her all the details of the trek which Nikos and I had undertaken to Trikousa and Kalahori. I tried to describe to her the people we had met—Paul, Chrysoula and Andreas, and my ventures with the mules. Finally I wished her a happy Christmas and told her that I would be home before too long, and that I missed her all the time.

I wrote a shorter letter to Tom Preston, thanking him for his tolerance, and again I told him to expect me back in the first half of the New Year. But there was one more letter that I knew I had to write.

I had to write to Maria to tell her something of what I had found out about Stephen, but how much should I tell her? It was obvious that Maria was still passionately fond of Stephen, but I could not tell her whether he was alive or not, and if I told her that he had been badly burnt this would cause her endless grieving.

I knew that I would never forget the kindness of Arturo Manzoni and his daughter, Maria. Certainly I still owed money to Arturo for my fares. I thought of Maria typing her children's' books whilst Arturo projected his oils onto another canvas. Maria, with that glossy black hair and deep-set brown eyes that could look so serious, sad or happy. She would never forget Stephen, I was sure of that. These feelings of hers would cast a shadow and would always cast a shadow over any other relationship she had with the opposite sex, and that included me. There would always be a penumbral region in any association between Maria and myself; she would, I felt sure, forever fantasize over Stephen, and in any case, I would never be free nor ever want to be free of my feelings for Lydia.

After much thought I did write a letter to Maria; apart from the usual pleasantries I told her of the villages I had been to, and that although I had traced Stephen's activities at one time to a certain village, the scent had then gone dead. I did not mention the horrific tragedy of Kalahori, but told her that Stephen must have been through some grim times. So that she would not give up hope altogether I told her that I was going to stay in Greece a little longer, but I had to explain that I could not tell her whether Stephen was still alive or not. I sent her my love, but I knew it was not my love she wanted or needed, and I think that with her feminine instincts she knew that my love was platonic. I sent greetings to her father, Arturo, whose painting had been the genesis of my search.

I realised suddenly that tomorrow would be Christmas Eve, so I ended my letter to Maria with Christmas greetings— 'Buon Natale' as I remembered it from service days in Italy.

I would not be involved in the exchange of Christmas presents this year, I thought—but in this I was proved wrong. I suppose I went to bed fairly early; the drive from Florina had been tiring and cold, and now fortified with the warming food and retsina I huddled under the sheet and blankets.

It would be a novel Christmas to be sure. I could not remember when I had ever spent Christmas on my own before; away from home, yes, but always in company.

As I fell asleep I felt sad about this. Perhaps I should have stayed with Nikos in Florina, but I suppose Kavalla had always been a lure for me since spending the last spring of the European War there, including VE Day.

* * *

Christmas morning was a bright cold, crisp day, and I walked down to the sea-front and then through the old part of the town of Kavalla. It was pleasant wandering through the old quarters, past the Turkish aqueduct which dominated the area, and then I climbed up Mount Simvolon to gaze back at the descending tiers of houses and harbour. Even at this time of year there was a sparkle on the sea, and certainly the red, yellow and blue of the buildings were happy colours for the region.

There was much evidence of the different cultures for it wasn't until after the First World War that the area became part of Greece; in Turkish times the women would have peered out from the shuttered windows of the houses and not been allowed to attend male gatherings.

I had worked up an appetite by this time, and so I slowly made my way back towards my small hotel.

Presently I pushed open the main entrance door to the hotel foyer, and there waiting to greet me were Bill and Zoe.

I could scarcely believe my eyes, but their Christmas greeting was so genuinely effusive that I felt elated in spite of my frustrated journeys looking for Stephen.

Bill and Zoe had brought me presents and fruit and wine, and that evening we celebrated by visiting a waterfront taverna. Carefully we trod our path down through the cobbled alleys and under archways; even if one closed one's eyes it was self-evident that we had reached the seafront with the smells of salt and tar and resin and fish.

It has to be remembered that we had not yet reached the era of jukeboxes and transistor radios, boutiques, souvenir shops and concrete tower blocks of hotels, and the general tourist invasion.

I could make out the outline of the restless caiques and their masts at anchor as we entered the taverna where the local fishermen greeted us with smiles and good humour.

The wine flowed, and presently encouraged by the musical accompaniment one of the fishermen acted out a slow dance on his own before joining the others with their singing.

Certainly the weather-beaten faces of the seamen were happy and friendly; there were high spirits and humour and a zest for singing, dancing and drinking—this Grecian zest for life and gift of laughter that's known as 'Leventeia'. The distinctive rhythms of the metallic bouzouki, the mandolin with three double strings, seemed to take over our bodily movements.

Bill and Zoe knew the traditional steps of the dance, and by degrees I was able to join with them in the Sirtaki, a group dance, accompanied by the bouzouki music. However, it was left to the local mariners to perform the pidiletos, and we finally ended our Christmas day watching the leaping agility of these physically well-endowed marine dwellers; the clicking of fingers, the anti-clockwise rhythmical movements, the feet stamping the ground and the pirouetting.

So my Christmas proved far more lively and enjoyable than I had any reason to anticipate.

On Boxing Day Bill and Zoe went to visit her brother's grave in a cemetery near Drama. Zoe's brother had apparently lost his life in the Greek civil war when he had been in the Greek national Army, and I did not intrude on their private visit inland to the Drama region. Bill still possessed the jeep of course, and I realised that without transport it would not be long before I would have to abandon my human quest.

★ ★ ★

We were drinking the usual thick black coffee that evening in the hotel; we were somewhat subdued, partly because of Zoe's sorrowful reminder of the loss of her brother and partly because the next morning they would return to Salonika, and then Bill would drive south to Athens.

Zoe had been thoughtful, but I put this down to her sad day. Her grey eyes reminded me of the pewtery winter sea near at hand.

I had told them in detail of the mule journeyings that Nikos and I had made from Trikousa to Kalahori, and of the grim tragedy of Kalahori.

"So your trail went dead at Kalahori?" Bill asked.

"Yes, I suppose so. It seems that Stephen was badly burnt when he rescued the two sisters from the inferno of the school building, but they don't know what happened to these three survivors after that," I replied.

"Always assuming that Stephanos was the Stephen you are looking for," cautioned Bill.

"Quite, but I think it must have been, although God knows what he was doing in that area anyway." I sipped my brandy and the spirit coursed through my veins.

"The guerrillas moved around much when they were in the mountains, David," Zoe spoke for the first time. "I will speak to my father again. He is, as you know, a chemist. It is just possible that he heard at that time of someone requiring treatment for burns, but it is unlikely."

I also gave Bill the telephone number of Ken and Sofia in Athens. Perhaps they could make inquiries at the hospital where they worked, but like Zoe, I did not think that there would be any positive outcome.

Unless I made any progress early in the New Year I would have to leave Greece behind, and resume my normal life. Yet I was growing an affection for Greece, for their Leventeia and for their generous sympathetic attitude to all things English dating back historically to the Byronic influence. Certainly Byron's death at Missolonghi had been a calamity to the Greeks at the time of the Greek War of Independence against the Turks; he had become a heroic Greek figure and Greek children had been baptised in his name, Vyron or Vyronos.

How sad it had been, therefore, that during the E.L.A.S. troubles with the British forces, the E.L.A.S. had set ambushes at Missolonghi. There had been casualties, and then the E.L.A.S. had laid mines at the entrance to the port. This resulted in further casualties when two landing craft were blown up. E.L.AS. had laid the mines after the Royal Navy had swept the area.

In any event I suppose the former tender feelings towards the English were later to be partially extinguished by the Cyprus troubles, but for now it seemed that these country and sea folk were welcoming, and the festering wounds had not yet occurred.

The following morning was overcast and grey as I waved farewell to Bill and Zoe. I wished them a happy journey, 'Kalo taxidi'. Their jeep brought up clouds of dust in the distance, and I soon retreated indoors in the face of a bitter wind off the sea.

★ ★ ★

That evening, somewhat reluctantly, I took up pen and paper and wrote to Margaret Hardinge. I explained to her in detail about my meetings with Arturo Manzoni and his daughter Maria in Urbino. I confirmed to Margaret Hardinge that I had made arrangements for the painting of Stephen to be sent direct to her, and I intimated to her the sum I had agreed that she would pay to Arturo.

For some reason best known to myself I did not give her the further information about my searches in Greece. Why did I not do so, I wonder? Perhaps at this stage I wanted Stephen's sister to remain convinced that Stephen had been killed in action in Italy—at least until I had any further substantial evidence as to whether he was still alive and if so where he was living. Also, I imagine I did not want to distress her about the serious burns it appeared that Stephen had been subjected to in the Greek mountains.

Then there was also Eric to consider, Stephen's illegitimate son. Why at this stage give the boy any hopes, which might turn out to be false, that his father was still alive? No doubt he thought of his father proudly and envisaged that his father died in the war in Italy.

I did not, therefore, give much information to Margaret Hardinge; I remember making some platitudes in the letter in the form of encouraging her with her piano concerts and lesson-giving, and hoped that Eric was happy and contented at his boarding school. Was any boy happy and contented at that age to be away from home? It seemed to me to be too early an age at nine years to be left all the time, apart from school holidays, in the harsh realities of school life, confined to school precincts.

Of course it was the easy way out for Margaret Hardinge so that she could give all her attention to concerts and piano lessons, and yet there was an aura of adequate wealth in her Chelsea home with its substantial furniture and furnishings. I felt sure she could easily afford help in the home and companionship and learning for Eric without thoughtlessly dismissing him to the portals of a boarding school at his early age. Perhaps when I returned to London I could help the boy in some way.

I looked out of the hotel window which would soon be shuttered for the night. The flakes of snow were haphazardly descending to the ground in the darkling scene like small white grains in closed bottles one used to shake as a child and then they clouded up.

Then I looked around the small lounge where I had been writing my letter; there were only three other people, all middle-aged men, sitting there quietly. They were all reading newspapers—Greeks read newspapers so much, it was as if they had to know the latest dramas and crises as soon as they emerged. The chances were that it was a political impasse of some kind about which they were reading. No doubt I would miss the company of Bill and Zoe now that they had gone.

As I dozed off to sleep that night I thought of the German folklore that whatever you dream during the twelve nights after Christmas will come true. My mind fantasized over being with Lydia again, and I drank deep of her imaginary consoling nearness. By dreaming of her I kept alive my dim hopes of holding her in my arms again.

The next morning the snow had ceased, but it was still very cold everywhere. Although Spring often came early in Greece, it would be some time before Kavalla could look forward to mild days and the flowering of cistus, tamarisk and thyme. There was a Greek saying that 'once the lambs hear the cuckoos we know that we are all right', but the days of cuckoos were a long way off yet.

Although the weather was raw I felt that this should not be allowed to keep me indoors, and each morning I strode out for exercise. One day I climbed the hilly road towards Kavalla airfield where during the War we had hung on grimly against the odds, hoping that the E.L.A.S. would not open fire; the E.L.A.S. guerrillas had been dug in on the surrounding mountains and could have picked us off like ninepins if there had been an eruption of shooting, as indeed there had been in Athens. It had been an unpleasant wintry time, and the Royal Navy had taken us back to Salonika until the so-called peace was established.

The snow had been compressed by passing vehicles, and was now freezing solid. My ascent of the road back towards the hotel was slitheringly dangerous in the circumstances, and I resolved to buy some suitable footwear for these journeys in Northern Greece.

After three days spent in this fashion I was sitting in the hotel lounge one evening; one of the Greek guests, I remember, was explaining the headline of the newspaper to me. During this explanation there was a telephone call for me, and to my great pleasure it was Nikos Solomos from Florina.

He enquired about my whereabouts and how I had spent Christmas, and I told him how fortunate I had been with the visit of Bill and Zoe.

"And your search for Stephen, Kyrie. There is no more you can do, is there?" Nikos asked disappointedly.

"There doesn't seem to be, Nikos; if you have any ideas perhaps you will let me know," I answered.

"I have no ideas, I'm afraid, but if you need help at any time I can take some time off work again and we can use the car like last time together. The museum is quiet at this time of year."

"That is very kind of you, Nikos. I will bear it in mind. I think you are missing those mules."

We both laughed, and after I had thanked him for telephoning, I returned to the staid air of the hotel lounge. I doubted if in fact I would ever see Nikos again.

On New Year's Eve I returned to the waterside taverna where I had enjoyed the music, singing and dancing at Christmas in the company of Bill and Zoe.

The grey-green waters were darkly slapping against the quay walls as I entered the taverna, and I renewed friendships made at Christmas in the taverna. However, the songs of unrequited love put me in mind of Lydia again.

I suppose it was only to be expected that I missed Bill and

Zoe that evening, in spite of the hearty welcome from the local fishermen. In trying to shake off my somewhat gloomy attitude towards the New Year I drank more wine than was good for me, and had it not been for the friendly assistance of two burly mariners it is probable that I should have strayed in error off the quay and into the embrace of the Aegean. My two ouzo-soaked friends were quite steady compared with myself, and having ascertained where I was staying, they obligingly steered me back to my hotel in the small hours of the first day of the New Year. The skies were clear and darkly blue, and the moon shone brightly, but alas I had no thought or true vision of this, as I crawled between the sheets of my bed.

Rigorous bonhomie on such occasions is so often regretted in the light of the next day, and I felt in a truly sorry state for the first day of the New Year.

A letter that day in fact arrived from Tom Preston; how far away seemed those legal cases in the office.

Tom explained in his letter that he was keeping the office work moving (was he perhaps hinting that my contribution to the workload was not that great or was he working into the night to keep on top of things?). He did not seem too perturbed by my absence and extra time off which it was apparent he condoned. There was a caveat however at the end of his letter to the effect that he expressed a Wordsworthian wish to see me back in the office in London by the Spring.

There was no letter from Lydia although in one of my letters to her I had given her the address of this Kavalla hotel. Indeed, Tom Preston had made no mention of Lydia in his letter; there was no particular reason why he should have written about her—he had not known the extent of my involvement with her before I left England, and he had not known in fact that Lydia had gone with me to Italy. Lydia and I had discussed this, but without wishing to be subversive we had deemed it expedient to be discreet at that stage. Still, I was somewhat puzzled; it was as though a veil, like a spidery screen, had come down over Lydia and she seemed to move mistily across my London habitats. There were times when I felt that I could see her clearly, the whole outline of her body and the texture of her skin, those eyes of Mediterranean blue and full seductive lips. Then the scents of her musky perfume—were they like the fruity odours of apricots?—wafted through the wintry cold of my bedroom, and the moonlight would shine on her long strands of auburn hair.

But it was not always so, particularly when my searches were not going well. Then I seemed to lose Lydia in my dreams and fantasies, and she would be lost to me in the London crowds; just as I followed her up the wide, stone steps of Earls Court tube station and out into the Earls Court Road the press of people of mixed nationalities cut off my view of that graceful Afro walk of hers.

The phone rang in the foyer. It was a call from Zoe in Salonika. Apparently her father, Constantine Sophoulis, had looked up the shop records and had asked around both his pharmaceutical colleagues and medical friends at hospitals… but he had advised that there was no trace of any treatment or medication in the past years either for Stephen or the two sisters Anna and Elena Katsimbalis. Zoe explained that the search into such records could only be partial in any event, and it had proved inconclusive.

We wished each other a happy New Year, and in spite of my frustrations I did sincerely hope that Zoe's future with Bill would be one of joy and contentment.

Next morning the intermittent falls of snow continued, the soft whiteness feathering mournfully the steep alleys below the hotel and then dissolving into wetness and nothing.

At one point it made me think of Joy Mitchell and her soft beauty weaving intricate webs before dissolving away. That episode in Rome and her presence then seemed insubstantial now. I could still remember her wistful smile as she quietly said, "I don't know how long we shall be here. We are really only in transit for some field hospital."

So many 'ifs'. If I hadn't contracted dysentery I doubt whether Stephen would ever have met Joy, yet there was something fascinating about their similar physical qualities. They were both tall and fair, and they both struck the observer quite forcibly with their bearing and demeanour when they entered a room. Usually I could enter company almost unnoticed with my unremarkable features, and I ought to have realised that, in the short term at least, Joy would be far more attracted to Stephen than to me. Had she been homesick for Canada, I wonder? Nursing in the field would scarcely have given her time for thoughts of home.

Another 'if'—If I hadn't been poorly at that time, Eric would not have been born. Perhaps Joy would not have died. These conjectures of course led me to consider whether if I had been well I would have had sexual intercourse with Joy. As transitory beings near to the war zone it was quite likely that Joy and I would have ended up together for sex in one of the hotel bedrooms—but I am making too many presumptions. Just because Joy fell into bed with Stephen does not mean that she would have been equally obliging to me.

And then there was that white shirt that I had lent Stephen; had she embraced him whilst he was wearing my shirt? The one that was eventually found on the field of battle, soaked in blood.

Later in the day the snow stopped, and carefully, to avoid slithering down the cobbled lanes, I edged slowly towards the salty tang of the sea front.

The bright colours of the houses had taken on a mantle of whiteness, slowly melting away.

There was a scattering of cirrus cloud far up in the heavens, but a deep Delft blue was now predominant in the sky, and I strode confidently towards a nearby secluded bay that I remembered from my army days,

I suppose I would always associate Kavalla and the island of Thasos with happy days as the European war ended, and one's thoughts had turned to the realisation of possible survival and return to England. My thoughts came true, and in due time I was demobilised, I had gone to see my parents in Dorset, and then I had returned to my career in law.

My parents had known that I was visiting the Continent at present, but they had assumed that it was a holiday. I had not disillusioned them in their rural quietude. My father would soon be retiring after a lifetime's teaching. I sometimes thought that he was disappointed that he had risen no higher than housemaster of a famous public school, but he had never shown any disappointment. There is no doubt that I have been somewhat spoilt, being an only child, but maybe it had all been a little suffocating.

I clambered down off the road and over the rocky dunes to the small quiet bay where I had known peace after all the years of war.

This time I had no responsibilities, no ties; but the widening vacuum needed to be filled.

The tide lapped quietly at my feet. Some gulls flew overhead, casting wintry green shadows on the water; the shadows turned to deep inky blue. It was getting colder now and the dampness seemed oppressive.

I walked back along the road to Kavalla, and then up the hill to the hotel.

I would have to make plans to leave and return home. There seemed no further avenue I could explore regarding Stephen, whether he was still alive, and if so where he dwelt.

My present inactivity had only given me time to think too much of the 'might-have-beens', and I had indulged in too much nostalgia. The Pandora's Box was best left not to be opened further.

I would no doubt continue to sleep and dream and have fond memories of Lydia until I saw her again—like Voltaire I had to place sleep on the same level as hope. Despondency could only lead to destruction.

★ ★ ★

The next morning the sky was leaden and heavy with snowy dampness.

I told the hotel manager that I would be leaving the day after, and I phoned the Sophoulis family in Salonika to expect me later on the following day as I was abandoning any further search for Stephen now. Constantine, or Costos as I now called him, and Zoe were both out at work, but Costos's wife Marina answered the phone. I told her of my plans and she kindly confirmed that the bedroom would be ready for me in their Salonika home on the next evening. I had no intention of being a burden to them, so I explained to Marina that my stay with them would be a short one. She told me that it had been a bitterly cold winter so far in Salonika. Strange how one always used to think of winters in this part of the world, especially in towns, as being mild, but I knew and remembered how cold it had been at Christmas time in Salonika during the last Christmas of the European war. In fact, I had been caught up in heated arguments with a local resident at that time over what he had been charging us for fuel, but the civilians often thought the army were fair game to make some profit out of without anyone being personally financially hurt.

★ ★ ★

I spent the remainder of the morning in desultory fashion, although in browsing around the local shops, I found an appealing coral bracelet which I bought with the intention of taking back to England for Lydia.

I had a light lunch of cheese and wine on the waterfront, and then returned to the hotel to start packing for the morrow.

I suppose it must have been almost tea-time, an English tea-time that is, when Calliope, the small yet strong young Macedonian girl who each day had cheerfully tidied up my bedroom, knocked on the door of my room to say that I was wanted on the telephone by a man who had apparently tried to telephone me in the morning when I was out shopping for Lydia's present.

I wondered who it could be; I had already only a short

while ago been telephoned by Zoe from Salonika telling me of the negative results of the search in Salonika.

To my surprise the telephone call was from Ken Dacre in Athens. It was a bad line and we both had to shout to make ourselves heard.

"I have some information for you, David," he called down the line from Athens.

"Information of what sort?" I asked loudly.

"Sofia and I have been making inquiries at the hospital. As far as I can tell, your friend Stephen never came to Athens for medical treatment." Ken's American drawl had an air of mystique about it.

"So?" I queried briefly.

"However, there are records of a woman called Elena Katsimbalis being treated for bad burns in the latter part of the World War."

"But not Stephen or Stephanos, or Anna Katsimbalis?" There was now more crackling on the line.

"No, but Sofia traced an address for the sister called Elena from the hospital records. The name of Katsimbalis was not in the telephone book, but from the medical records Sofia saw the address of an apartment on the outskirts of Athens. Are you still interested?" Ken chuckled at the other end of the line.

"Of course, go on." Naturally I encouraged him.

"Sofia visited this apartment; the sister Elena still lives there. She seems to have made a fairly good recovery with plastic surgery, but she is very reticent about the past. However, she did tell Sofia that Stephanos and Anna never came to Athens for treatment."

"Does this Elena know where they are?" I asked excitedly.

"Only that the last time she had heard anything about them, Stephanos and Anna were living in the Meteora."

"The Meteora—where all the monasteries hang like ships in the sky overlooking steep, precipitous cliffs?"

"That's right, David. I understand you will have to go to Kalambaka. You will have to find out at Kalambaka which of the monasteries is your destination. There are several monasteries there, and Elena could not give Sofia any further details. Some of the monasteries are occupied by a few monks or nuns, but others are not."

It was only after I had put down the telephone after thanking Ken for this surprise information that momentarily I thought of my vertigo and dislike and apprehension over sheer heights.

However, excitement was now strong within me, and I wasted no time in telephoning Nikos in Florina. I realised frustratingly that he was out at work, probably in the museum, and I had to wait until nightfall to contact him.

I reminded him on the telephone of his kind offer to help further if I obtained any more information, and I then explained to him the gist of what Ken had said to me.

"Then we must go to Kalambaka to make arrangements." Nikos sounded equally excited. "You realise that the weather will make travelling in that area difficult just now. We are still wrapped in winter," he added more cautiously.

"Yes," I answered, "perhaps we shall need our four-footed friends again." I laughed happily.

"I will meet you tomorrow evening in Salonika at Zoe's." Nikos was already making plans.

I thanked him again, and then I telephoned to Salonika to speak to the Sophoulis family once more.

It was Zoe who answered the telephone this time. She was surprised to hear my voice. I told her that I was still coming to Salonika the next day, and then I gave her the news from Ken in Athens.

As I anticipated, she was very pleased for me, but she warned me not to be over enthusiastic in case there were further disappointments ahead. Needless to say, she was very welcoming at the thought of Nikos going to Salonika where we would all meet again.

★ ★ ★

It made much sense to return to Salonika first before proceeding to the Meteora region. Meteora was in the province of Thessaly and across the Macedonian border.

I had read about the Meteora and certain unconfirmed reports had led me to believe that the weathered monasteries were perched precipitously on rocky outcrops in the valley of Meteora. The Greek word Meteora conjured up otherworldly manifestations, hovering in the air.

At least it would seem to be not quite like the precipitous Mount Athos, which was entirely a male preserve, and which required at that time letters of introduction from the consulate to the Greek Ministry of Foreign Affairs or the Ministry of Northern Greece in Salonika.

It was likely that our plan would be to proceed partly along the main road from Salonika to Athens, and when we reached Larissa we would head for Trikala inland and then briefly north to Kalambaka.

★ ★ ★

The morning after these telephone calls I left the hotel as planned after settling my hotel bill. I gave Calliope a generous tip; after all, it was Calliope who had brought the message of cheer that Ken had some positive news for me.

However, as the bus jolted along the road from Kavalla towards Salonika, I remembered Zoe's words of caution. There could well be further travails and disappointments ahead.

There were icy patches on the road which caused a hazard to our journey. To add to my concern the bus driver was constantly gesticulating and waving his hands whilst conversing with the passengers near to him. Greeks cannot talk without using their hands, and I thought that at one point of our route he would decimate a goat herd. Perhaps the icon with its Saint swinging on his windscreen had saved him and the goats.

At various villages the bus put down some of the passengers, but at the same time several fresh passengers came on board as we neared Salonika.

I was quite hungry at the end of the bus journey at Salonika and I decided to have some lunch at a taverna before proceeding to the Sophoulis family home. In any case, Costos and Zoe would probably have been out at work at that time.

Although I was tempted to visit one of the waterfront tavernas, I remembered the pleasant hilly suburb of Salonika appropriately called Panorama, and I luxuriated in a taxi as the car climbed the steep road.

There were indeed several tavernas from which to choose in Panorama, and I settled on a pleasant small one which had impressive views over the city and the sea.

It seemed appropriate, being near the Aegean, to have

barbonni or red mullet, and as Salonika was famed for kolouri—baking, I decided to have one of the koulouri or hard-crusted circular rolls with central holes and dotted with sesame seeds. Having washed all this down with some retsina—talking myself into believing that the Greeks were correct in their claim that it aids the digestion—I ended up with a horn-shaped pastry which apparently was called trigonas and again was identified with the Panorama area.

This wining and dining, even at lunch time, was a boost to my morale as I gazed across the wintry waters.

Our Battalion had been reasonably comfortable here in Panorama before we fanned out to search and garrison the towns and villages in the hinterland. Why hadn't Stephen been content with his lot in Italy, and then perhaps he could have enjoyed all this? Instead of which he had ended up in guerrilla raids and internecine strife in Northern Greece, and the Germanic scorched policy. There seemed no logic in it all, and I wondered if, even now, I would ever resolve the enigma.

It was a pity that we were still in the midst of winter; it would have been pleasant to have watched or joined in the evening stroll or volta along the waterside in Salonika when the evening sun went down; to have seen the summery frocks and animated gossip and the interchange of greetings.

Now people walked hurriedly to escape the cold wind off the waters. The gossip and greetings would have to await the coming of spring.

Even though there had been a peace agreement signed in Athens following Churchill's visit during the war, life thereafter had not been easy. It had been not far from Panorama that we had encountered a town of strong Communist tendencies. I remembered the harangue I had been engaged in with the local E.L.A.S. leader in front of the Mayor; of course the E.L.A.S. leader had not wanted his local force to give up their arms or their barracks. I bluffed pretence that there would soon be tanks arriving in the town; the E.L.A.S. then reluctantly gave up their arms, and I settled for cleaning up another barracks on the edge of the town for us to occupy—it proved strategically better also.

However, it had not ended there; I received clandestine visits from local rival political parties, and although I repeatedly told them that I could not get involved in their politics, such visits were reported in the local press, causing umbrage all around.

The waiter put down my coffee on the table in front of me. There seemed to be a resumption of normality now, at least in the cities, but the hubbub of conversation in the taverna gave the usual undertone hint of politics, and surreptitious reading of political newspapers.

After my impressive lunch it did not take long by taxi to reach the Sophoulis household, and I found that Zoe had arrived home early from work and was helping her mother, Marina, to prepare the evening meal.

There was the usual genuine welcome, and then Zoe guided me to the same bedroom which I had used on my previous visit.

"This time you will share the bedroom with Nikos, not with Bill," she smiled.

"Thank you, Zoe. How is Bill; is he down in Athens?" I asked.

"Yes, David," she replied—sadly I thought. "We always seem to have this separation. It is not good." Her English speaking occasionally had an alien brevity, mixed with a little French and Greek.

I tried to speak encouragingly to her as I emptied my battered suitcase of its essential clothing and kit.

"Cheer up, I expect you and Bill will be together again at Easter."

There was a pause, her grey eyes focused on me, and as those long eyelashes of hers fluttered, her sadness seemed to lift.

"I've agreed to marry Bill in the early Spring." She volunteered this information, and I kissed her lightly on the cheek.

"I'm so glad. You must both be very happy." Suddenly I remembered our visit to the island of Thasos, and how I had advised Zoe to keep her tree evergreen. Smilingly I recalled how she had touched the Satyr's statue at the Silene Gate and the accompanying hope for fertility.

I looked at her. She was as tall as I was.

"Strange, I thought you looked a little sad just now, but I can see the happiness in your eyes," I told her.

"The sadness is because last evening I told my parents that they would lose me in the Spring."

"I'm sure that they are not sad at your happiness, Zoe."

"No, David, but you see they have lost a son in the fighting, and now their daughter will be leaving. They realise that Bill will not be in Greece indefinitely, and that I will go with him to whatever country he is assigned—if that is possible, of course. So you see, as they get older they will be alone."

"But they will have each other," I argued.

"I hope so." Zoe closed the door quietly behind her, and I was left to rest for a short while before Nikos arrived.

It seemed to me that Bill and Zoe were on the road to happiness and a joyful life together. In fact, if it hadn't been for my long standing friendship with Bill, I could perhaps easily have fallen for the attractions of Zoe. Perhaps it was the thought of the unobtainable, such as Zoe, or the current non-availability of dearest Lydia—what was the saying? 'The grass is always greener.'

Was I being prudish in my attitude towards Zoe? The truth was that instinctively I knew that there was no one else for her but Bill. Once more I was an 'also ran'—but not really—not as long as Lydia was there. Too many leaves must not be allowed to fall from my tree.

★ ★ ★

Nikos arrived just as the light was fading, and Costos, looking somewhat tired after his day's work, came home shortly afterwards.

I think Nikos enjoyed conversing in English and improving his command of the language. "I have brought black beetle," he laughed.

"Black beetle?" I queried.

"Yes, you remember you called my little car 'black beetle'."

"Of course I did. Well, your car certainly didn't let us down before, and I don't suppose it will this time," I spoke encouragingly.

"It will be all right, but you will need to have warm clothes. You will recall that the car has no heater," he warned.

★ ★ ★

The evening progressed in a similar fashion to the previous evening I had spent in the Sophoulis household.

Near the stove fire we enjoyed a fish soup, and then the moussaka with cheese. It was appropriate, I suppose, that as we were in this particular part of Greece, Costos producing bottles of Chateau Carras; the full-bodied red wine caused a mellifluous tide of conversation, and yet underlying the aura of bonhomie I could sense a tinge of melancholy from Costos and Marina. I put this down to the news that they had digested a day earlier about the marriage in the forthcoming early part of Spring of their daughter. It was not a selfish sadness, but a realisation, I felt sure, that their daughter would soon be leading a peripatetic life a far distance from Salonika.

Zoe and Nikos were discussing mutual problems with their respective museums. Suddenly Costos stood up and proposed a toast.

"To my daughter's future happiness when she marries Bill in the Spring." There was a pause as we toasted Zoe. "Also," added Costos, still on his feet, "let us drink to the hoped for success of David finding Stephen, and a safe journey for David and Nikos."

Much later, as Nikos and I prepared for bed, I asked him how much time he could take off from the museum at Florina.

"A fortnight at most," he answered. "We shall need all this time, especially as there will be preparatory work to do at Kalambaka before tackling the Meteora. We shall have to see—maybe it will be best for me to remain in Kalambaka as…"

"As a base," I added.

"Yes. Anyway, after our journey by road through Larissa and Trikala, we will be too tired to make any further preparations tomorrow for ascending the Meteora."

"Apart from being completely chilled, there being no heater in the car," I added cheerfully.

I was soon asleep, but occasionally I would awaken; there was an anxiety and stress within me at the thought of ascending giant crags to the mountain eyries of the monasteries, and I dreamt of falling through snowbound ravines to death below.

I knew, however, that I would endeavour to see matters through to the end, whatever the final scenario would reveal.

The wind howled against the shuttered windows as January struggled towards its finale.

★ ★ ★

The next morning it seemed like meeting an old friend as I climbed into the small black car.

Once more we bade farewell to the Sophoulis family, and as if to remind us of its frailties, the car engine took its usual three attempts before bursting into life; the familiar cloud of smoke enveloped us as we waved goodbye, but soon the little 'black beetle' was weaving through the traffic.

Both Nikos and I were only travelling with our essential kit, hoping that we could obtain any necessary supplies at Kalambaka before advancing and climbing to the Meteora.

Our journey was likely to take five hours, and as forewarned by Nikos we were soon feeling the cold temperature in the unheated vehicle. I seem to remember Mount Olympus in a haze to the east of us, and a welcome stop at lunch time at Larissa for lunch. Fortified by the local cheese and wine and coffee, we left Larissa and turned inland towards Trikala.

"We are crossing part of the plain of Thessaly," Nikos called out above the noise of the engine, but my eyes were scanning the snow-clad Pindus Mountains to the west. The mountains seemed to overshadow our movement, even though we were, in fact, turning northwards towards Kalambaka.

As we neared Kalambaka it was just possible to see the spiky, barren rocks soaring hundreds of feet into the sky, the eerie and weird isolation of the weathered crags, and the faint vision of monastic walls atop; this was the Meteora.

I shuddered involuntarily as I stamped my feet on the floorboards of the car in order to maintain the blood circulation; but it was my hands that seemed to suffer in the cold, and they felt increasingly numb.

Nikos did not seem to feel the cold so much. I suppose he was more used to it.

We entered the streets of Kalambaka just as a snowstorm had reached its zenith; the snow was drifting in the cold wind, and it was not surprising that there were few people about.

At the appropriate times of the year shepherds would no doubt drive their flocks of sheep along the roads of Kalambaka, but now the sheep would be in their wintering pastures on the plain of Thessaly. The monasteries seemed wreathed in snow on their dizzy heights. I thought I heard the ringing of distant bells, but my imagination could have been playing tricks with me in this region of eerie wilderness.

Nikos parked the car, and it was soon enveloped in a sheet of snow. He decided that he would make inquiries regarding accommodation at a nearby grocer's shop, and the friendly shopkeeper directed us to the house next door which he also owned. Apparently his wife ran the 'pension' part of the joint enterprise whilst he looked after the shop.

The accommodation was fairly basic, but the house was at least warmer than the car; we had separate bedrooms, and we were able to arrange for food as well, as long as we were prepared to eat the same food as the owners.

I remember the owners, Zena and Yanni Diamanti, as being hospitable. After all, they did not normally have paying guests at this time of the year. They spoke a little English, but mostly they spoke in Greek, and then usually of course to Nikos.

Nikos and I rested for a while on our beds. I think I dozed off with the tiredness of the journey and the sight of the sunless white tone of the landscape.

I woke up just before dusk and gazed out of the window at the rising rocky columns of the Meteora. The smooth rock spirals seemed remote and detached. Nikos had said that when I approached these isolated mountain-top eyries they would seem to be floating in air and watched over by eagles.

We had a simple, but warming repast that evening with Zena and Yanni. They were a couple in their forties I suppose, so that their ages fell between mine and that of Nikos.

Yanni (the name in Greece was as common as Tom in England—it was really a shortening of Ioannis) was of medium height but stout with the familiar olive brown complexion. Even at his comparatively young age his face was weatherbeaten and crinkled when he smiled, like an old apple-skin. He seemed strong and thickset as he handed glasses of raki to Nikos and I after the meal. He put his lips to the mouthpiece of his narghile, and I heard the familiar bubbling noise. At the same time he offered us some snuff which he had made from powdered tobacco and herbs and spices.

The room was large with heavy old-fashioned furniture, consisting of a sideboard, cupboards and a long sofa.

It was only natural as we talked with Zena and Yanni that they should extol the grandeur and isolation of the Meteora and its monasteries. I thought how marvellous it would be to see the impressive rocks and crags spiralling and spiking to the sky with the monastic dwellings atop if the weather had only been spring-like or summery. Then, no doubt, to have seen the majesty of these eerie outposts of the heavens, especially against the setting western sun, and to the accompaniment of the bells ringing the Semantra from the chain of monasteries would indeed have been unforgettable.

It was Zena who first raised the question, asking the reason for our presence in Kalambaka at this wintry early February time. Zena was taller than her husband, but more slender with smiling brown eyes. Again, her face was tanned with the sun and winds of the country, and framed with soft, black, short curly hair.

She had been listening to the description Nikos had given her of our road journey from Salonika; he had proudly told her of the trouble-free performance of his small car. Quietly she asked:

"Why do you come to Kalambaka now when it is so cold? You would enjoy the Meteora and the mountains so much more later on in the Spring or Summer, especially with all the wild flowers and the warmth in the air."

Nikos and I looked at each other for a moment. We had not really discussed exactly how we were going to explain our presence here in the latter part of winter.

Nikos, no doubt correctly, decided to explain to Zena and Yanni the true purpose of our visit, at least in the essential outline. Our hosts appeared to nod their heads in the appropriate Greek manner as though they understood what was being said. Their equable, smiling faces did not change until Nikos specifically raised the names of Stephanos, a British officer working with the guerrillas, possibly as a medical assistant, and a Greek woman named Anna Katsimbalis. As Nikos went on to describe them as best he could, I could detect a certain look of privacy and understanding pass between Zena and Yanni.

"They were apparently badly burnt—at the time of the German occupation," I added.

There was a pause of taciturnity, and then Yanni launched into a description of the monasteries. I remember he explained that distances between the monasteries were not as great as we might think when we looked at these solemn heights from the lowly plains.

Some of the monasteries, he went on, were occupied by a few monks, or abbots and deacons; one was even occupied by a few nuns; and then he explained the history of the decay of the Greek monasticism, and why some of the monasteries had now crumbled away, being no more than inaccessible shells in the air of the heavens.

Zena intervened to explain that there were now probably no more than a dozen monks in the region when in earlier times there had probably been hundreds.

"Are there only monks or a few nuns there?" I intervened.

"There are also a few shepherds who come and go and possibly one or two peasants," Yanni answered, again looking meaningfully at Zena. Then he added sadly, "A monastic life does not appeal to young Greeks when they see all the material attractions in Athens and other cities imported from the West. Also, you have to remember the tragedy of Greek history, the wars, the burning and looting, and the self-destruction of our homelands by rebels and guerrillas. Our Eastern Christian monasteries do not have the rigidity of your Western ones; some monks here tend their domestic livestock or cornfields or olive trees, and then only wear their black garments when they come here to purchase provisions."

There was another pause.

"So you know nothing of this Stephanos or Anna?" It was Nikos this time who diverted Yanni and Zena back to the crux of our visit.

Once more Yanni turned to Zena who shrugged her shoulders at him. He refilled our glasses with raki. The bubbling of his narghile was the only disturbance in the silence of that dark wintry evening.

"I have always promised not to tell this to any strangers who come here asking for them. They wanted to be cut off from civilization like the monks, but they have to rely on provisions from my shop. One of the monks from a nearby monastery, or sometimes a peasant, comes down from their eagle's nest, and they drop off or take supplies to them, but they themselves never come here." Yanni stopped for a moment.

"Who do you mean by 'they'?" I asked.

"It is your friend Stephanos who is up there with the woman of the house, Anna," he replied.

"You mean you can tell us exactly where they are?" Nikos could scarcely keep his excitement under control.

Again Yanni stared meaningfully at his wife, and this time it was he who shrugged his shoulders.

"Because you are obviously an old friend of Stephanos and you have had a long search for him, I will give you the information you want. Although I promised I would not reveal where they were, I do know from the last time the donkey-laden supplies were taken up to them that Stephanos is, how do you say, struggling to keep alive this winter. Therefore, it may be helpful for him to see you again, kyrios David, after all these years." Yanni looked away sadly.

I nodded sympathetically, and allowed Yanni to continue.

"There is one small monastery. It is not occupied by monks. When Stephanos and Anna went there some years ago, there was only a shepherd who of course was not there all the time. He was usually tending his flock, and there was also an elderly peasant and his wife."

"What is the name of this place in the sky?" Nikos looked at Yanni.

"It is called Saint Nicholas." It was Zena who answered his question quietly.

★ ★ ★

Later that same evening I was lying in bed; there were no stars and the moon was hidden behind cloud.

I should have gone to sleep fairly quickly after the daytime travel to Kalambaka, followed by the evening meal and the raki and the Greek hospitality.

I suppose it was because of the descriptions and blurred outlines of the Meteora and their steep, remote monasteries and their sheer precipitousness that caused my restlessness.

Once more I was back in my waking nightmare; I was on a visit to Austria just after the War. I had joined a few old school friends for an early summer holiday in the Tyrol. I suppose none of us were skilled mountaineers, but the clean mountain air had been exhilarating and the quietude had been such a contrast to the recent mountain warfare I had endured.

When you have fought in the mountains it is as though the mountains enfold you and you become part of them.

Our little holiday had been a cheerful one, and after an evening of much revelry and wine, we embarked on the last morning of our stay towards a high peak unexplored by us.

I remember the profusion of mountain flowers as we climbed up the mountain path. Eventually, of course, we left the path and the tree-line behind. We had just negotiated one side of a ravine, and had moved towards the other side when I felt the shale give way beneath my boots. I slithered towards the ravine and managed to hold on to a clump of vegetation.

"Hold on! Hold on! We'll go and get help," one of my friends called out.

I was now sweating on my wooden-slatted bed in Kalambaka as I dreamily recalled the incident.

"Can you hold on? It won't be long now," they encouraged me.

In the meantime my grip on the undergrowth was weakening; as I changed my grip to the other arm in order to clutch another small piece of scrub I slipped further. I could see the valley and village like dolls' houses several thousand feet below; there would be no way to break the fall.

Every time I tried to climb a little I ended up nearer the edge of the ravine.

My imagination and half-sleep in the quietness of the Greek house were playing tricks with me. I thought I heard again a distant bell ringing out in the night, and summing me through the mists of time. Just when all strength was leaving my arms and I knew that I could no longer hold onto the vegetation, Karl, the experienced climber from the hotel, had arrived equipped with ropes and gear. It took Karl a long time before he could safely climb down to me with ropes, but slowly I was able to ascend the shale with his help. My back was to the ravine, so at least I did not look down at the world below. We finally made it to the rest of the party, and our last night at the hotel was a subdued one.

Gradually in my hard bed at Kalambaka I realised that I had endured another nightmare caused by that Austrian holiday. The sweat was trickling down the brow of my face. Ever since that holiday I had been apprehensive of heights and steep mountains, and yet I felt that it had been the mountains that had sheltered me from the shelling and mortaring during the War. The mountains surely were my friends. Now the realisation that I would soon be ascending the barren rocks of the Meteora had brought on this veiled fear of heights. Yet I knew that I must carry out this mission. What was the Greek word I was thinking of? 'Philotimos'— that was it. I must ask Nikos and Yanni to translate and tell me about 'Philotimos', it was to do with honour I felt sure.

So gradually my mind diverted towards the Greek 'Philotimos'. It would be interesting to have a discussion with my Greek friends about it, and with this in my mind I finally drifted off to sleep.

★ ★ ★

The next morning after breakfast Nikos and I accompanied Yanni to his grocery store, and although I could not follow the interchange of their conversation, Nikos eventually explained to me the arrangements he had made with Yanni.

Apparently the elderly peasant who lived at the tumbledown monastery of St Nicholas was due to arrive that day to collect provisions. Yanni would arrange for this old man, Georgios, to guide us the next morning to the monastery where Stephanos was living. Yanni would arrange for Nikos and I to ride donkeys alongside the donkey-borne Georgios who would also have a spare donkey laden with supplies.

As my Greek friends were making these arrangements I gazed up in silence at the weird cones and perpendicular spikes of the Meteora, wreathed in snow and winter stalagmites.

"How were they formed in these weird masses?" I asked Yanni.

"Probably from the stones and sand and mud transported by river water into a lake, and then the stones and debris of sand and mud remained there when the waters receded," Yanni answered.

"But how did the bare rocks obtain this peculiarly impressive form?" I searched their faces for an answer.

"Probably the elements; the wind, rain and earthquakes would most likely have been responsible." It was Nikos proffering the information this time.

This tragic country, I thought. Not only did they have to contend with all the different wars, but they had earthquakes as well.

When there was a silence in the air and everything was still, the Greeks would shrug their shoulders and talk of earthquake weather; Greeks have no fear of life or death. There were terrible earthquakes on the islands of Zante and Cephalonia in that very year of 1953; there had been several earthquakes in Volos, and the disastrous earthquake in Santorini was still three years away.

Strangely, as I looked up at the snow enveloped monasteries in their sinister eyries, I felt no recurrence of the Austrian nightmare of the previous night. I felt a buoyancy and confident expectancy for the morrow.

Nikos made some further arrangements with Yanni for me to take some provisions and medications for the monastery of St Nicholas.

Briefly the sun explored the heavens, but these cold February days were cheerlessly cold.

Much of the day was taken up with these preparations and finding suitable donkeys, and making a list of the supplies which we would be taking.

The old peasant Georgios arrived about midday. He exchanged greetings with Yanni, but looked suspiciously at Nikos and I when he was introduced to us. Georgios was grey with age and sucked his lips through his toothless jaw; his beard was grey and his mountain clothes were dusty with age. He still cut quite a good figure with his tall well-built frame.

A short argument proceeded with much waving of arms; Nikos joined in, and eventually poor Georgios, whether overcome by numbers or age, agreed to the plans. I think he felt great loyalty to his friends in the monastery, and it was only when Yanni explained that our visit might bring happiness to Stephanos in his condition of bad health that Georgios reluctantly agreed to escort my journey on the following morning.

Meanwhile he made arrangements to quarter himself in a shed near the donkeys so that he could tend to their needs.

Later at dusk that day Zena prepared a moussaka dish. I thought it as well to have a hearty meal, especially as I had no idea what food would be available to me up at the monastery. Clearly, Zena had a well-earned reputation as a good cook, and I can remember the almond-tasting pastries which we enjoyed after the moussaka.

The flow of retsina encouraged the flow of our conversation, and I asked Nikos to explain 'Philotimos' to me. I had heard it referred to so often before—'Where is his Philotimos?'—as though one's reputation was at stake. As so often when what appears to be a simple question is asked, there is a long discussion between my Greek colleagues. Nikos and Yanni spoke quickly with waving of arms:

"It is to do with a man's honour, but it is more than this. A man's excellence, whether say concerning his physical or moral standards or concerning his intellect, is the value; we are concerned with what a person loses, if others do not give a good esteem on his excellence." Nikos seemed pleased with himself with this clarification.

"It is what is often referred to as 'loss of face' perhaps?" I ventured to say. But of course I then had to explain what I meant by 'loss of face', and so our conversation continued.

I suppose it was not unnatural during this discussion of 'Philotimos' that Yanni, who as usual was smoking his narghile, turned to his wife and said quietly:

"Perhaps I should tell Kyrie David about what happened when I was fighting with the National Army against the Communist guerrillas in the Grammos Mountains."

Zena nodded her head in agreement, although the different Greek interpretation of nods always seemed confusing.

The bubbling of the narghile ceased for a moment. Yanni explained:

"As you were in the infantry in the last World War, David, you will appreciate what it was like. We would clear one mountain stronghold, and then there would be another mountain stronghold and then another."

"I know," I nodded my head in a way in which I hoped was a nod of agreement." There was always one more mountain, or one more river.

Then Yanni continued: "There was usually the mortaring and machine-gun fire and grenades which made up the sounds of battle. Sometimes, the countryside would give cover in our advance or attack, sometimes there would hardly be any cover at all. Anyway, during one attack on a mountain strongpoint we were making our way upwards and taking cover where we could amongst the rocks and boulders. During the course of our stealthy ascent we were held up by machine-gun fire coming from the remains of a stone hovel. I was near enough to throw a grenade; a figure charged out with a machine-gun. Instinctively I flattened myself to the ground and used the last of my ammunition. It was fortunately an accurate shot by me; the figure spun around and fell onto a rocky outcrop." He paused a moment. "When I reached the body I found that it was a woman. To see a woman like that was horrible—she had been beautiful too. Perhaps if she had killed me people would have said 'Where is his Philotimos?'."

Nikos intervened, shaking his head. "The Simoritises no doubt." Before I could ask Nikos what he meant by 'Simoritises' he went on to explain: "They were gun-toting peasant girls usually, probably trained in Yugoslavia."

"But why?" I asked. "Why, for heaven's sake, did they join the Communist guerrilla bands?"

Nikos shrugged his shoulders. "It was like, how do you say, a fashion. They wanted to live a better life. When they joined the Communist Youth Movement they had a meeting place, and they would have dances."

Yanni continued: "They were promised a better world. You must understand that usually a peasant family would all live in one room. They thought that there would be progress if they joined the Communists."

Zena had seemed in deep thought, but she intervened to say: "You must realise that a girl used to be constantly chaperoned; it was a tradition that peasant women and young girls were not allowed to share the company of men."

Zena then left us to make some more coffee.

"How were these 'Simoritises' trained?" I asked Yanni.

"Usually their day would commence with Swedish drill and then they would be taught how to fire their weapons. There would be shooting practice, but apart from this limited military training, the peasant girls were taught how to read and write, and then of course they would be indoctrinated with politics. In the evenings there would be singing and dancing."

"Of course they became disillusioned," Nikos continued on from what Yanni had been saying. "They came to realise that in fact when they had been at home they had been treated well by their families. After they had joined the 'Simoritises' they soon understood that the 'Kapetanios' had all the advantages and took everything."

Finally Yanni explained: "Sometimes the 'Kapetanios' would threaten to shoot them if they were reluctant to advance further in any military operation."

He paused, and seemed to look towards a distant landscape—"I shall never forget the look of anguish on that girl's face. She was so young, so pretty."

Nikos nodded his head sadly. "It is surely something you will never forget, Kyrie. Now we must go to bed, David. We must have good sleep before we join Georgios and the donkeys for our journey tomorrow."

As I undressed to get into bed I realised that Yanni's story of the 'Simoritises' had reminded me of an incident in Athens in the earlier E.L.A.S. uprisings during the World War when a brave British paratrooper had been drawn to a window of a house in Athens by a cry of help from a dark-haired alluring female; he had not known that she had a gun concealed below the sill of the window. She had fired the gun, and the paratrooper had lost an arm as a result.

It was such a paradox that Greeks had such warm hearts, had such a love for their country and their freedom, and yet they continued to destroy their own country.

Strangely enough I slept well that night. There was no repetition of the previous evening's nightmare amidst the Austrian mountains. I fell asleep thinking of Lydia and all she meant to me. Hopefully we would soon meet again in the London Spring.

★ ★ ★

It was snowing early the following morning, but by the time Nikos and I had consumed an adequate breakfast and joined Georgios the snow had stopped. In spite of a pallid sun struggling through the clouds it was a cold day, however.

We helped Georgios to load the supplies onto the donkeys,

and in one of the panniers I ensured that a sufficient supply of wine would be transported with us.

I waved farewell to Yanni and Zena—I think they were still somewhat dubious as to the wisdom of my visit—and soon Georgios was acknowledging the greetings of local villagers as the three of us directed our animals towards the outlandish crags of rock.

There were chasms to circumnavigate, and as we plodded slowly forward our mountain destinations seemed not only far away but also soaring into the clouds.

Vaguely in the distance I could see the walls of monasteries, but there was no sun now, the road was slippery with ice, and the mountains seemed almost blue and menacing.

Eventually we started climbing up the cavernous narrow track; we were surrounded by rocks and boulders and stunted plane trees. We had left the plain behind.

I was surprised that Georgios spoke a little English, but Nikos thought it likely that he had learnt some essential words and phrases from Stephanos and other travellers to Kalambaka and the Meteora region.

At first Georgios had appeared somewhat sullen, just as he had done when Yanni had first told him of my intended visit to the monastery.

As we started the climb through the sheer rocks and bouldered terrain, however, Georgios's bearded features seemed to soften. He urged his donkey forward and seemed to enjoy the more rarefied air. Eventually we moved out of the sombre twilight of the stone-encrusted landscape, and the sun lit our path through the plane trees.

Georgios, who was leading, stopped for Nikos and I on our

uncomplaining donkeys to catch up with him. With his stick he pointed to the distant perpendicular cliff on which I could discern the outline of structures.

"The monastery we are going to is crumbling away, it is really in a ruinous state, not like the monasteries near at hand which have a few monks and visitors," he said.

We entered a dream world of silence, the only noise being the steady clop-clop of the donkeys' feet on the slippery snow. There was a surround of mysticism from the smooth genealogical structures, and I could now see more clearly an overhanging platform with a cable suspending a large hook. At certain points there were bulges in the otherwise perpendicular cliff formation, but the rock was incredibly smooth in appearance.

We could now see the jutting walls of the ruined monastery, and as we dismounted from the donkeys it was clear that the large hook was already in position. The supplies were taken off the panniers of the donkeys and secured to the large hook; these stores which we had brought with us then ascended to the platform above.

The base position where we had stopped contained some crude stalling for the donkeys, and it was at this point that Georgios said: "My wife Marika is now seeing to the supplies being hauled up." Then he laughed: "You are lucky, Kyrios David—in the old days you would have been hauled up in a net with the food. We must go on foot now."

Somewhat sadly I bade farewell to Nikos who was to travel back to Kalambaka from this point, a lonely journey it would be.

"I will return here in a week's time, David. Ten o'clock in the morning. Do not be late. We must then leave the Meteora." Nikos smiled as he started down the steep descent.

I then followed Georgios up what seemed an endless flight of steps.

"Don't look down," I kept saying to myself, but in truth I no longer seemed to feel dizzy at the height. I was more concerned lest I missed my foothold on the icy steps.

Eventually we reached a small doorway which led to a cavernous, rock-enclosed passage. Georgios then guided me up some more stairs, and as the light began to fade we reached the arched entrance to the monastic remains of buildings.

Surprisingly the entrance opened up to a quiet courtyard, and although there only appeared to be a low stone wall separating the courtyard from the sheer precipice of rock, I noticed a few cypress trees that seemed to be able to weather these high-altitude elements.

Georgios moved towards the platform to help his wife, Marika, handle the windlass, and the supplies were safely landed at our tired feet.

Leading off from the courtyard I could see some ruined monks' cells, and a small chapel, desolate in appearance.

Beyond the chapel and on the other side of the courtyard there appeared to be a garden, and a pillared arch leading to what perhaps were more monks' cells.

Georgios called me over, and I smiled at Marika, who was now regaining her breath expended on the winching task.

"This is my wife, Marika; she usually cooks for us. You will need to speak out loudly to her—she is becoming deaf now." Georgios looked fondly at his wife.

She certainly looked as elderly as Georgios. A black handkerchief was tied around her chin, but I could see a wisp of grey hair.

She had a bowed appearance and she was wearing the usual long, dark skirt together with a tunic coat as so often seen worn by Greek peasants.

"Chrysornou,"[2] Georgios put his hand around her shoulder. She seemed much shorter than him. "This is Kyrios Thompson—he has come to visit Stephanos and Anna."

Her first reaction was similar to the one we had received from Georgios in Kalambaka; she did not seem very pleased to see me.

I asked them both to call me David, and then I asked Marika for news of Stephanos and Anna. Speaking loudly to overcome her deafness my voice seemed to carry across the mountain tops towards the other monasteries.

Slowly I could detect a thaw in Marika's attitude towards my arrival. With Georgios explaining her Greek words to me she said:

"Kyrie Stephanos is not well, not at all well, you see. Anna keeps reasonably well, but it is very cold here until Spring. I will see that you have food this evening, the same as the rest of us, Kyrie David."

Marika then trudged off ahead of us as I waited for Georgios to sort out the different stores we had brought with us.

The clouds seemed to drift below us, so that even if I had gone to the parapets to look down I would only have seen a billowy soft grey cumulus movement. I looked up instead— there were a few large predatory birds hovering, vultures and crows I thought they were.

Presently Georgios guided me towards the other side of the courtyard towards the little garden which I had seen earlier. We walked over cobbles and paving stone, and we were both carrying the segregated stores. Passing under the pillared arch we came to a smaller courtyard around which were three low-lying stone buildings, one of which was smaller than the other two.

I suppose at one time these single storey buildings had been either monks' cells or ante-chambers of some sort perhaps. Although the stone walls seemed in poor repair, the red tiled roofs seemed solid against the mountain weather.

I followed Georgios into the middle building, and I was surprised to see that the inner stone walls had been white-washed, and the rooms were not as gloomy as I had anticipated. There were two rooms, one of which was used as a kitchen and the other room was the sleeping quarters for Georgios and Marika. If they had been monks' cells, any intervening walls had now been demolished or perhaps collapsed with age and climate.

Marika was already unwrapping packages, and she wasted no time in preparing food.

The light was now fading fast, and Georgios lit an oil lamp which soon cast dark shadows against the white walls.

I was about to ask Georgios the layout of the remaining buildings when the stout wood door was opened, and a woman much younger than Marika came in, greeting them both. Before she finished her greeting, however, she broke off to stare uncompromisingly at me.

"You are Anna Katsimbalis?" I asked.

"Yes." She lifted the oil lamp to look more closely at me. I must admit that I had half expected to see some physical blemishes after the tragedy I had been told about when the Germans had set fire to the village school in Kalahori, but in the dusky light I could not detect any history of facial burns.

Like myself, Anna was of medium build, but she did not

have my slight round appearance. She had quite a good figure and wavy, short dark hair which fell over a wide brow. There was a wisp of whitish grey in her hair, like morning rime on heather. She continued to stare at me with puzzled hazel brown eyes. Her lips were full but she wore no make-up.

"Who are you?" she asked.

"My name is David Thompson," I answered.

Before she could ask for explanations I told her as quickly as I possibly could that I used to be a friend of Stephanos and that I had come to see him.

"How did you know he was here? How did you know I was here?" she asked guardedly. Her English was better than I had expected.

"It has taken me a long time to find out exactly where I could find Stephanos. It is a long story too," I smiled at her.

There was just a hint of a smile on her somewhat tight lips, and then sadness entered her eyes. In her broken English she said:

"I do not know whether he will want to see you. Apart from all the bad burns, he is very ill now." She shrugged her sagging shoulders. "Perhaps he will see another Spring, perhaps not."

There was a pause as she continued to take stock of me and what my presence might entail. Finally she said she would go and tell Stephanos that I was here, and then return.

I saw her disappear outside, and then into the other larger building, so I waited as the appetizing aroma of food being cooked enveloped the small kitchen.

Georgios was taking off his heavy boots, damp from the melting snow. I looked at him thoughtfully:

"Didn't Anna get burns damage herself in Kalahori?" I asked him.

"Yes," he answered, "but at the time Stephanos had managed to cover her face and head with a blanket. Her legs and her back were badly burnt though. I believe time has healed some of it."

Marika broke into our conversation. I looked on amusedly as she was clearly admonishing Georgios over the mess his boots were making on the floor. He waved her aside and carried on speaking from his chair.

"The two sisters were not so badly burnt because Stephanos shielded them with a blanket and his body, but Stephanos himself suffered badly because of this. You will see, you will see," he repeated.

Presently Anna returned. There was still a look of strain and resignation on her face. It was an oval face weathered by the mountain air; the nose was small and slightly upturned, but underlying the tragedy of experience was a quiet attractiveness.

"I have spoken with Stephanos. As I have already told you, he is unwell and very tired, and when I told him your name first of all he looked away and shook his head. He did not want to relive his past. However, when I explained to him that you had come a long way and I reminded him that you were an old friend of his he turned to me more happily and said that he would like to see Kyrie David." When she smiled with her full lips her face seemed to light up, as though the shadows of the years gone by were erased.

I wondered if this would be an appropriate moment for me to go and see Stephen, but she must have read my thoughts as she continued:

"It will be best if you see him in the morning after he has slept, and in the light of day, although it might be a shock for you. He has not left his bed for some weeks now, and I fear he is growing weak."

To underline what she had said I heard some continuous wracking of coughs from next door. Eventually the coughing stopped.

"His lungs are weak and they cause him much loss of breath now," she added in explanation.

Anna then spoke briskly to Marika in Greek. The conversation was loud with Marika's deafness.

"Kyrie David, after we have all had some food, Marika will show you where you can sleep. It will be in the small building at the end. Sometimes our shepherd friend Vincentios comes from the mountains to stay there, but he is away at present. There is only a straw mattress on the stone floor, I'm afraid, but there are plenty of blankets," she spoke apologetically.

"That will be fine, and thank you." I tried to sound appreciative of Anna's good intentions. Then to help foster goodwill, Georgios proceeded to show Anna the provisions and wine which I had carried up with the help of the donkeys in the Meteora climb.

Anna's tawny brown eyes thanked me, and then she took some of the food which Marika had cooked to the building which she shared with Stephen. Before leaving Anna said goodnight to the three of us. A short time later I sat down at the plain table with Marika and Georgios to partake of the simple but warming food that Marika had cooked. The bean soup was welcome after the tiring journey, and I remember that we also had some goats' cheese and bread. The coffee was thick and syrupy, and I offered Georgios one of my cigarettes. He and I sat back contentedly whilst Marika busied herself in the shepherd's hut.

"You might see Vincentios before you leave here," Georgios said pensively as he drew on his cigarette. "The weather is bad mostly at present, and he would be wise to have shelter here until February has ended."

"He won't take kindly to my having his bed," I laughed.

"It is alright. The room is big enough for two beds on the floor. He likes company after he has been alone on the mountains," Georgios smiled knowingly.

Marika came back into the kitchen, and then with an oil lamp she guided me to the sleeping quarters prepared for me.

The palliasse type mattress was covered with thick blankets, but the white-washed stone-walled room was cold and damp. Still, I was lucky in all the circumstances to have a roof over my head.

Marika wished me goodnight, and presently I tucked myself into the comforting blankets.

The wind moaned outside on the rocky heights, but when it spasmodically subsided there was an eerie mountain silence. If I was nearer to Paradise in the Meteora I did not feel it, but at least I didn't have to sleep on wooden boards or directly onto a stone floor.

Occasionally I could hear a strange muted sound. Perhaps it was Stephen coughing again or the heavy breathing of Marika or Georgios.

Although St Nicholas had not been one of the monasteries that had been kept and maintained by the monks, it seemed difficult to understand why people at one time had given up the material attributes of life for this isolation in a mountain fastness. And why had Stephen come here with Anna?

Sleep overcame my inquisitive mind as the moon cast a lustre of gold on the chapel roof.

I woke the following morning as daylight seeped into my sleeping quarters, and I could hear the sound of the voices of Georgios and Marika through the adjoining walls.

I had brought shaving kit and a small mirror with me, and by the time I had shaved and dressed I was feeling reasonably fresh again.

As I walked from my sleeping quarters to join Georgios and Marika I ventured under the pillared archway to the larger outer courtyard.

It was strange looking down at the billowing clouds below; it was like being on a ship floating on the clouds. I could hear the bells ringing in the other monasteries as though they were sending out distress signals in ice-bound seas. I surveyed the sad monastic remains of buildings. It seemed that it was only the chapel here that remained in a recognisable form, and even the chapel looked forlorn in isolation.

The cold air forced me to retreat to the inner small courtyard. Now that it was daylight I could see that our habitations consisted of former monks' cells; there was the one in which I slept, and the other two dwellings where stone walls had been demolished to make larger accommodation.

Marika's coffee and bread were very welcome. The combination of Marika's deafness and Georgios' lack of teeth made conversation difficult. There didn't seem much for Georgios to do when he was not fetching supplies from Kalambaka. Marika seemed to do all the cooking and the carrying of cooked food to the room occupied by Anna and Stephen.

I had marvelled at the stalactites of icicles hanging out

from jutting rock formations in my brief walk before breakfast. I was commenting on the sheer size of the icicles and Georgios enthused as he said:

"When the thaw arrives the icicles crash into the valley with a thunderous noise." He paused, and then added, "But it is nice when the Spring comes. I wish you could see my garden in the Spring and Summer, the cistus and tamarisk and thyme."

"You look after the garden then, Georgios?" I asked.

"I do, and we have a few goats and hens which also I attend to," he added.

Anna came into the room. Her smile seemed friendlier this morning.

"Did you manage to sleep?" she asked.

"Yes, thank you," I answered. "But I think I awoke early with the sound of bells."

"That is the Semantra of the other monasteries. Now if you have finished breakfast I will take you to see Stephanos." She started to lead the way to the next chamber.

"How is Stephanos today?" I asked.

"He seems a little better this morning, Kyrie David, but please do not tire him too much at first." Her brown eyes looked at me pleadingly.

It was snowing heavily and my feet had difficulty in keeping a grip on the ice-packed surface of the stone pathway as Anna opened the door of a large room which had been surprisingly well furnished. I suppose I had anticipated some truly spartan conditions, but there were a few comfortable chairs and the floor was rugged.

There was a straw-filled mattress in one corner, similar to the one that I was using; from here my eyes lifted to the proper bed and the face on the pillow.

I should have prepared myself for the charnel house shock—the scorched residue. I had been told several times about Stephen's rescue mission in that inferno at the school in Kalahori, but that tragic incident had been some years ago during the World War.

I had, of course, heard of the burnt airmen in the Royal Air Force during the World War, and how they had first looked in the early periods of their treatment. I remembered the great work of Sir Archibald McIndoe in the famous Queen Victoria Hospital at East Grinstead, and how the skin grafts eventually took on a fairly natural colour. I remembered the disfigurements and the mutilations of young men, and how sometimes their wives and girlfriends had stood by them—and sometimes they had not.

I think, therefore, that I had instinctively prepared myself for a shock, but I could not disguise the fact that I was completely appalled by the horrifying face lying before me.

The fire had obviously destroyed his eyelids, but surprisingly his hands seemed all right. His hair had been burnt away up to the middle of his scalp, but behind this it had grown thick in a stand-up fashion. His neck and jaw were seared, and his mouth was misshapen so that he could not close it properly; the nose was so burnt that it had a squashed appearance. Poor Stephen had not undergone any skin graft operations, and the burnt and affected skin seemed a purplish yellow.

He must have sensed my inward horror—he covered his eyes with dark glasses which he kept on the bedside table.

He seemed quite pleased to see me, although he was somewhat apprehensive at first.

"It's taken me a long time to find you, Stephen. I'm glad

to see you even if you have chosen a most inaccessible place to live—to keep visitors away no doubt." I smiled at him encouragingly.

"I don't know what brings you here, David, but as you can see I am very much a wreck now." As he spoke he seemed to control a fit of coughing with difficulty. "Sit down." He pointed to a chair near his bed, and then he signalled Anna to leave us. "The woman of the house, she is very obedient you see." His charred mouth framed itself into a grotesque grin. Then he rested his head on the propped-up pillows.

The air was silent except for the distant monastery bells. It seemed that Stephen had disowned all material possessions and material ways of life; he had left the world behind in coming to the Meteora. A 'moving cloud' seemed an apposite name for the place where he dwelt. What right had I to disturb his final peace? Oh! Yes, I could see—it wasn't only the horrible burns—there was a difficulty in breathing; his lungs were clearly under too much strain even at this altitude—he could not be long for this world.

"Well, David, why have you come to St Nicholas? Not just for the view in February's winter, I'm sure."

Bravely he tried to smile with his disfigured mouth; and seemed to scratch the remains of his nose. Momentarily I thought of Stephen with his once proud Roman nose—and what had Maria said in Urbino about the portrait of Federico Montefeltro? Hadn't the Duke Federico lost his sight in combat and then he had removed part of his nose so that he could see better with his one good eye?

Poor Stephen could certainly see better presumably without his Roman nose, but he hadn't wanted it incinerated in this way. Duke Federico had wanted part of his nose removed. It was only too apparent that any previous envy over Stephen and his good looks and power to attract the opposite sex was all washed away. In its wake was a shoal of pity, and self-doubt as to whether one had been fair to Stephen in the past.

Perhaps Stephen had been reading my thoughts. He seemed to stare at me through his dark glasses:

"I lost my eyelids, they were burnt away. It means that you can't close your eyes."

"Is it very uncomfortable?" I asked.

"No, but it is not good for the eyes. Perhaps I shall go blind before I die, perhaps not. We shall see." He seemed resigned to anything that lay ahead.

He waited for me to begin my explanation as to why I had searched for him. I decided it was best to tell him everything, so naturally I started by giving him an account of how his photograph appeared in a London Daily newspaper that I had been reading some months ago.

"Knowing you, I can imagine which newspaper it was, David," he interrupted with what seemed to be a slight sneer on his face. "You're an old die-hard, aren't you? Still, let's not talk about politics, right?"

His slightly challenging tone began to intimidate me, especially when I recalled his somewhat left-wing sympathies.

"I certainly haven't come all this way to talk politics, Stephen," I countered.

He apologised, and then I carried on telling him not only that I had recognised the photograph in the newspaper, but also that the Italian artist who had painted the original portrait had been trying to locate him after the War in order to let him have the portrait painting. "You see, Arturo

Manzoni, knew you as Major Stefano, but…"

"But he didn't know my surname, and certainly I wasn't going to tell him what it was. And then there was Maria of course." His interruption ended with a sigh.

"You always instinctively knew where to find the most lovely girls," I spoke enviously.

"Yes, you were envious in those days I don't doubt," he paused, "but not now." He ended quietly.

"Anyway, Stephen, surprising as it might seem to you, at the same time as that late summer in London when I saw the photograph, I fell in love with a South African girl who was working in London in our office."

"Spare me the details, David."

Ignoring this remark I went on. "Her name is Lydia, and eventually she came with me as far as Italy."

"But no further?" It wasn't a very friendly laugh, but I ignored it.

"Before Lydia and I left for Italy I went to the Public Records Office."

"Did you now? How did that help you?" His questioning became more defensive.

"I thought at first that the records would give me a lead as to what exactly had happened to you after we attacked north of Urbino during the Gothic Line operations; originally I had thought perhaps that your portrait had been painted at Benevento when I came across the name of that town."

"God, Benevento, that was a good course, David. No worries either."

"Not really, except I do remember that it was in Benevento that you told me how your parents had been killed in an air-raid. In fact I remember it well, as it was the first time I had ever seen you sad. We drowned our sorrows in wine that evening."

I paused whilst a spasm of Stephen's coughing filled the room.

"But Arturo Manzoni and his daughter Maria didn't live in Benevento, they lived in Urbino as you know."

"What did you do after leaving the Public Records Office?" Stephen asked with curious impatience. "I assume the Public Records Office was of no help to you?"

"It seemed to me that a part of the War Diary was missing, a vital page. Anyway, I went to see Justin Townsend in the Cotswolds. You will recall that he had been our Commanding Officer at that stage of the War," I answered as I stood up to stretch my legs and walk slowly around the room.

His dark-glassed scarred face followed my movements.

"I suppose old Justin was his usual vague self. Somewhat surprised to see you, I imagine, after so many years."

"I phoned him first of course, and he and his wife, Daphne, were quite hospitable. He was surrounded by dogs in his retirement."

"Did he spout poetry at you?"

"Only once, as I remember."

"He would call it poetic justice if he could see me now." His voice was beginning to sound tired. Anna came in with some coffee. It was only as she was leaving us again that she spoke:

"Only a half-hour more, David. He should sleep then."

I nodded my agreement, and felt the thick treacly coffee course down my throat.

"Anyway," I continued, "Justin confirmed that you had been posted as missing, believed killed in the Gothic Line operations; he also hinted that there were unconfirmed reports that later you had been involved with E.L.A.S. in Greece, and possibly taken prisoner by them. Frankly I didn't give much credence to the unconfirmed report at the time, and Justin professed no knowledge of the missing page from the War Diary. It seemed to me that Justin was apathetic when I visited him, but his health was not good after the War."

"So then you went to Italy?" Stephen's voice was raspily hoarse now.

"Not directly. Lydia sensibly suggested that I should try and contact some member of your family. It was then that I remembered that you had lost your parents in the Blitz, but that you had a sister living in London, a sister with whom you were not exactly on cordial terms."

"You went to see Margaret? You poor old chap. Did you come away with your tail between your legs?" His voice was now more sympathetic.

"Yes, I went to her Chelsea home. She is like you—in looks I mean," I answered.

"*Was* like me in looks, you mean."

"Yes, of course. I'm sorry."

"Was Margaret as devious as she usually is?" he asked.

"I had the feeling that she was holding something back perhaps. Certainly I would not describe her welcome to me as warm."

"What did she tell you, if anything?"

"She had heard about what she called 'unsubstantiated rumours' that you might have been in Greece, but she seemed convinced that you had died in Italy."

"So you see, my dear sister is not always right." It was a hollow laugh.

"She told me that you had in fact qualified as a doctor just before the War started. I asked her if she knew why there should be any part of the War Diary missing, but she denied any knowledge of this."

"You don't seem to have achieved much with Margaret, David old man."

"Ah! But there was the letter," I smiled into his dark screened eyes.

"Letter, what letter?" he questioned me agitatedly.

"Margaret told me of the letter you had sent her about that Canadian nurse, Joy Mitchell. You remember Joy—our mutual friend in Rome? Apparently you told Margaret that Joy had died in childbirth, but that there was a son. Your son, Eric, is nine years old now."

Anna came into the room, and she made it clear that I must leave Stephen to regain his strength.

Certainly he was looking very pale and worn. Because of the dark glasses I could not see his reaction to what I had been saying about his illegitimate son. I would have to let it rest until the following day.

As I left he said, "Did you know that Margaret is certainly better than me at one thing?"

"What's that?" I asked.

"She plays the piano beautifully. Strange, when there is no beauty in her soul." His breathing became deeper as he floated off to sleep.

★ ★ ★

Marika offered me some dark bread and goat's cheese and apples for lunch, but in truth I was not hungry. I had taken no exercise all morning, and the shocking appearance of Stephen had undoubtedly upset me.

Anyway I toyed with the food and ate a little in order to satisfy Marika, and as it was no longer snowing I ventured out into the small courtyard. I strolled under the pillared arch and then into the main courtyard. The wind was chill.

Certainly the monks' cells in this part of the monastery were in an abandoned and ruined state. The small chapel still had a desolate appearance, but the structure was intact.

Then I entered the chapel itself and in the gloom I was beginning to regret that I had not brought a candle to lighten up the dark voids. However, as my eyes became accustomed to the light I could see a candlestick and holder by one of the miserere-stalls near the chancel. With my matches I lit the candle, and shadows formed across the lectern and altar. I was surprised that these monastic chapel fixtures and adornments were in such a reasonable condition when compared with the adjacent monks' cells.

The silence and the peaceful aura were profoundly affecting. It almost seemed that I had been too quick to criticise the withdrawal of Stephen and Anna to this remote place in the heavens, their abandonment of the materialistic world where no one could respond hurtfully to their charred bodies.

It was as though the clouds floated through the chapel; in fact, a misty cloud seemed to blur my vision temporarily. I started suddenly as something brushed my legs clingingly. I looked down at my feet and in the dimness I could see a tortoise-shell cat. A strange companion in this holy place.

It seemed sad that historical economic factors and destructive wars had contributed to the desolation of some of these ruined monasteries. A few of the monasteries still thrived, but there were not many monks in them, and they had lost their mountain farms. We had brought materialistic advancement from the West, so perhaps we had much to answer for.

There were still one or two frescoes on the walls, but alas these were in a sorry state. One appeared to be a Nativity scene and the other of a dark bearded figure in a long cape.

"That is a fresco of St Nicholas; it is said that he built this monastery."

The unexpected words piercing the silent gloom startled me, until I recognised the voice of Georgios.

"I try to preserve what is left here. I have been buttressing one of the walls. Anna likes the chapel to be looked after. This is another of my jobs, you see." I could sense a smile playing on his bearded lips.

"The tortoise-shell cat?" I asked.

"Ah! You have seen Mitso. He often comes here. I expect you will meet the female black and white cat before long. She is called Marina," answered Georgios.

"How did the cats get to this isolated place, Georgios?"

"Zena and Yanni in Kalambaka gave them to me one day when I was in Kalambaka getting food supplies. I think the cats were worried during the journey up the mountains," he laughed, "But once they settled in here they seemed to like it. After all, they have no competition from other cats or dogs."

We had wandered out into the main courtyard and Mitso was following us across the snowy cobbles. The world below was screened from us by the vast clouds full of snow, and I could only dimly discern the parapets.

The light was fading, and I accompanied Georgios back to his stone-walled home.

Marika was adding various pieces of kindling to the fire, and soon she had a warming blaze to prepare the cooked meal.

Then Georgios produced some ouzo, and at last I felt as though I was sufficiently hungry to enjoy a meal.

Normally I would have found the meal that Marika had prepared too oily, but the cold outside air had sharpened my appetite and the cooked minced meat was very welcome.

"It is strange," I said to Georgios, "that the chapel is in fairly sound condition, but so much of the remainder of the monastery is in ruins."

"There were a few monks here—and an abbot—until a few years ago. During the Civil War, the Communist guerrillas attacked the monastery. I think there were a few National Guard here. The E.L.A.S. guerrillas cut their throats. The National Guards couldn't even escape by throwing themselves over the parapets. The guerrillas had heavy weapons and they caused much destruction. They even beat up the abbot." Georgios shook his head sadly. "I suppose the Monastery of St Nicholas was in a state of decline anyway, but the Civil War hastened the end in a bitter fashion." His face was pale against the shadows of the oil-lamp.

★ ★ ★

Later on I went to bed next door. It had been a strange day; it seemed a pity that I had been forced to discontinue my discussions with Stephen just as I had started to talk about Joy Mitchell and Eric, their son. I wanted to know what really happened, but it would have to wait.

It seemed the sensible course was now to give Stephen a

full account of my search for him in the first instance before I asked him to explain what actually happened to him since he and I had last been together in the Gothic Line battles.

I pulled the blankets closely around my shoulders and, sighing, wished that Lydia was still with me in these precipitous mountains. Lydia and my normal life seemed so far away. Soon I was fast asleep.

★ ★ ★

The next morning Anna once again discreetly left me alone with Stephen. I still found it a deep shock to visit him in his present state. I tried my best not to show any feeling on the matter; in fact, for this second visit of mine, Stephen seemed more rested and cheerful, even though his breathing was erratic.

"I expect it came as quite a surprise to you when Margaret told you about Joy Mitchell and that I had a son?" Stephen pushed his dark glasses over the staring eyes.

"Yes it did," I admitted, "although my first reaction was one of sadness that Joy was no longer alive."

"You always were a bit jealous over that affair, weren't you?" It was that sneering look again.

"A pity it was only an affair as far as you were concerned, Stephen." I checked myself from going further. I had to make myself realise that I was with a sick man, not the laughing, all-conquering heroic Stephen. "I remember lending you a white shirt," I remarked, changing the subject.

"You did indeed," he confirmed.

Then, remembering my thoughts of the previous evening, I embarked on a description of my search for him.

"I obtained the address of the Italian artist from a Fleet Street contact, and Lydia and I travelled by train through France and into Italy to reach Urbino."

"You were surprised, no doubt," he interjected, "that the portrait was painted in Urbino."

"Yes I was. After all there would certainly have been no time for a sitting as we drove northwards during the War, and you went 'missing, believed killed' shortly afterwards. Lydia and I settled into Urbino and we contacted Arturo Manzoni and his daughter Maria."

"Ah! Dear Maria. A pity she was so possessive," he interrupted again.

"She was in love with you. She still is," I protested.

"Not now, David. She wouldn't be in love with me now if she could see how I am—you know that as well as I do."

The silence that followed was broken by the quiet approach of Anna with our coffee. I thought that Anna looked even more tired than the previous day, but she smiled at me and quietly reassured me that she was glad that Stephen was able to see an old friend at last.

After Anna had left us alone again I resumed, "You did not leave your surname with Arturo Manzoni, nor with Maria. Presumably that was deliberate. You had led them to believe that you were actually working in the military medical field. Anyway, it was now clear to me that you had not been killed in the battles north of Urbino. Maria had given me the address of a farm."

"The Salvati farm." He seemed to gaze into the distance, although this was conjecture on my part—the dark glasses disguised the objects of his vision.

"Yes." I paused before adding, "Lydia went back to London then."

Perhaps he sensed the underlying disappointment in my tone of voice. "You never could hang on to a girl. You lacked charm or something." His chuckle sounded almost obscene.

The silence was interrupted by the melancholy calls of birds of prey above us in the heavens.

Anyway, I chose to ignore these latest remarks, and described to him how Giovanni Salvati at the farm had shown me evidence that he, Stephen, had reached E.L.A.S. territory in Trikkala in Greece.

"So you hadn't been killed, and you hadn't been wounded." I started to walk around the room in a restless fashion.

"Then you came to Greece on your own?" he asked.

"Yes, but I had two previous connections. You see, our Battalion was posted to Greece from Italy to help clear up the E.L.A.S. troubles. I had kept in touch since the end of the War with Bill Wyatt, a war correspondent, and Ken Dacre who had worked in U.N.R.R.A. They are still in Greece; Ken Dacre now works in a hospital and he is married and they have a daughter. Bill is engaged to a girl from Salonika."

I don't know why I gave him the details of the private lives of my two old colleagues. After all Stephen was not going to see them presumably, but it seemed that I wanted to maintain the full picture in my mind of the realism of my journeying.

Before Stephen had time to interrupt I went on: "Bill and I went by road to Salonika, and then Zoe, Bill's fiancée, joined us for a further road journey to Kavalla. They were able to combine business with pleasure. Our Battalion had been in Kavalla during the troublesome time with E.L.A.S..." I looked over at Stephen, but he gave no indication as to whether he knew of this or not.

"How did you get on from there? I should have thought that you reached a dead-end at Kavalla." Stephen was clearly puzzled.

"I thought that the trail had gone cold," I admitted, "but then Zoe introduced me to Nikos Solomos. He was the curator of a museum in Florina, near Mount Vitsi. Nikos told me much about the Civil Wars, and I questioned him about the time of the German occupation of Greece. It was only near the end of our initial talks that Nikos mentioned Kalahori."

I looked at Stephen. He did not say anything, but I saw his hands clutch the blankets of his bed in a frenzied grip.

"Nikos had heard of a Stephanos who had apparently saved two women in the school house fire at Kalahori. I thought that this Stephanos might possibly be you; but it was a long shot. I arranged to stay with Nikos in Florina, and then he and I went in his car to Trikousa. It was early December then. We stayed with a peasant friend of Nikos' in Trikousa. Her name was Chrysoula. From here a guide called Paul directed us up through the rocky mountains by mule. There was much snow on the mountain paths as you can imagine."

"So you eventually reached Kalahori," Stephen spoke in a whisper. Again there was silence until his whole body shook with a rasping cough.

"Yes. At Kalahori we met Andreas, the village patriarch. Eventually, after I had learnt all about Kalahori, Andreas described how an English doctor with a Resistance group had saved two sisters from the fiery furnace, how the three of you had been badly burnt. Andreas referred to the doctor as Stephanos, and then described you, Stephen."

I was going to add 'especially your nose', but this time I

was able to check myself as I looked at his charred and smudged face.

"There was further suffering later on in Kalahori," I went on, "but, of course I expect you know about that."

"What else did you learn at Kalahori?" Stephen asked.

"Nothing, I'm afraid. There was no lead as far as you and the two sisters were concerned. It was a big disappointment to me after so much progress. I was back in Kavalla for Christmas; I had a cheery visit at Christmas from Bill and Zoe."

As I spoke I realised that all this seemed a long time ago.

"Leventeia," Stephen whispered over his blanket cover.

"Yes. I was resigned to planning my return to London when my American friend, Ken Dacre, phoned me. Through the hospital in Athens where he worked he had been able to trace Anna's sister Elena. Apparently Elena had been treated for burns. Ken's wife Sofia visited Elena's apartment on the outskirts of Athens. Elena had recovered well after the plastic surgery. I believe Elena was reticent over telling Sofia anything about your whereabouts, but eventually Sofia obtained the disclosure that you and Anna were thought to be living in the Meteora region."

We were both then silent with our thoughts. After a while, Anna brought in our lunch. Obviously today she thought that Stephen was well enough for me to stay and for us to eat our food together. The soup was welcomingly hot, and we had the usual dark bread and cheese. Outside there was a further fall of snow, but the room was relatively warm with oil stoves.

After a long pause I added: "So Nikos and I came to Kalambaka."

"And then you came here," Stephen sighed audibly.

"Yes. We stayed with Zena and Yanni Diamanti in Kalambaka. We told Zena and Yanni why we were in Kalambaka at this time of the year," I continued.

Suddenly his body stiffened and his hands shook; there seemed to be a trembling rage within him.

"I made them promise that they would never tell anyone, never tell any visitor where Anna and I were staying." His anger caused a long fit of coughing.

"I assure you, Stephen, that Zena and Yanni were very reluctant to tell us where you were, but they appreciated that I had come a long way to find you. Also, they thought that as you have been so poorly it might cheer you up to see an old friend, an old Army friend of yours."

Stephen seemed to be more relaxed now.

"Are you concerned about your 'philotimos'?" I asked smilingly.

As far as he was able, with that distortion of a mouth, he grinned at me.

I went on: "Nikos came most of the way with me. We travelled on donkeys; Georgios was our guide."

Anna came into the room to take away our plates, and I knew from her look that it was now time for me to leave Stephen once more.

Marina, the black and white cat, had followed Anna into the room, and settled at the foot of Stephen's bed.

At least I had given Stephen a reasonably full account of my travels to reach him here on St Nicholas. Perhaps tomorrow he would tell me more about himself and what actually had happened to him all those years ago. Although sometimes the 1939-1945 War seemed like yesterday.

I walked around the monastery grounds amidst the

disintegrating stonework and rotting timbers. It was like being on another planet, supported by smooth rock-grey pillars, mossy and damp. It seemed to me that we were on a level and just as high up as the other monasteries. Sadly I looked at the snow-blanketed garden.

"I wish you could see the crocuses and anemones. It all looks so different in the Spring and Summer."

It was Georgios speaking with a grumbling voice as he cleared the snowbound stone pathway.

"Had I known my journey was to take me to the Meteora I expect I would have made different plans, Georgios," I smiled encouragingly at him.

"Perhaps Stephanos will be well enough to take wine with you one evening," he suggested.

"I hope so. Especially after having brought the wine all that way up the mountainside." Laughingly, I looked into the distance; there was the faint sound of bells ringing from one of the monasteries across the ravines and chasms. Eagles and kestrels flew overhead with graceful movements.

Slowly Georgios and I returned to the warmth of the kitchen. Marika was already preparing the evening meal, and Mitso the cat had sensibly taken up a position near the warm stove.

Anna had been helping Marika, but she had now returned to Stephen. I tried to conjecture at the relationship between Stephen and Anna. Had they merely been, say, comrades-in-arms, if that was the right expression, or had there been a more intimate relationship? Perhaps I would never know.

It was as though Marika had sensed my thoughts. She didn't volunteer any information about the past, but she turned to Georgios and asked him quietly if Anna was making plans to join her sister near Athens if anything bad should happen to Stephanos. At least with my smattering of Greek I think that was Marika's question to Georgios. Georgios shrugged his shoulders; obviously he was fatalistic about the future, but for him, living at the St Nicholas monastery had become a way of life.

Later on Georgios joined me in drinking some ouzo, and soon after our meal I decided to go to bed. Leaving their warm room to venture into the cold outside was not an easy decision. The evening darkness and passing clouds gave the impression that we were floating once more cocooned in an icebound liner. I was soon under the blankets in my own little room, and the mountain air brought an early sleep in this eerie dreamworld.

In my dreams I was back with Lydia, but I could only dream of her, I could not hold her in my arms. So let me dream.

★ ★ ★

The following morning Stephen seemed more agitated when I went to see him, but I attributed this to whatever he was going to tell me of himself which would no doubt be a painful reminder of the past. Anna had accompanied Marika to the small chapel; apparently they made regular visits there to maintain an air of cleanliness before lingering dust surfaced over all. I daresay too, that Anna and Marika prayed there from time to time. The heavenly clouds no doubt would merge with their entreaties in the dust-moted stalls. So Georgios maintained the structure whilst Anna and Marika kept it clean.

I sat down once more in the chair facing Stephen expecting him to begin by describing the last time we had been near one another just north of Urbino during the Gothic Line Battles and what had been the sequence of events in his life from then.

However, he went further back than this. At first I thought he was just describing one of his many past conquests with the female sex, but when I heard his murmuring about her blue eyes, fair hair, luscious lips and tall slender figure I knew he was recalling his time with Joy Mitchell; his time with her in Rome. Perhaps he wanted to recall his memory of her and the pleasant time they had experienced together. Perhaps he just wanted to remind me of what I had missed that time in Rome.

He looked at me with a grain of sympathy:

"She wasn't right for you anyway, David."

"Why not?" I asked.

"I don't know. Too brash perhaps."

I started to walk up and down the room.

"So you knew that Joy was pregnant and eventually you knew that she had died in childbirth, and that you had a son?" I asked for confirmation.

"Yes. I met Joy once or twice after our time together in Rome. She was posted to a hospital not far behind the lines where we were operating. Before I left the Salvati family in Italy I wrote to Joy. I told her in my letter to write to the Salvati farm and that news of her would reach me. You see, for once, I had really fallen in love."

"And yet you went to another country?"

"Yes, well, there were reasons—" he paused, and then speaking of himself again he said, "It didn't seem to be me—

I mean actually loving someone this way. I'd always been so self-centred before, hadn't I, David?"

He had put his dark glasses on now. I was glad of this as the staring eyes were scary somehow. As if anticipating my question he continued:

"Some time after I had joined the guerrillas in Greece I heard from Signor Salvati. Joy was apparently pregnant. I was caught up in all the Greek troubles at the time, but I managed to get word back to Italy. Joy knew that I loved her, and that I would marry her as soon as that was possible."

Stephen's agitation increased, and the anxiety showed on his face again. He paused whilst a fit of coughing swept through him.

"And then later you learnt through the same Salvati link that Joy was no longer alive, and that you had a son," I spoke for him now realising what had happened.

"Yes. By this time I was a burnt hulk of a man. Communications were difficult, and then much later—I think it was about May—about V.E. Day—I heard what had actually happened."

"Wait a minute," I ventured. "Your sister, Margaret, when I went to see her in London, told me that the last time she heard from you was in a letter from Italy. I remember her saying that it was unusual to get a letter from you, but that she had heard from Italy."

"Actually I wrote to her from Greece, but I used the Salvati address. I sent all my letters to Signor Salvati for him to post for me in Italy."

"So no one of your family or friends knew you were actually in Greece?" I asked.

"Not at that time. My middle name is Eric, and I wrote to

Margaret about my son." He seemed to regain some pride in his voice.

"You asked for your son to have the name of Eric?"

"Yes," he answered. "I asked Margaret to look after Eric whilst I was overseas." There was another long pause before he continued. "Long before I became a father—some years ago in fact—I had a formal will made out in England before going overseas, leaving all my estate to my sister. My parents at that time seemed to think it was for the best. Anyway, I managed to remember this, and just as the Civil War in Greece was starting—you remember, Greek against Greek."

"The third round?" I interrupted.

"Yes. I sent word in a letter to Margaret asking her to get my will annulled. I told her in my letter that everything I had was to be held in trust for Eric. You have to understand that my estate became quite substantial when my parents lost their lives in that air-raid."

"I see." I hoped that I was beginning to see through a little of the fog of mystery that seemed to surround Stephen. I suppose it was my legally trained mind that caused me to store up this last piece of information about wills. Perhaps I would need it at some future date, although up here in the Meteora it all seemed a far distant piece of the jigsaw puzzle.

Anna came in with some coffee, having no doubt finished the chapel cleaning. Anxiously she asked me how I thought Stephen was today. I reassured her, but inwardly it seemed to me that his strength was ebbing away.

I was prepared to leave our future discussions until later or even until the following day, but after sipping his coffee, he looked at me and said, "Do you remember that white shirt you lent me in Rome?"

I knew then that he was going to tell me what happened when he went missing, believed killed, just north of Urbino during the Gothic Line Battles.

"Yes." My laughter was hollow and strained. "It was lent for one of your evenings with Joy, although you never returned the shirt."

"Sorry, old man, but it had its uses. It looked rather impressive, I thought. Something different. A white shirt instead of the usual khaki drill."

"You kept that shirt of mine a long time. I suppose you kept it to remind you of your successes with your sex life." Why did I always have to sound a note of bitterness when thinking of Stephen's relationship with Joy?

"When I said the shirt had its uses, I was thinking of that action north of Urbino," Stephen spoke quietly.

I could hear once more the distant ringing of bells from the nearby monastery. I think I will always remember the peels floating across the mountain clouds.

"What actually happened there, Stephen?" I asked in a low voice.

"You remember how the Jerries were waiting for us on the next ridge after we advanced from Urbino? I was probing forward with my company and with the Carrier Platoon towards the village with its church and campanile. I had gone forward to the leading Bren Gun Carrier. We were sitting ducks for target practice for a couple of Tiger tanks. I had just left the Carrier in order to return to the Company position when the Carrier suffered a direct hit. I ran back to the Carrier. They were all dead except for the driver. That white shirt. Yes, your white shirt. I tore it off to try and stop the flow of blood of that poor driver. He died in my arms."

Then I interrupted him: "I came up shortly after with my Company. A young boy in the Carrier Platoon handed me the bloodied white shirt, but there was no sign of you. Naturally you were posted as missing, believed killed. What happened? Where did you go?" I asked.

"I remember it all only faintly now. I'm not sure whether I ever remembered it clearly. It is like a permanent blur. Perhaps it was…"

"Shell-shock?" I interrupted him. We were both groping for the right words.

"Temporarily, maybe. We had a word for it, 'bomb-happy' wasn't it? Anyway I think I wandered off in a daze. You remember how I always used to wear a blue forage cap instead of a steel helmet, much to Justin Townsend's annoyance? Anyway, I left my blue forage cap with that bloodied white shirt. I suppose I thought that the powers that be would assume that I had been killed."

"I don't think that they ever found your blue forage cap. As I suspected, you hadn't actually been wounded then?" I persisted with my questioning.

"Not physically anyway, but the long war trail from Africa and up through Italy must have taken its toll. I couldn't think straight anymore. I remember staggering off down one of the many tracks into a shadowed valley. I crossed a stream and followed a path to a stone farmhouse. There were the usual farmyard noises and dogs barking. I must have presented a strange sight."

"What was so strange?" I asked.

"No longer was I wearing that shirt, and I had no headgear. Signora Salvati thought that I was trying to loot the farm at first. That's not surprising in the circumstances.

Fortunately her husband soon arrived on the scene. He thought I was some sort of spy, but we conversed in English and after they realised that I was harmless, they provided shelter for me. I suppose, looking back on it, that Il Signor Salvati was more concerned as to whether I would be of any use to their Communist cause." He paused to regain his breath after another fit of coughing, and then continued: "Nevertheless they provided me with a temporary home and plain food—they even managed to find me a khaki shirt of sorts."

"How long did you stay with the Salvatis?"

"I'm not sure now. Some weeks maybe. I remember their son, Giovanni; the father was trying to get him to learn English. I was the reluctant teacher. Naturally after a while I began to realise the enormity of what I had done. My nights were sleepless agonies. The more I became myself again so the impossibility of the situation impressed itself on me."

"Because of your desertion, you mean?"

"Yes, but desertion—that wasn't me, you know that."

"I know that," I confirmed quietly.

"I tried to forget what happened. The War had moved on so I ventured into Urbino. As you know so well now, I met Maria several times. I think she was in love with me, but all my love was for Joy really. I asked myself a thousand times, 'Would Joy ever forgive me for what I had done?'…" His voice trailed off.

"Then Arturo Manzoni painted your portrait. You were wearing a white shirt for your sittings, I remember. For some reason this seemed symbolic to me, although I knew of course that it couldn't be the same white shirt that I had lent you so long ago."

"Symbolic? Why?"

"It was as though that bloodied white shirt that I had given you and which was found on the field of battle was the end of one life. The fresh white Urbino shirt represented the start of a new life, a clean break."

Stephen laughed. "You shouldn't read too much symbolism into events, David. I suppose I had been fortunate to see Maria stumble and twist her ankle. I had to make up a story quickly when I went to help her. I told her that I was a Doctor which was not untrue, and the Army Casualty Clearing Station near the town gave credence to my story. I was able to take Maria and her father some food from the farm, but Il Signor Salvati did not like my visits to the town."

"She still loves you, you know." I had to say it.

"Who, Maria? She wouldn't love me if she could see me now, David. Nothing but a burnt wreck, eh?"

As in Shakespeare's *Twelfth Night*, perhaps he had been in love with love, or in love with melancholy, or in love with himself, I thought.

Anna came in with Stephen's lunch and her own, but I didn't stay with them. I joined Georgios and Marika next door for some midday food.

It had been enough for one day, for both Stephen and I. Also, after some food and coffee, I felt I needed some fresh air, however wintry it was.

It wasn't snowing, but the air was raw and biting in the outer courtyard. There was no sign of the cats who presumably had wisely considered that it was too cold to be outside in the open.

I proceeded to walk around the courtyard at a quick pace, and after a while I took refuge from the low temperature in the chapel. There was a deserted darkness in the chapel, but the peace and quiet attuned with my deep-felt thoughts. I sat for a while in the hard-backed stall below the low wooden roof and thought about Stephen Hardinge, that heroic, swashbuckling military commander, the man whose physical presence had turned so many female heads. Eventually the strain of war had become too much for him, but only in a temporary manner. The irony of it was that his defection had only led to worse horrors as he would surely tell me in the days to come.

And what of Anna? How exactly did she fit into all this? Seemingly content in this isolated mountain eyrie, and yet saddened by what the future would hold.

I left the darkness of the holy place, and walked alongside the garden in its winter clothing. Suddenly I realised that it was St David's Day, and sighed to think that I would probably miss the sight of the first daffodils in England that year. Spring would not reach the Meteora for some time yet. Somewhat sorrowfully I entered the kitchen and dining quarters of Georgios and Marika.

Marika was busy adding more kindling to the fire in the sooty kitchen; Georgios was pleased to see me back inside their home—it meant that he could take down the ouzo from its shelf and pour some for me and charge his own glass as well. Certainly the water was too cold to drink on its own.

They led a lonely life in this Polar wilderness, scarcely ever seeing anyone except when they journeyed to Kalambaka for provisions. It was a decaying, isolated hermitage, and yet no one here seemed to complain. It was as though they had given up all material aspirations, as though the outer world below this blue-pillared rocky domain had been tried and tested and found wanting.

"In the old days you could only get here by a rope ladder." Georgios stroked his thick beard. "You had to be fit and healthy for the climb then, Kyrie David." He chuckled through his hirsute nest. "Now everything is crumbling away. The monks who lived here before the War will never return now."

I could hear the clanging of the distant bells again.

Suddenly Georgios brightened up. All his features seemed to sparkle. He poured us both some more ouzo.

"Remember the words of the Greek Testament, Kyrie. 'Wine makes glad the hearts of men'."

We clinked our glasses together. I hadn't noticed that Anna had been listening to what Georgios had been saying.

"Not if you drink too much," she laughed, and then turned to me: "Kyrie David, the shepherd, Vincentios, will be staying here for a few nights. He will be arriving later today, but you should be able to manage together the space next door."

"Thank you for telling me, Anna. I'm sure we shall be able to cope," I assured her.

Later on that evening the door opened with an inrush of cold wind, and Vincentios arrived clutching a tall crook. He seemed to be wearing moccasins of a sort, and his body was mainly wrapped in sheepskin clothing. At first he had a wild appearance, but the main contrast with Georgios and Marika was in his youthfulness.

It was quite refreshing to see someone in this mountainous retreat who was young and friendly. His blue eyes shone out of a weather-beaten countenance, his flaxen hair thick and tousled over a chubby face. He was quite tall, but not broad, and I could foresee no difficulties in our having to share accommodation.

Vincentios greeted the news that he had a cell-mate with

cheery matter-of-factness. Clearly he was a favourite of Marika's, and she plied him with much hot and plain food.

Presently an aura of peace descended. Georgios smoked his narghile, and Vincentios appreciatively accepted one of my cigarettes. We sipped glasses of raki and ate some walnuts that Marika had produced like a conjuring trick out of nowhere.

For a moment the only sound was the coughing next door of Stephen. Sadly this reminded me of what I had learnt that morning. In some way I took comfort from the ordinariness of my own life, and I felt disturbed and almost apprehensive as to what I should learn on the morrow.

As anticipated Vincentios and I had no difficulty in settling down on the mattressed floor. I suppose it was the healthy air that sent Vincentios off to sleep almost as soon as his head hit the pillow.

There would be a long tale to tell Lydia when I next saw her. The thought of Lydia in the London Spring suddenly seemed such a wonderful fantasy. Not too long before we met again, I hoped—and prayed.

★ ★ ★

"So you probably think of me as a deserter," he said it as a statement of fact.

My silence was another form of cowardice. Had he been a deserter? Not the Stephen that I recalled. Temporary shell-shock or bomb-happiness maybe, but then he had quickly recovered himself. He went on:

"The longer I stayed at the Salvati farm, the more I felt sure that somehow I had to exonerate myself in Joy's eyes. Besides, Maria was taking our relationship too seriously.

Arturo Manzoni had finished painting my portrait." He started to cough, and so I interrupted:

"Perhaps no one has ever loved you like Maria, you know," I spoke quietly across his bed to his haggard and wrecked face.

"Maybe so, but it was a love too stifling, too much for me." He paused, his staring eyes looking down at the cat Mitso curled up at the foot of his bed.

Putting on his dark glasses he continued: "It was clear to me that Signor Salvati was engaged in some clandestine business, and gradually I obtained his confidence. He had been active in a partisan cell, and also he had links with the Communist cells in Yugoslavia and Greece. I felt that with my military training I would be an asset to any guerrilla formation. Several times I hinted at this to Signor Salvati. At first his wife was suspicious of my motives, but eventually they agreed for me to go to Greece and join the E.L.A.S..."

"So you thought that this line of action of working with partisans behind the lines would not only give you back your reputation as a brave soldier, particularly in Joy's estimation, but no doubt you also visualized an exciting role for yourself. Was that your reasoning?" I asked.

"Something like that. Also, I knew I must get away from there, from visiting the Manzonis. I told Maria that I was going to Greece and she asked me how she could write to me. I told her to send any letters to the Salvati farm for forwarding to me."

Then I told Stephen how the Salvati son, Giovanni, had shown me an extract from a wartime letter he had found in the farm in Italy which confirmed that he, Stephen, had arrived safely at E.L.A.S. headquarters at Trikkala in Central' Greece.

"Apparently you then operated in the Mount Vitsi region and Kozani to the north west," I added.

"Yes, that's right. We had a terrible sea journey from Pesaro first of all. They gave more importance to the weapons and ammunition than they did to me," he added bitterly. "Our schooner had to take shelter in the island of Vis off the Yugoslav coast for a time because of the German E boats, and we could only move safely at night."

"Vis? I don't know anything about Vis. Tell me about it," I encouraged him.

"Vis was an island surrounded by German held territory in Yugoslavia, but the Yugoslav partisans and some British Commandos defiantly hung on to Vis." He paused whilst Mitso changed position on his bed. "They certainly fought against the odds there; their supplies were limited and there were practically no medical facilities. Added to this there was the usual red tape from up above. Maybe it was seeing how the medical staff tried to overcome their difficulties on Vis which finally led to my medical work in Greece. Or maybe it was just Fate."

We had been talking for some time, and both of us I think were glad to have a break for coffee. It was Anna who again brought us our refreshment, but she quickly withdrew once more. I could faintly hear her talking to Vincentios next door.

"Eventually I reached Trikkala in Central Greece. I think the E.L.A.S. headquarters there thought that I had been sent as a British Liaison Officer from the British Military Mission who were trying to bolster the Resistance groups in the mountains during the German occupation."

"So it was as a Liaison Officer that you joined the E.L.A.S. partisans in the Mount Vitsi region?" I asked.

"Yes, at first that is. The E.L.A.S. groups were much stronger than the rival E.D.E.S. groups, but I hadn't expected the rivalry between the different Partisan outlooks. I hadn't been prepared for that."

"Somewhat disillusioning, I imagine," I smiled enigmatically.

"Yes, rarely would the Groups cooperate together, unless they thought in any particular action against the Germans that one group would get all the credit if they didn't act with one another. However, it was later on when I assisted at parachute drops that I became angry with the E.L.A.S. partisans. A Halifax or Wellington bomber would wait for the recognition signals and then the containers would be parachuted down. If arms were dropped the E.L.A.S. partisans would use them against the rival guerrilla forces, or store them for future use against their rivals; if any golden sovereigns were sent by cylinder drop the E.L.AS. kept this bonanza for themselves, although the villagers had also been entitled to gold sovereign allowances. Also after the Italian surrender, many Italian soldiers agreed to fight the Germans, and not suspecting any deviousness, they instructed the E.L.A.S. partisans as to how to operate Italian weapons. The E.L.A.S. then stripped the Italians of their clothing and boots and their weaponry."

"So what did you do when you became so disillusioned?" I seemed to be questioning him all the time this morning.

"Looking around me in the mountains there seemed to be fighting on all sides, against the Germans, against the Italians, between different Partisan groups, and there was the ruthlessness of the E.L.A.S. against the mountain peasants. The British Military Mission had obviously hoped to give such support to the Partisan groups that their harassment of the Germans in occupation would be severe, but it was not as effective as it should have been, as I've explained. It seemed to me that I could give most help now as a Doctor."

"So you turned from the fighting role to a medical role?" I asked for confirmation.

"Yes," he said." As you know I qualified just before the War, but I had always wanted to be in the thick of the fighting. Then there was that incident north of Urbino and my temporary bomb-happiness. I came to Greece to fight with the guerrillas, but as you now know they fought amongst themselves.

"I think what finally convinced me that I could serve best as a Medico was an incident I witnessed one day in a Greek village—in fact I was forced to watch as the E.L.A.S. commander I was working with ordered the torture and death of a non-communist partisan. It was terrible. The poor man was splayed out and tied to a table in the open square of a village. Very slowly he was then hacked to pieces."

"My God! What bestiality," I exclaimed.

Stephen continued: "I couldn't bear to watch it all and to hear the screams of agony. I put the victim out of pain with my revolver. The E.L.A.S. were of course furious with me. One night the E.L.A.S. group with whom I was working suddenly found themselves without a British Liaison Officer. I had slipped past the sentries, and set off on foot towards Florina."

"Florina? I recently met the curator of the museum there, Nikos Solomos. He has been a good friend to me, and as I have already explained he came as far as Kalambaka with me and up into the Meteora." I wanted to talk and think of my friends away from this place. There were times when it seemed so doom-ridden here.

It was time for a break—time for Stephen to rest again.

When I walked past the garden after lunch and exercised myself in the main courtyard, a fitful sun broke through the layers of white cloud and cast peaceful shadows on the stonework. The sun burnished the rock and I caught the shadow of a hawk hovering overhead. There was the comforting distant ringing of bells and far away I could faintly hear the bleating of sheep. Truly there were moments when it was a heavenly place, and the air was always crisp and clear.

It was at times like this that I could understand why Stephen had come to St Nicholas, and why he had turned his back on the world. He would no doubt continue his story on the following day. There were really only a few days left before my expected rendezvous with Nikos and my return to the materialistic world.

Later on that day the sun disappeared, the clouds darkened and snow again began to feather the landscape.

We had eaten well of a hot meat stew, and around the kitchen fire I joined Georgios and Vincentios to drink the now familiar ouzo. Marika was busy preparing some dishes for the following day, whilst Anna as usual was sitting next door with Stephen.

I was enjoying the evening Greek warmth of hospitality after the morning's sombre account of Stephen's experiences with the Communist guerrillas.

The wind was getting up again, and started to moan and whine around the stone walls and rocky outcrops.

"Georgios sometimes used to join me on the mountains as I looked after my flock of sheep, but he does not visit me these days, Kyrie David," Vincentios sighed, as he stretched out his long legs before the fire.

"I am too old now, Vincentios, but I used to spend many days on the mountains with you, sleeping in your hut and drinking your wine, eh?" Georgios laughed as he stroked his beard. "Do you know, Kyrie David, that during the German occupation Vincentios hid two British soldiers in his hut on the mountain for several months."

I looked towards Vincentios.

"Yes," he said. "I managed to keep them hidden before they were able to escape South towards the sea."

"How did they manage for food?" I asked.

"Goats' cheese and apples. I shared my bread with them. After they left it was some time before I met Stephanos and Anna, but you must allow Stephanos himself to tell you of that."

I offered him a cigarette hoping that he would tell me more, but I sensed that he and Georgios had been schooled to be as reticent as possible when talking of Stephen and Anna.

"Stephanos will tell you all you need to know, or all you should know," Georgios gazed sadly into the fire until Mitso jumped onto his lap. Smilingly he soothed the tortoiseshell furry cat who purred obligingly.

"Stephanos is not long for this world, Kyrie. I'm sure Anna knows this." Vincentios stood up and went to say goodnight to Marika.

I said goodnight to Georgios and Marika myself, and went outside briefly before retiring for the night to my makeshift bed.

It was no longer snowing, and the moon had gilded the Basilican chapel. The silence of the mountain peaks was overwhelming.

★ ★ ★

I was up early the next morning and exercised myself in the restricted courtyards and garden before breakfast. The garden was beginning to show the promise of the Spring to come, but the surrounding mountains were all snow-capped still.

It was curious that my vertigo weakness seemed to have left me on these rocky peaks. I suppose it was like travelling on a plane which also held no fears of giddiness for me.

The two cats were gambolling on the snow-compacted cobblestones, and in turn they brushed my legs seeking favours; they followed me inside to the kitchen hoping for tit-bits from my breakfast, plain though the meal was. Marika gave me the usual coffee which coursed through my cold body, and soon Anna came in to say that Stephen was sitting up in bed and waiting to see me again.

This time Anna came with me, maybe because Stephen was no doubt coming to the part of his narrative which concerned her as well, or it could be that she was afraid that he might tire himself out. Although I had now stayed with Stephen in his room and its comfortable plainness for several days and many hours, it was always a dreadful shock each time I saw him initially. If only he had been given plastic surgery treatment perhaps his life would have been quite different.

"There was something I didn't tell you yesterday, David. I was saving it up for today." He sounded reasonably cheerful this morning.

"And what was that, Stephen?" I asked.

"When I left the E.L.A.S. in the mountains, Anna came with me." There was an air almost of challenge in his voice.

"Anna?" I looked over in Anna's direction. She had seated herself in a wide-backed wooden chair softened by an old rust-coloured cushion. Her hazel eyes seemed animated. She was undoubtedly attractive when her face and body showed life; it was the remembrance of a former life perhaps. My eyes wandered over her slender figure to her crossed legs encased in thick black stockings, and remembered that her legs had been badly burnt in that bygone tragedy.

She looked towards Stephen, propped up in bed, and I could see that there was a deep love for him.

"I met Anna in the E.L.A.S. group with which I was working. I was acting as a Liaison Officer, but Anna was one of the guerrillas working under the kapetanios." Stephen smiled at me.

"Anna was a Communist guerrilla, working with E.L.A.S.?" I asked, unable to disguise the surprise in my tone of voice.

"Yes, like many other partisans in Greece and Yugoslavia, Anna carried a rifle. At that time, Anna was a so-called progressive; she believed that Communism would be for the good of Northern Greece, Macedonia and Thrace and for all the Balkans. It was later on that she became disillusioned." Stephen had started to cough, so Anna carried on for him:

"Not all the E.L.A.S. groups were fighting other partisan groups, nor were they all so cruel. Some of the E.L.A.S. guerrillas did fight and sabotage the German troops. but our Group was led by a sadistic and ruthless egoist. His one thought seemed to be to strengthen his forces and armaments for the day when he thought the Russians would help them to bring Greece into the Communist fold."

"So, Anna, you also became disillusioned by the Communists, by the E.L.A.S.?" I asked.

"Yes," she replied. "Our Group was not really acting in the interests of Greece, and they were ruthless against village peasants who stood up to them, and they took the animals and food from these poor people."

Stephen interrupted her: "Anna and I had become good friends. She would often come with me to help to lay out the recognition lights for an incoming R.A.F. plane so that the dropping zone for supplies could be picked out, and for a time we tried to ensure that these supplies were properly used.

"It was during this time that a letter was forwarded to me from Signor Salvati in Italy. It was a letter from Joy, telling me that she was pregnant."

"What were your feelings about that?" I was curious to know.

"Mixed really. On the one hand I felt pleased and proud, and yet it seemed as though it would be some time before Joy and I could be married. You see, I really did love her, and I wanted her to be mine for ever." Stephen spoke convincingly, almost defiantly.

Of course since those days we have lived through and experienced the permissive society, co-habitation without marriage and all the other modern ways of living, but at the time of Stephen's tragic life, marriage not only brought responsibilities but also legitimacy was very much an essential part of parenthood.

"I remember Stephen telling me about Joy and the future childbirth," Anna said. "He was very happy about it, and I was happy for him too. We left our mountain hideout that evening, and went to a village. Together we found some wine and celebrated." Anna laughed, throwing back her curly black hair.

"A few others came with us to the village," Stephen went on. "I don't know if they really were amicably prepared to celebrate with us, or whether they were only interested in the possibility of finding some wine. Anyway the next morning Pavlos summoned us."

"Who was Pavlos?" I asked wonderingly.

"Pavlos was the kapetanios, the cruel leader of our group," Anna explained. "They always had a political instructor with them, and Pavlos learnt from him about our escapade."

"The E.L.A.S. were becoming disenchanted with the British anyway; the British began to realise that their air drops were not being used for the intended purpose, so supplies to E.L.A.S. were reduced. This meant that I was no longer in favour with Pavlos. Also, he disapproved of my association with Anna. Just as with the Communist partisans in Yugoslavia, any serious fraternisation between the sexes in the Group was frowned upon. I think Pavlos thought that Anna and I had been more than intimate behind his back, but we hadn't—not at that stage anyhow." Stephen momentarily took off his dark glasses to look at Anna—I was expecting a look of affection—I think this is what I would have seen had it not been for those fixed staring fire-damaged eyes, eyelashes and eyelids.

"It was all right for the kapetanios to have sexual intercourse with any of us girls he fancied, but not for anyone else," Anna laughed bitterly. "Pavlos was always trying to, to…"

"Seduce you," Stephen helped her out. "So that was another good reason for leaving."

"And taking Anna with you," I added.

"Yes. By this time Anna was also disillusioned by the E.L.A.S. and Communism. We decided to head for Florina

213

together. It was near the other Balkan borders of Yugoslavia and Albania if at any time we considered it was prudent to 'disappear', and also Elena was living and working in Florina," Stephen continued.

"Elena is my sister," Anna explained.

"Yes, I know. It was through your sister, Elena, that we learnt that you were both living in the Meteora."

"We escaped from the E.L.A.S. band—quietly we descended the mountains, travelling at night, and staying during the day in villages that had been friendly and partisan towards E.D.E.S., the National Republican guerrillas. The village peasants took us into their homes at great risk to themselves." Stephen spoke as though that night-time passage brought back a happy nostalgia.

"I felt closer to Stephen than I had been in the mountain guerrilla warfare, but I knew I could never displace his love for Joy. Sometimes he would be deep in thought, and I realised that he was thinking of Joy and his forthcoming parenthood," Anna spoke candidly.

"And how I could one day hopefully be reunited with them—without any loss of esteem following my aberration in the Gothic Line Battles. I felt that in the eyes of the world I had now exonerated myself, but the War Office would no doubt think otherwise." Stephen began his retching and coughing, straining his poor wretched lungs. "I conjured up a picture of a court-martial and Justin giving damning evidence against me. That depressed me, and Anna comforted me as best she could."

"Did you manage to contact your sister, Elena?" I asked Anna.

"Yes. Prior to the War Elena had been a schoolteacher and

I had taught music, especially the piano. Our parents had been taken by the Germans and our other relatives were well scattered. We had worked in Florina, and had made our home in the suburbs of Florina."

"You must have been young when you lost your parents," I commented. "Was it part of the Holocaust?" I asked. I had not previously considered Anna as being Jewish—she just looked like an attractive Greek girl to me.

"The Germans rounded up so many with Jewish ancestry, our parents amongst them. They never survived the Haidari SS Concentration Camp near Athens. The Germans must have destroyed the lives of approximately eighty thousand Jews in Greece.

"Anyway, I thought then that I would join the Communists, the E.L.A.S., and try to get my own back on the Germans, but as you now know I defected from the E.L.A.S." Her laughter was mockingly sad.

"And your sister, Elena?" I enquired.

"She thought that she would be safer from any German witch-hunt if she left the school, and worked in the hospital at Florina," Anna explained. "Our small house was still there in the outskirts of Florina, and that is where Stephen and I sheltered for a while. Elena cycled into the hospital most days. She became quite experienced in nursing, how do you say it?"

"Qualified." I helped her with occasional words, but her English was quite good.

Stephen had been quiet for a while. Again I could sense that mutual understanding and remembrance of a loving, happy time they had experienced together in Anna's old home.

"Elena brought us food on the way back from the hospital, and in the evenings Anna and I would play the piano together.

Life was almost civilized again," Stephen sighed. "I managed to write a letter to Maria in Italy. I thought this was the least I could do. But our new temporary way of life had to end; it was too good to last."

"So what happened?" I asked.

"There is no doubt that at that time in some instances the Germans turned a blind eye to the activities of E.L.A.S. if the latter were engaged in fighting other guerrilla partisan groups. After all, it meant that E.L.A.S. was doing the job for the Germans. The feuding between E.L.A.S. and the other Greek groups suddenly became intense in the area where we were living in our pre-war home," Anna explained.

She went on: "It became dangerous for us to stay where we were, and dangerous for Elena at the hospital. It seemed the best solution for the three of us was to move further away from Florina."

"So we decided to go back to the mountains again. I thought that I could give medical help away from too much German presence. But our move proved eventually to be a big mistake"—He hesitated as he looked cynically towards me — "to say the least."

It was time for a break and Marika brought in coffee for the three of us. I wondered how painful the remainder of their story was going to be—how painful for them to recall after the intervening years. And yet the pain would always be there, both the physical and the mental anguish.

Briefly I stepped outside into the clear air; there was a stiff breeze and the pale sun was fragmented like broken glass. Perhaps when Stephen took to the mountains with Anna and Elena he had thought that the air would purify or sublimate the danger, I don't know.

I smoked one of my few remaining cigarettes before returning to the comparative warmth of their room. Stephen was beginning to look tired, but I knew that he wanted to carry on with his narrative. A burst of lung-strained coughing greeted my entry, and Anna went to put her arms around him and hold him closely until the brief attack wore off.

Presently Stephen said, "The three of us—Elena had decided to come with us now—obtained a lift by lorry driven by a friendly local dealer in groceries, and he dropped us off at Trikousa."

"Trikousa?" I repeated the name animatedly.

"You have been there, David?" he asked.

"Yes, in my search for you. By this time I had heard something of the dreadful tragedy at Kalahori, and my friend, Nikos, knew people in Trikousa. So we went to Trikousa first of all," I answered.

It made me think of Chrysoula and her kind hospitality and her question as to whether we would come back. Well, I wouldn't be going back to the Grammos mountains now.

Stephen expected me to continue so I added:

"We had a guide with mules for the mountain climb along the track to Kalahori, and he was able to tell Nikos and I about what happened there and your part in it."

I was prepared to leave matters there as regards the incidents at Kalahori—I didn't wish to remind him of it—but I knew he wanted to speak about it. I hoped it would not be too hurtful after the intervening years for him and Anna.

"We would have liked to have stayed in Trikousa, but it seemed that the Germans scoured the village at intervals. In any case there were little or no medical supplies there, and we could not have done much good. Like you did, David, we rode by mule up the precipitous track. It was Autumn, but the sun was still warm across the back. I expect you encountered snowy, hazardous tracks when you did the climb?" Stephen seemed to look at me through his dark glasses.

"Yes—and I never did like heights." My laughter seemed forced in the silence.

"When we came to Kalahori perched on its mountain cliff it seemed to be a village sufficiently inaccessible from too much interest by the Germans, and for once we found an E.L.A.S. commander for the area who seemed genuinely to want to work with all Greek parties and the British in the cause of overthrowing the Germans. His name was Bessarion, but he was commonly referred to as 'Nonda'," Stephen explained.

"At least 'Nonda' is shorter." I bit my lip, and told myself not to be so light-hearted about it all. There was no way that one could alleviate the memory and suffering of Kalahori.

Sensing that Stephen wanted to conserve his breathing for a while, Anna continued:

"Nonda was tall and bearded. His hair was sandy coloured. He looked strong with his piercing dark grey eyes. He provided us with a house in Kalahori, and a quantity of medical supplies. At least there were some air drops that didn't get spirited away. Stephen's name soon travelled amongst the neighbouring villages, and Elena was able to teach me some basic medical knowledge. The two of us were then soon able to help Stephen in a practical way."

"Is Elena like you?" I asked.

Anna paused. "She was then, but I was more fortunate than her in the fire you see." Her sad voice lingered in the air.

Stephen became livelier again, and sitting up more in bed he said, "We not only treated wounded and sick guerrillas that came in from the mountain skirmishes, but the village peasants soon came to us as well. Believe it or not, I managed some minor operations and a few births. You see, they trusted us."

I could believe it all right. Once Stephen put his mind to something there was probably little he couldn't do—or couldn't have done, I thought looking at his charred appearance.

"The school building had a piano, and after a day's work we would go to the school, the three of us, and play the piano, classical music mostly, for about an hour at a time. One evening some of the local peasants came in and Anna played some Greek music." Stephen was remembering his time in Kalahori in every detail as he continued:

"The Greek villagers started an impromptu dance and at the height of this Nonda came striding in. He took me to one side and his wide top lip curved into a grin over his beard that he habitually stroked. He told me that some of his recent ambushes and raiding parties had caused many casualties amongst the Germans. A few of his own men were waiting for us in our home; they needed urgent medical attention, but what I particularly remember Nonda saying was that we should now be extra vigilant in case the Germans carried out reprisals."

"And were you extra vigilant?" I asked.

"We certainly tried to be, but of course there was no real military armed group actually stationed in the village. The guerrillas usually attacked at night, and dispersed in the mountains by day.

"However, it was decided that if someone was badly wounded and it was not too far from Kalahori then I would ride out by mule to the encampment rather than bring the wounded person into the village. Nonda hoped in this way that there would not be too much activity in and around Kalahori, and we would not draw too much attention to ourselves."

Stephen waited for Anna to continue:

"Sometimes Elena and I would go with Stephen to encampments to attend to the wounded, but if it was only one person, say, that needed attention he would probably go on his own. So I didn't think that we drew attention to ourselves or the village." She seemed decided on this point.

"It was just bad luck," added Stephen. "At the time I felt that I was really doing some good, that my future would be in medicine and then…"

"Ah! Yes—what happened then?" I asked.

There was a silence whilst Stephen steeled himself to continue:

"I received a message from Nonda to meet him up in the mountain at a shepherd's hut—I had been there before. Apparently his second-in-command was badly wounded and could not be moved. I thought that it was best to leave Anna and Elena in the village. If only I had taken them with me."

"It was no different from any other occasion—there was only one person wounded, and in these conditions you went on your own. Nothing could be helped," Anna was quick to interject.

"By the time that I reached the shepherd's hut Nonda's second-in-command was dead. There was nothing I could do, so I retraced my steps towards Kalahari. I was approximately halfway down the mountainside towards Kalahori when I heard much firing of shots. It sounded like machine-gun and rifle fire. I remembered what Nonda had said about possible German reprisals, and my sense of foreboding unfortunately proved accurate." Stephen drank the cool water at his bedside.

"That was when they took all the men to the cemetery and shot them." I was remembering what Andreas had told me in Kalahori.

"Yes, that's right," said Stephen. "I had made my way as quickly as I could towards the village, using any available cover of copses and scrub. I thought the firing had come from the direction of the cemetery, but by this time as I reached the outskirts of the village my attention was diverted to the schoolhouse." He paused.

His coughing had erupted, but with a further drink of water he was able to continue: "I'll never forget the shouts and screams of the women and children in that school. The last of the Germans had left by lorry on the road out of the village. And then I saw the flames of fire leaping into the sky.

"I rushed to the school building, but the heavy doors were locked. I couldn't move them. I found a small side window and broke through the stained glass. Anna and Elena were at the back of the building—they had been the last to be rounded up."

"We had told the Germans that we were medical orderlies," Anna explained. "They stood at our house arguing amongst themselves, but eventually they marshalled us with the others at the school. That is why we were the last and at the back of the building."

"As the fiery beams crashed down on some poor victims and others suffocated with smoke, I pushed Anna and Elena through the side window. I went back to try and help others—I found an old blanket and we managed to get out a woman and two children, but our further efforts were of no use. It was all over so quickly. I felt I was suffocating with smoke as Anna and Elena pulled me to safety away from the school. The other woman and the two children then died."

It was certainly not surprising that the memory of that day was upsetting to them both; the permanent physical reminders would always be there.

"Stephen and Elena were more badly burnt than I was." Anna's voice was sad. "I had burns on my back and legs, but Stephen and Elena had severe facial burns as well. We struggled back to our house where we had some basic medical supplies. We tried to salve the wounds, but the pain for us all was intense."

"The Germans were always very thorough. It was possible that they would have come back to check that they had not missed anyone in their lethal destruction of human beings. We had to get away from Kalahori. That was our best chance of survival. We were not far from the Yugoslavian and Albanian borders, but we wanted to stay in Greece. We packed as much as we could onto a couple of mules, and headed away towards the Mount Vitsi region. We were still very much in the north, but I thought that we might be able to join up with a friendly guerrilla group or take refuge in an isolated village somewhere. It was already Autumn, and I did not fancy our chances if we were on the mountains without food and supplies in the Winter." He rested his head on the pillow which Anna had bolstered up.

"Couldn't you have stayed in Kalahori?" I asked.

"As I've said, the Germans could have returned at any time.

Besides, after what we had witnessed, the very name of Kalahori was synonymous with a nightmare of fire and fear and death, and man's inhumanity to man. No, we had to get away.

"Fortunately for us, after we had been travelling for two or three days, we found by chance an isolated farmstead. There were some of Nonda's men there. They said that Nonda had been killed in further German operations against the guerrillas. I did not altogether trust these men—without their leaders they were never slow to pillage and rape, but I felt that it gave us a little protection against any hostile elements."

"We gave them some of our food, and I thought that we could rest here, and try to recover from our burns," Anna explained. "But then they received news that the Germans had quit their country and that the British had landed in Athens. For all of us it seemed sensible to descend from the mountains once more. We had heard that the British had cleared the retreating Germans from the town of Kozani, and we thought that it would be sensible for us to go there. I thought perhaps that we could then get proper medical attention."

"But it was not to be," Stephen shook his head sadly." Nonda's men had heard of the E.L.A.S. resistance to British Forces, and these Communist guerrillas started treating us like prisoners, especially as I was British. They took us to a village called—like many other Greek villages—Arachova—it was some miles from Kozani. There were other E.L.A.S. guerrillas in the village."

"Presumably it was because of this that eventually the Regiment, possibly Justin himself, received unconfirmed reports that you had been taken prisoner by the E.L.A.S.," I suggested.

"Yes, that is possible," mused Stephen.

"It is strange to think that we were part of a Division sent to Greece to help restore order after the German evacuation, and all the time you were in Greece yourself." I stood up to stretch my legs and walked slowly around the room.

"I expect there were times when I was close to the Division and the Battalion if one all but knew it"—-Stephen's laugh was mirthless—"although with my charred face I doubt if anyone from the Battalion would have recognised me.

"I realised that we would somehow have to get away once more from the E.L.A.S. guerrillas, and apart from being prisoners I knew that there was no Nonda with us to prevent…" He hesitated.

"To prevent Elena and I being raped, you mean to say." Anna stood up, and added, "I must get Stephen's lunch now, David."

"Yes, of course." I turned to Stephen: "I expect you will be able to finish your story and all its adventures tomorrow."

"They were adventures I would dearly love to have missed," he paused. "Except for Anna of course." His face smiled grotesquely. Perhaps his eyes were twinkling like stars on a frosty night, but in reality they just seemed to stare into space.

I stumbled out into the small courtyard and walked past the garden plot into the outer courtyard. I felt bemused by all this subterfuge and intrigue that had taken place across the Greek countryside, in its mountains and plains, and I was desperately saddened once more by the tragedy of Kalahori.

As though in a clouded mountain dream I entered the little chapel of St Nicholas. Once more I felt one of the cats brush against my legs as I knelt on the stone floor facing the altar. I prayed for peace in the world and peace for Stephen's soul, but I was not overtly a religious man, and I could not foresee with confidence any peace in the world nor peace for Stephen within himself.

Later that day I learnt that Anna suspected that Stephen had caught a chill to add to his serious condition, and I saw that she was adopting the customary Greek remedy of using glass jars on his back. Periodically, with Marika's help, the glass jars would be changed.

Vincentios told me that he had brought a gift of some lamb for Stephanos and Anna, and it seemed that Stephanos wanted to get up the following evening to have a farewell cooked meal and party with me. It all sounded incongruous in this mountain eyrie, but I hoped that Stephen would be well enough to get up just for this once.

It seemed strange to think that I would soon be leaving this towering hide-away. I felt that I could rely on Nikos to meet me at our rendezvous; certainly I owed much to him.

I was actually beginning to look forward to being in civilization again, to enjoy a change of diet and to see Lydia and perhaps with time to forget all this tragedy. Yet perhaps Stephen and Anna had been right to reject the materialistic world after their prolonged traumas.

That night the wind increased in strength, to remind the few inhabitants of St Nicholas that the mantle of Winter was reluctant to depart.

★ ★ ★

Perhaps the remedial glass jars were effective or perhaps the possible advent of a chill was a false alarm, who could say, as on the next morning I found Stephen not only sitting up in bed, but vowing that he would get up later in the day so that he and I could celebrate as in old times. What we had to celebrate I couldn't imagine, but it would be pleasant to take away from this monastic height a memory of the Stephen I once knew.

Anna brought us some coffee, and took up her station in a chair near to Stephen's bed. She told me that Stephen had coughed too much during the night, and certainly he looked pallid in the early morning light filtering through the small windows. Impatient to learn the remainder of their sorry tale I was soon prompting them:

"When we spoke yesterday you were telling me how you were in effect prisoners of the E.L.A.S. group not far from Kozani," I started off.

"That's right," Stephen confirmed. "I was anxious, particularly as there was confusion within their own ranks without proper leadership. Arachova was a small village, and like other Greek villages which you have seen, it perched on a steep hillside. It was like terraces or rows of cottages where the roof of one cottage was level with the ground floor of another."

"Eventually the E.L.A.S., realising that Stephen could help with the sickness and ailments of their Communist band and with the villagers as well, treated us more humanely," Anna explained.

"It was like being under house arrest," added Stephen. "Then Christmas came, and the visit by Churchill to Athens, and it seemed as though life might become better for us all."

"We were staying in a small white-washed cottage and there were vines all around us," sighed Anna. "There seemed little reason for us to move on from Arachova now that E.L.A.S. had become friendlier. We even had a glass of wine with them on Christmas Day."

"But you will appreciate that the British forces in Greece at that time were not large, and were very much spread out." Stephen looked at me, his eyes now shadowed by dark glasses.

"I remember that only too well," I spoke bitterly.

"I knew that all was not right. The E.L.A.S. in our village had not handed in their arms. In fact I knew that in addition to the arms with which they strutted about, they were concealing caches of arms in isolated farm buildings and in camouflaged country hideouts." Stephen paused as he fought to stifle his coughing.

"We used to search villages for arms, but it was an impossible task," I recalled to them. "Often the Mayor of a village would be young and surly, offering us greasy food on the one hand, whilst his henchmen hastily hid all traces of arms."

Stephen had regained his breath: "Perhaps if the British had stayed in Greece, the third round, the Civil War of Greek against Greek wouldn't have happened."

"We had our own economic problems then because of the long war we had been through. We had to pull out in order to help fashion world peace. The Greek dilemma became an American problem," I interjected. "We were not long in Greece after V.E. Day."

There was a marked pause before Stephen willed himself to speak:

"There were two occurrences which not only changed my life, but made me determined to give up the inhuman struggle to live in the ordinary work-a-day life where peace was never secure.

"I had managed to send my Arachova address to Signor Salvati in Italy. Perhaps it would have been better if I hadn't done so.

"It was just about the time that you would have been celebrating V.E. Day, David, that a letter came for me. I learnt that Joy had died in childbirth. The news was shattering, you understand?" He spoke quietly as he looked in my direction.

"It was very sad," I agreed," but you had a son, you had Eric."

"A son who was illegitimate, who had no mother, only a disfigured and embittered father. I knew I wouldn't return to England to see him. I wanted him to remember me as a brave soldier, not as a burnt deserter. I've already told you that I had made financial provision for Eric," he argued. "I had quite a tidy sum of money left me in trust, and I had told Margaret in my letter to see that it all went to Eric."

"You could have gone to Athens or England and had plastic surgery. You remember what Sir Archibald McIndoe had done for the RAF crews?" I spoke questioningly.

"We did persuade Elena to go to Athens for treatment, but I stayed with Stephen. After all, my face hadn't suffered," Anna explained.

Then Stephen continued: "For me it was too late, David. In any event, I had now lost Joy."

Anna helped him to sit up more comfortably on the bed. He went on: "The second momentous occurrence was that I could see that a Civil War was coming to Greece. Everything we had tried to achieve in Greece now seemed to be in vain; my whole life seemed to have been in vain, but I still had Anna." He gripped her hand firmly as she smiled encouragingly and lovingly at him. "And the combination of the burns and wintry conditions had affected my lungs. Oh! Yes! I have been lucky to have had these last years in the mountain air, but it cannot last much longer."

Anna sighed, fulfilling the proverb that a woman sighs who has an ill husband.

Stephen seemed to want to continue, and Anna obviously did not think that he had become overtired. His voice, however, was whispery hoarse as he spoke:

"In 1945 the foundations had been laid for a new Greek Army, although recruitment and training in a mountainous country like Greece with primitive communications was very difficult. By the beginning of 1946, on the one hand the activities of left-wing armed bands were increasing, but so also were the actions of armed civilians of right-wing sympathizers and of right-wing extremists, the 'Monarcho-Fascist Terrorists'. Thousands of ex-guerrillas were arrested, and some were murdered. Even some National Guardsmen joined the 'White Terror' campaign against the Communists. Prime Ministers came and went, and a compromise between the Right and Left became impossible. Violence loomed ahead."

"I suppose the vacillation of the British Government at that time didn't help. It was decided that British troops would leave Greece after the elections, I remember," I added. In fact I myself had already left Greece at that time I recollected.

"Yes, but the Communists wouldn't take part in the elections, so the Royalists had a handsome victory, and King George II was also given a majority in the plebiscite."

"Hardly surprising," I muttered.

"Already the third round, the Civil War, had in fact begun with raids on villages and insurrections in rural areas," he continued. "By 1947 any hope of a peaceful settlement disappeared. King George II died, and he was succeeded by King Paul and Queen Frederika. The rebels and their government were never recognised by the Soviet Union. In that same year, 1947, the British Government indicated that it could no longer supply arms and equipment for the Greek forces, but the Americans provided the necessary funds instead. The British military Mission remained in Greece, but it was now the Americans who really bolstered the Greek armed forces. At first the communist-led so-called 'Democratic Army' was the strongest until the National Army had been reorganised with outside help."

"You stayed in the village of Arachova?" I asked.

"For some time, yes. And after all we had been through we witnessed the toil and the tears and the tragedy of the Greek peasants. Elena had now gone to Athens for treatment. With Anna I started a small surgery in the village, but it was difficult to overcome the suspicions of the villagers. The Communist guerrillas became quite ruthless, and were armed from other Balkan states like Albania and Rumania. I heard of an incident not far from Arachova where the Communist guerrillas caused a young girl to flee. They had beaten to death her grandfather and then seized the girl's dowry." Stephen was drinking from his customary glass of water.

"A Greek girl cannot hope to marry without her dowry," Anna explained.

"A woman came into my surgery one day. She had been badly injured by a mine."

Stephen had temporarily removed his glasses, and stared apparently into space." I learnt that it was the Greeks peasants' custom during mine clearing operations for a peasant woman to lead a donkey on a long rope, whilst behind her, her husband sat in comfortable safety on the donkey. Their reasoning was that if the woman stepped on a mine she would be blown up, but the man and the donkey could well survive."

"The man and the donkey were more valuable in the eyes of the Greek peasant family," Anna sighed, and arose from her chair to fetch Stephen's lunch.

I was surprised when she indicated that we could continue our discussions after lunch, but clearly this was to be the day when they had decided that all would be told, and that we would have a small party in the evening. I hoped it would not be all too much for Stephen, as I joined Marika and Georgios for some soup and cheese.

After lunch I walked around the outer courtyard again. The overnight snow was now freezing, and I nearly fell onto the hard surface, using my arms to break my fall. Everyone was pleasant enough up here in the Meteora, but I was beginning to yearn for my creature comforts.

Did it all really make sense? Seeing the photograph of a wartime colleague in a Daily Newspaper in England and ending up here in these monastic heights, concerned at the same time that I might have lost the love of Lydia—to be reminded of all these Greek tragedies that cast their spell in Italy as well? I have heard it said that beneath ordinary chat we are scavengers, gnawing at each other's histories, for scraps of hope. Could there be hope for me after all this scavenging and searching? Certainly I felt that I must be as determined to find happiness when I returned to England as I had been resolute in this Continental search.

★ ★ ★

"The peasant women were bowed and silent as they drew their water from the wells." Anna was describing life in Arachova when we resumed our conversation after lunch. "They would wear their traditional costumes, the long dark skirts, their embroidered tunic coats, and with the black handkerchief tied under the chin. Food was scarce."

"They did not like the American army rations anyway." Stephen's laugh was derisory.

He then continued: "A few days after I had treated that Greek peasant woman who had been badly injured by a mine, a young boy of sixteen was brought to me. He had been taken to Albania and armed by the Communists. When he was back in Greece he tried to escape, but he was caught and tied up with a rope."

"What happened then?" I asked.

"He was hung, head down, over a fire of coal, and kicked and kicked. I did what I could for him, but it wasn't much."

"Were there Communist groups in your village, in Arachova, Stephen?"

"Eventually they came, David. We had heard how villages were burnt to the ground, so we were all fearful of what might happen. However, I supposed they considered that Arachova, perched on its craggy outcrop, was a good vantage point. From Arachova you could observe all movement in the plain below. So they occupied the village, although they did not destroy it."

I tried to think what had been in his mind at that time. "You felt that having given up fighting in Italy, you were being frustrated in trying to bring peace and medical help in Greece?"

"Yes, David, but it was more than frustration. Anna and I

had endured that terrible experience in Kalahori on account of the savagery of the German reprisals. We then witnessed and heard about the E.L.A.S. attacks on British forces who had come to Greece to help in the rehabilitation of the country; and then we were caught up in a ruthless Civil War."

It was no wonder that he felt bitterness towards mankind, I thought to myself.

"One hundred and fifty thousand Greeks died in the Civil War, and another hundred thousand were made homeless. Both sides in the Civil War perfected the German art of burning houses and setting fire to complete villages." Anna's soft voice sounded equally bitter.

"The Communist so-called Democratic Army eventually became strong enough to launch attacks on large provincial centres such as Florina, but they were not successful, and they reverted to guerrilla tactics. Towards the end of 1948 the Greek Government declared a state of martial law, but the guerrillas were active in the Grammos Mountains and Vitsi— when they had a severe reverse they simply withdrew over the frontier to Yugoslavia, Bulgaria or Albania, where they soon found new recruits." Stephen spoke so clearly about these tragedies it was as if it all had happened yesterday. He didn't seem to tire as he was wont to do.

I looked at Anna; she had a serene look as though Fate could not deal her any more blows.

Stephen's voice cut into my thoughts. "Then American aid began to pour into Greece, and the Greek National Army increased in numbers to a quarter of a million men. Even so the mountain warfare might have gone on for years had not two events changed the situation."

"What were these events?" I asked.

"You probably remember when Tito in Yugoslavia was expelled from the Comintern. That was in the Summer of 1949. Consequently Tito closed his Yugoslav border to the Communist guerrillas who thus lost an important supply source. That was one event—the other was the indifferent leadership of the Communist forces; their leaders decided to create larger formations when they should have operated in small units. This was a big mistake. When Grammos fell the Communists agreed to a ceasefire. By the end of 1949 the Civil War had ended. Can you understand all that, David?" His dark glasses turned in my direction.

"Yes, I think so, Stephen." My mind was recollecting some saying I had heard before, possibly in a military lecture—'The path of duty lies in the thing nearby, but men seek it in things far off.'

It seemed to me that Stephen's path of duty had been in Italy in the attacks through the Gothic Line, but he had sought his path in Greece and then had been embroiled in conflict for another four years or so after the end of the World War.

It was Anna who then spoke. She always seemed to be able to sense when Stephen was about to start his retching and coughing. I'm sure he was bringing up blood. She handed him a glass of water. "Stephen has told you the general picture. Although the Communists did not destroy Arachova we thought that they might do so if the fighting near at hand went badly for them. They had a grudging respect for Stephen and the medical work he was doing, but knowing that he was British they treated him with suspicion. Some nights when the Communist guerrillas had been drinking tsipoura, the strong vodka drink, we would hear them pass our cottage. I would cling to Stephen in the darkness. Always their footsteps frightened me. Then after all that had happened to Kalahori when the Germans were there, we heard that Kalahori had now been looted by the Communist guerrillas, and they had set fire to the police station and post office. It was too much."

In recalling the fate of Kalahori I saw that tears had started to trickle down her bronzed face. Her words had brought back to me a memory of Andreas, the patriarch, who had lost his wife in all this looting.

Anna wiped away the tears and started speaking afresh: "The old men and women of Arachova would peep at the guerrillas from behind closed doors; these simple mountain people were worn and resigned, as they watched the guerrillas on the outskirts of the village train the young village girls to fire their rifles, to lay ambushes and to prepare booby-traps— young girls who did not know what they were fighting for. Perhaps they had just liked to be on an equal footing with the boys. Boys were keen on war games."

Stephen then spoke: "So you see, parents would hide their children if they could. Some of the villagers in that part of Greece were Slav-speaking. One day two women were brought to me; their legs had been blown off. Later I found out that it had happened when one of the Communist Slav women had been concealing an anti-personnel mine in her knickers. It was all so incongruous.

"You can imagine, perhaps, a Greek or Slav peasant girl trekking up a mountain, hoping for excitement and joining the Communist guerrillas. No longer would she have to wait at home under the continual eye of her parents until they married her off. The so-called Communist 'Democratic Army' were strict as far as these girls were concerned. There was no loose living or free love, and any man accosting these girls was shot by the Kapetanios. The girls were checked regularly to see that they had behaved. Part of my job." Stephen was naturally cynical as he voiced these matters. "I remember one girl from Arachova who fell in love with a Kapetanios. Eventually she was able to marry the Kapetanios, and during their guerrilla raids together they managed to have a wedding feast with wine and Greek songs and dancing. Later on, her Kapetanios was captured by the Greek National Army and executed."

"What happened to the girl?" I asked.

"I think she died a little later of a fever. There was much fever in the guerrilla bands as you can imagine—they had forced marches, hiding in ditches and little or no food, with the milk probably tainted." Stephen paused before continuing. "The guerrilla bands simply left these girl Amazons behind in woods if they had been wounded. Sometimes the girls were shot if their weeping made so much noise that their positions would be given away. Many of these girls were brought to me with ugly mortar and shell wounds; some of them were no more than ten or twelve years old."

"They were grateful to you for the medical treatment you gave them?" I looked at his face which was now showing tiredness.

"Not especially," answered Stephen. "They usually looked sullen and surly. Perhaps too they half shunned my physical appearance after the burns I had endured. Some of the villages including Arachova where we were staying were one day in the hands of the guerrillas, the next day in the hands of the National Army, and then sometimes in the hands of the guerrillas again. It was all too much. I told Anna that when the snows began to melt we would leave Arachova and move south towards Thessaly. The fighting was bound to last longest in the Grammos and Vitsi Mountains. We had endured enough of wars and civil wars and fighting and intrigue. We planned to leave Arachova in early 1949."

"And we did," added Anna. "We left Arachova and passed through the mountains as the thaw in the weather began. We came across peasant women who not long before had helped to carry supplies on their backs to the Greek National Army on the mountains, who had repaired military roads, and were now tending their small wheat patches. They would carry their sheaves of wheat down off the mountains for threshing in the lower reaches. The wheat was all-important to them, and they thought not of the minefields. Some of these peasant women had already seen their children abducted and sent to neighbouring 'friendly' Balkan Communist countries. These peasant women had endured the worst of everything, especially as some of the husbands and children had already gone to the United States." After a short pause she continued with their story: "As we trekked southward through the mountain villages I remember one night we stayed in a humble cottage in a run-down village. This peasant woman's name was Calliope and she made us welcome for the night. She told us that to prevent the guerrillas from abducting her children she had hidden them in the country ditches at night; the guerrillas sought retribution on her and other mothers in the village—the mothers were tortured. Calliope had been hung from a tree, her feet were burnt and she was continually beaten. But she survived, and so did her children." Anna had spoken at some length, probably to save Stephen from strain and tiredness.

"So you see, David, civilization was no more. I decided that we would go away as far as we could from all this strife," Stephen explained.

"But you both needed treatment yourselves, you could have had your burns dealt with," I protested.

He shook his head. "It was too late, and we had learnt to live with ourselves, but I knew also my lungs were now weak. The mountain air would suit me best."

"Sometimes I would think of Elena, my sister. I knew that she had reached Athens, and had received plastic surgery. I was happy for her, and I imagined her, as the days grew warmer, sitting outside a pavement cafe in Athens, looking at the fashions in shops and living in a comfortable apartment once more." Anna smiled at me, and her brown eyes came alight.

"Did you not want this for yourself?" I asked her.

"No, David. I was always happiest wherever Stephen was. We were in love, you see, and I knew that I would never leave him. Eventually we travelled south as far as Kalambaka. Originally we thought we would head for Trikala, but at first we sought refuge in the mountains near these monasteries. One day we met Vincentios with his sheep. He gave us shelter that night in his shepherd's hut and he told us all about these barren rocks, these eagles' nests. He mentioned that one of the desolate and partly destroyed monasteries was not occupied by monks, but only by Georgios and Marika. Yes, he guided us to Saint Nicholas, and we have been here ever since."

"Didn't the Civil War end in 1949?" I questioned Stephen.

"Yes by the late Autumn of that year the Civil War had ended, but we knew not what the future would hold for us— or for anyone else. What permanent peace would there be for anyone, anywhere? Now, my friend, I must rest, for this evening you and I will have a party—like the old times," he ended cheerfully.

"Like the old times," I repeated in a dazed fashion.

"Yes, in your honour, I will get up and join you and Anna and the others—we will kill the fatted calf, or lamb to be precise," he chuckled quietly, and before long he was sleeping deeply.

Sadly I looked at Anna, and silently I left their presence.

★ ★ ★

If Stephen was going to be anything like his old self again for the evening party I thought that it would be as well if I also had a restful afternoon sleep, leaving Stephen and Anna in peace for a time. Vincentios must have been with Georgios and Marika as our cramped sleeping quarters were empty and cold. Soon I had the oil heater alight and the glow sent shadows across the floor.

I lay down on the makeshift mattress; it was only natural that I should now begin to look forward to a proper bed again. Motes of dust danced before my eyes.

Sleep would not come that easily after all I had heard from Stephen and Anna. I closed my eyes, but just as Arabs say that their camels never sleep even if they close their great liquid eyes, I turned restlessly amidst the blankets.

Perhaps I had stayed here too long. Again thinking of Arabs I thought of the Arabian Desert courtesy being extended for two nights and a day only; but it had not been possible to leave earlier; I needed to know everything before I left.

I cast my mind back over all the events which had led to Stephen and Anna spending their lives on St Nicholas. It was easy to say 'if only'—if only, for instance, he had not been temporarily so shattered mentally in the Gothic Line Battles in Italy, and had not just simply walked away from it. But if he had stayed the course in Italy, perhaps he would have been killed in action. Then he had regained his personal honour, if that was the right expression, by joining the guerrilla forces in Greece, firstly in a liaison capacity and then by using his medical qualifications to help the insurgents.

How was he to know that the Germans would be so ruthless as to burn down that school with women and children inside it? How was he to know that the E.L.A.S. Communist bands would turn against the British forces? How was he to know that there would then be a civil war between the political factions of Greeks themselves?

It seemed that wherever he had turned there had been strife; the bravery he had witnessed had been more than counterbalanced by the atrocities.

In all this maze of tragedy his only comfort had been Anna. How loyal to him she had been, but then women had always been fascinated by Stephen, and it seemed that his disfiguring burns had not weakened that magnetism.

I visualized Stephen and Anna in their last Winter in Arachova, being desperate in their repugnance of all the strife that they had witnessed, and eventually finding Vincentios amongst his mountain sheep. Vincentios had taken them to the haven of St Nicholas. Here at least, no doubt they had felt that they could leave behind 'man's inhumanity to man' and indeed 'woman's inhumanity to woman', and live out the remainder of their lives in peace. Alas, Fate had one more unkind trick to play on them; Stephen would not be long for this world, his health could resist the onset of death for only a little while longer. Like Icarus he had flown too near the heat of the sun.

As finally I fell asleep I thought of Anna, and what would become of her. My thoughts became blurred in a nightmarish dream and visual fantasy of bodies preserved in snow on the Meteora.

* * *

I must have slept for several hours and it was dark when Vincentios came into the building.

Gently he woke me up, and then I noticed that he was sprucing himself up more than he usually did. Then I remembered the party that Stephen had promised for the evening, and I too tried to smarten myself up although my clothes were by now somewhat roughed up and travel-worn.

I shaved carefully in the dim light, and presently we were both ready to move next door and join Georgios and Marika.

In the kitchen I caught the anticipatory aroma of the roasting lamb. I could sense the delight and excitement within my mountain friends. This was indeed a feast for them—and for me also after all this time.

Marika, speaking loudly because of her deafness, encouraged me to 'listen to the smell', this being the common Greek phrase, likeable in itself, but beyond understanding.

Georgios poured out some glasses of ouzo for us, and for a meze to accompany the ouzo, Marika had prepared some olives and sliced cheese.

Clearly, Marika had been working hard; their quarters were very clean, and for that evening a brightly patterned rug covered the stone floor.

It was whilst we were sipping some ouzo that Stephen and Anna came in. To see Stephen, once more on his feet, even though walking unsteadily, was a joyful scene for all of us. He seemed rested and cheerful. As far as he could he had tried to lessen his facial blemishes and the dark glasses helped to give him a more normal appearance. He was wearing a grey light-weight suit with a red tie, and his fair hair shone with the light of the fire.

Then I looked at Anna. She had tidied up her short wavy hair, and it was the first time that I had seen her with a little lipstick applied. Her hazel eyes sparkled, and she wore a warm red-coloured woollen dress, close fitting and underlining her pleasing figure. Although the light was dim and diffused I could see that beneath her tough and fatalistic veneer, Anna had a feminine elegance of Grecian charm and attractiveness. I suppose that the mutual devotion between Stephen and Anna would be my lasting memory of that evening.

Presently we sat around the low wooden table; Marika had found a sufficient number of stools for us to sit on, and the table was covered with a light blue cloth.

It was, of course, Marika who had prepared everything, and slowly she took the grease-paper off the roasted leg of lamb. Healthy portions with potatoes were lavished onto our plates, and the smell of garlic, thyme and rosemary rent the air. Marika must have saved up these items, and there were also cloves permeating the lamb.

The retsina, with which I had laboured up the Meteora with the help of a donkey, was poured into the glasses. We held up our glasses and touched the rims of the glasses of our friends; there were many toasts, but speech became muted as we attacked our meal with all seriousness. Marika was insistent with her second helpings. The knives and forks flashed beneath the oil lamp, and the quietude was not disturbed until the lamb was completely devoured apart from the basic bone.

I can remember the apples soaked in retsina, and then Stephen laughing and thanking Vincentios for bringing the lamb. Playfully he kissed Marika for cooking it.

Presently Stephen was engaged in animated conversation with Georgios and Vincentios; I think they were talking about Georgios' next visit to Kalambaka for supplies and what was needed. Marika was clearing away the debris from the meal.

Anna spoke quietly to me. We could not be overheard by the others. "Are you glad you came to St Nicliolas?" she asked.

I looked into her frank and earnest eyes. "Yes. Truly, very glad," I answered.

She hesitated and then said, "Do you not think it would be best if when you return to England you do not say too much about all that has happened to Stephen since he came to Greece? Perhaps it is best to say nothing. Let them all think that he died in Italy. After all…"

"Yes, after all it was a long time ago now. Is that what you were going to say?" I smiled at her.

"No, not quite. I was going to say that after all he has not long to live now." A single tear slid slowly down her cheek, but she banished it away.

I tried to marshal my thoughts which had become slightly befuddled with ouzo and retsina: "What will you do if Stephen dies?" I asked directly.

"Not 'if', David, 'when'."

"Will you join your sister, Elena? You could live comfortably in Athens," I suggested.

"No. That is not for me. I have learnt to live with the burns on my body and legs, but above all I have come to love it here. The freedom, the air, the quiet, my life with Stephen. Even after he's gone, I will always have his memory here. This is where we turned our back on the world, on the fighting, the bickering and the quarrels. I expect you find that difficult to understand?" I hadn't seen her so animated before and so obviously sincere in all that she said.

"I can understand," I murmured in response. "Whenever anything happens to Stephen, would you please let me know? You could send word to me through Yanni and Zena in Kalambaka."

"Yes, I will let you know." She looked at me with her sad tawny eyes. "I'm glad you came. You see how cheerful he is tonight. Tell me something, David…" She hesitated a moment. "Was Joy very beautiful?"

I suppose it was a natural question for her to ask, and yet I knew that Anna was not jealous. After all, there was really nothing for her to be jealous about now, at least that is how it seemed to me.

I knew I had to be candid with her. "Yes, Joy was very beautiful." I wanted to say more, to tell her that Stephen had not known Joy for long, that I had known her for even less time, but I could see that this did not matter.

"I'm glad she was very beautiful," Anna smiled with her full lips. "I wouldn't have wanted anything but the best for Stephen, you know? That is how it must always be."

Such a glib statement, and yet so meaningful.

★ ★ ★

244

Eventually the party broke up. I thanked them all in turn, and Vincentios ensured that I reached my bed through a high altitude alcoholic haze.

It had been an evening like old times with Stephen being in a happy mood, and giving his opinion forcibly on a wide-ranging number of topics; he had sat mostly in the shadows, but the outline of his face and imperious chin was as I remembered it in earlier times.

As I sank into a deep sleep I remembered Anna's words of wanting everything for the best for Stephen and I thought back to her satisfaction in the knowledge that Joy had been beautiful. There had certainly been a consistency in Stephen's magnetism for women; this magnetism even extended after all his suffering and experience by fire.

It was an enviable love but not one which I could ever want to try to emulate in the future.

★ ★ ★

I think we all woke a little late on the following morning, and as I dashed into Marika's kitchen for some reviving coffee I noticed that there was a further fall of snow in progress. Winter was yet defiant of the Spring.

Later in the morning I visited Stephen and Anna. The party of the previous evening had not been unbeneficial to Stephen's health it seemed, and he was not too tired to talk to me.

Once more his thoughts, outwardly expressed, ranged far back to his youth, and his parents, and the blow when they were killed in an air-raid. He talked about his early days in the Regiment, and how he had never really seen eye-to-eye with Justin Townsend, our Commanding Officer. He also spoke critically of certain other officers who had been glory-seekers; he hastened to assure me that I was not included in this number, but when he spoke of others being steady plodders I'm not sure that I felt particularly flattered.

However, he reminisced with light-handed pleasure of the off-duty times we had spent together, the oft-acknowledged rivalry whether it be our prowess with women or wine or physical strength.

Suddenly he asked: "Will you see Justin when you return to England? Will you tell him everything?"

It seemed to me that he was following up Anna's question at the party on the previous evening. "I think it is best to let sleeping dogs lie after all this time, don't you?" I replied. Anna looked at me gratefully, but I realised as soon as the words were out that they were ironic.

Bitterly he responded, "You're right. I am a sleeping dog now, and there isn't much more time."

But his moods changed, and after a fit of coughing had ceased, he teased Anna and as she tidied up his bedclothes he confessed to being a bad patient. "But I have a good nurse you see David, don't you think so?"

"I'm sure Anna does all she can for you. You have been through so much together."

"Yes, we will always be together as well," he spoke confidently for the future. Then again, once more his mind moved back to England, and looking at me through his dark glasses he asked, "Do you intend to see my sister, Margaret, when you get back to London?"

"I may do. I daresay you would like me to try and ensure that all your wishes are carried out, especially for Eric," I replied.

"Yes, but it is probably as well if you let her continue to think that I was killed in Italy. After all, I will soon be dead anyway." He paused, and then grabbed my arm forcibly. "See that the boy, Eric, is all right; I want his future to be happy and assured. I can rely on you, David, can't I?"

"Of course." I released my arm from his firm grip. I knew then and there that I would always let Eric believe that his father had been killed in action in Italy, however brave Stephen had been in Greece.

"Watch your step with Margaret," he added. "I've always had to."

I think during that particular morning he was happier talking about Italy than he was of Greece. I suppose the events of Greece had been nearer in time and so traumatic for him.

"They have such a love of life in Italy, David. We had some good times together, you and I—Naples, Benevento …"

I broke into his train of thought: "That portrait of you—I arranged with Arturo Manzoni for it to be despatched to your sister in London." And then I knew that I had been leading up to this: "Maria, what am I to tell Maria?" I looked at him and Anna in turn.

They seemed to whisper together in a quick flow of Greek, and then Stephen spoke: "She knew that I went to Greece. You know that I will not return to Italy. Perhaps it is best—if you are not too impatient—you can wait a short time, and tell her that I am no more. You see it will not be long now."

Poor Maria, I thought. Would she ever get over it?

I wanted to cheer him up and say all the things one says to sick patients to try and give them an encouraging future, but I was a layman—Stephen was a Doctor and Anna was a nurse.

Weakly I responded, "I will try and carry out all your wishes when I am back in England."

He settled back on his pillow and with an air of contentment and trust he dozed off into his intermittent dreams. What did he dream of, I wondered? Battles in Italy, battles and civil war in Greece, his parents, his sister, his son, the women in his life, Joy, Maria and Anna?

The snow had stopped falling when I left their company and I sought the warmth and comfort of Marika's kitchen.

It seemed strange to think that this would be my last lunch with them. It would be the last time that I would have Marika's kind but fussy attention ensuring that I should eat sufficiently in the cold weather. Certainly Georgios and Vincentios needed no encouragement as far as food was concerned. Vincentios was telling Georgios that he would return to his mountain sheep within a couple of days whatever the weather. Georgios was trying to reassure Vincentios that Spring would be early that year.

After lunch I thought I would visit the chapel for the last time. Quietly I sat in the dark interior of the religious sanctum. Across the years and continents I thought of Lt. General Montgomery's brief personal message on the eve of Alamein: "Let us all pray that 'the Lord Mighty in battle' will give us victory." With all the suffering in wars that Stephen had seen it was difficult to believe that God's hand was in every endeavour including war. Surely war was excluded?

Yet it seemed to me that religious beliefs had weakened since the war; during the war we had sought strength through religion.

I felt something brush my arm. I thought at first that it was one of the cats again, but looking round I saw that Anna had quietly slipped into the chapel and sat alongside me. As though reading my thoughts she whispered, "God is amongst us in our lives, but not on any side."

Strangely I thought of Tennyson's lines from 'The Passing of Arthur':

'If thou shouldst never see my face again,
Pray for my soul. More things are
wrought by prayer
Than this world dreams of.'

I suppose we both had our private inner thoughts, but I'm sure that we both prayed for Stephen's soul that day amidst the mountain snow-packed clouds.

★ ★ ★

I had a fitful sleep that night. This was hardly surprising in view of the leisurely way I had spent my day, and the anticipatory feeling of returning to Kalambaka and civilization the next morning.

The distant monastery bells seemed to pierce the dark and silent gloom, and it wasn't until the half-light of another dawn that I fell into a chasm of deep sleep wherein it seemed that I had joined Stephen and Anna in trying to escape from a world enveloped in wars and hate.

I must have slept for some hours before I regained consciousness as a result of a vigorous shaking from Vincentios. As I peered at him through a dazy mist he pointed to my wristwatch at the side of my warm bed.

I had overslept, but I made up time with a quick wash and

shave. Marika was waiting anxiously for me, and I wasted little time over a sketchy breakfast.

Soon I entered Stephen and Anna's quarters where Anna was standing at Stephen's bed. She had her fingers to her lips beseeching quiet, and looking at Stephen I could see that he was in a peaceful sleep. Perhaps it was as well that he was sleeping; to part for the last time in such strange surroundings would have entailed some hollow and forced conversation, a meaningless dialogue. It was much better to remember him as he was on the night of our little party, and his relaxed mood on the morning after the party when we reminisced on our time together in Italy. Strangely, considering that I had left the Army some years earlier, I saluted him. To me, he would always be the brave soldier and a chivalrous gallant. I remembered how he had inspired his men in battle, the respect he engendered.

Now, in the early morning, he had the great devotion and love of Anna, perhaps a love more profound than if they had been man and wife.

Quietly I moved into the open air. There was no snow falling, and the sun was rising in a pallid sky. Anna came and stood beside me. Her tawny eyes were weary looking. I expect Stephen had coughed his night away as she had comforted him. There was nothing further I could say, but quietly she whispered: "He'd never want you to feel sorry for him; he couldn't bear that you know." Instinctively I gave her a heartfelt kiss as I clasped her body to mine.

As I joined Marika, Georgios and Vincentios and we made our way towards the outer courtyard, I looked back just once for a second. I lifted my arm and waved to Anna; she waved back with both arms as though she was bidding farewell from both Stephen and herself.

The precipices of rock seemed to hold no terrors for me now. Perhaps my vertigo had at last been cured.

We passed through the arched entrance and down the stairs. Slowly we trudged along the rocky passage and emerged from the doorway at the far end. The long flight of steps was easier to negotiate on the descent than they had been on the climb a week ago, and they were not so icy now.

We began to move more quickly. I looked at my watch, and breathing a sigh of relief I realised that it had only just gone ten o'clock.

We came out into the clearing where the donkeys were stabled, and there to my joy was the reliable Nikos. Laughingly we shook hands as though it was a formal occasion. His white hair danced in the wind.

Now it was time for more farewells, and embracing them all I thanked the three of them in my stilting Greek for all their help. Georgios asked Nikos to tell Yanni that he would come to Kalambaka in three days' time for some supplies. And so Georgios, Marika and Vincentios started their climb back to the ruined sanctuary of St Nicholas. I don't suppose I would ever forget their kindness to an unexpected foreign stranger such as myself.

Nikos and I hitched ourselves onto the two donkeys and slowly we began to descend from the mystical heights of the Meteora. As the animals slowly and carefully plodded downward we did not talk animatedly as normally we would have done after the week of adventurous separation. The perpendicular precipices and dark smooth rocky formations cast a spell of silence on us.

Eventually we passed through the rocky terrain and dark chasms into a landscape of plane trees and more established paths. We paused for a short rest. I looked back up into the misty clouds for a last look at the ruined St Nicholas Monastery.

The well-worn track was no longer covered with ice, and shortly our donkeys headed towards the plain and the town of Kalambaka. Far away behind us the mountains reached for the sky; I could still hear the faint ringing of distant bells.

It was a clear day, and the sun had a hint of Spring within its temporary bright warmth as we reached the town once more.

We were tethering the donkeys as Yanni came out of his shop and greeted us with a smile and an air of relief.

"Kyrie David, Zena is waiting for you in the house to give welcome with food and coffee," Yanni spoke rapidly, unsaddling the animals.

"Come, David, you will have much to tell me," Nikos put his arm over my shoulder and guided me towards Yanni's house. It was strange how we had kept our thoughts to ourselves throughout the journey from the Meteora, but those granite outcrops seemed to mantle us in silence—now we were back amongst familiar friends and environs.

We were back in the material world.

We entered the house alongside the shop and there was Zena smiling anxiously at us. She brought us bread, cheese and coffee explaining that she would cook for us for the evening meal.

"Stephanos and Anna—they were not upset that Yanni and I had been able to direct you to them?" There was still a note of anxiety in her voice, a fear that she might have betrayed a trust.

"No, Zena, they were not upset. At first, of course, they

were surprised and puzzled to know how I had tracked them down, but then we had many friendly conversations—about the past mostly." I paused with my answer. "But Stephanos has not long to live. After I have gone, when you hear of any information regarding the well-being of Stephanos and Anna please let Nikos know in Florina so that he can communicate with me in London."

Zena nodded her agreement to this, and left Nikos and I to have our lunch.

In the quiet of that over-furnished sitting-room I told Nikos of all that I had learnt at St Nicholas about Stephen and Anna. Several times Nikos interrupted me to clarify some points, and I remember how I finished up by telling him of Anna's great love and care of her patient, Stephanos, and her constancy that triumphed over despair.

"They have found true love in adversity you think?" Nikos asked.

"I'm sure of it," I replied. "It is strange, Nikos, to think that up in the Meteora, Stephanos and Anna have little of the material advantages of this world, that Stephanos has not long to live, and yet in a curious way I was envious of their mutual love and their peaceful calm."

"What about all the burns they had suffered?" Nikos looked inquiringly at me.

"They were bad. Fortunately so far as Anna was concerned they were not visible to the public eye, but those of Stephanos were not only visible but horrible to witness at first encounter. Gradually I became used to his savaged face, and his wearing of dark glasses helped. Would that they had perhaps received plastic surgery, but they were caught up in so much fighting and civil war." I looked out of the window; already the light was fading. "In any event it came to a point where they had lost faith in mankind's humanity. By chance they were led to St Nicholas. At least there they thought they could encounter no further tragedy."

Nikos finished for me what I was going to say: "But even there they could not escape the ironic twist of life; his health; his weakening lungs."

"Yes," I confirmed. "But you see, they have had a little time together, a little peace. The mountains are their friends."

Zena cleared away our plates, and indicated that she had prepared our sleeping quarters. Soon we were resting on the hard beds, and it wasn't long before fatigue set in after the arduous journey.

I think we both slept for several hours, and then, having refreshed ourselves, we hastily descended the stairs attracted by the smell of Zena's cooking.

I believe that it was another tasteful moussaka dish that Zena provided, and Yanni was generous with the retsina. In the middle of the meal Nikos explained: "Kyrie David and I will be leaving Kalambaka tomorrow morning."

"You go so soon?" Yanni seemed disappointed, but I supposed they had little company in the Winter.

"Yes. I have to be back at work in the museum at Florina, and Kyrie David has a long journey back to London," Nikos spoke gravely in Greek.

Yanni spoke wistfully to me: "Perhaps one day you will come back to Kalambaka, in the Spring or Summer when you will enjoy the Meteora so much more."

"Perhaps Kyrie David will be happy to be back in London." A tentative smile played on Zena's lips as she looked at me.

The lamplight glowed in my raised wineglass. An image of Lydia momentarily crossed the glass. "Yes, I think I shall be glad to return to England now," I answered. "I have been away quite a long time. Don't forget to let Nikos know if there is any serious news about Stephanos or Anna."

Once more we sat back contentedly with the mellowness of the wine as my Greek friends smoked their narghiles. I could no longer see the monasteries nor hear the ringing of the bells, but I could visualize Marika, Georgios and Vincentios huddled around the kitchen fire—and most of all Anna comforting Stephen in the darkness of the night.

Eventually but reluctantly we went to bed. The sky was unclouded and the moon was clear; a myriad of frosty stars watched overhead.

★ ★ ★

We said goodbye to Yanni and Zena, and cleared the snow covering the car. But would the 'black beetle' start up again after the idle week in the open it had endured?

Certainly Nikos seemed confident; at first the engine seemed to protest with intermittent groans, and I thought perhaps that the battery was tired out. Nikos muttered a few words of Greek, probably an ancient curse, whereupon our little motor spluttered into life with the usual dark clouds of smoke. It had taken more than the usual three attempts this time.

The smoke eventually cleared and Nikos smiled cheerily at me. Temporarily he released his hands from the wheel to wave them in the air in a gesture of farewell and we left behind the streets of Kalambaka. There was an early morning quietude around the streets, and the working day had not yet truly begun.

Unlike our first entry into Kalambaka it was not snowing, and as the sun began its Eastern rise I looked up for the last time at the monastic crags in their isolation.

Although, of course, the little car still had no comforting heating, it did not seem so cold on that return journey. Perhaps the first days of Spring were now at hand.

"Are you glad that you came?" Nikos shouted above the noise of the engine.

"Yes," I answered loudly. "I have the answers to so many questions now."

"Do you think that we should always seek to find answers? Sometimes it is best not to know, sometimes the answers are misleading, sometimes the answers only lead to more questions."

"You should have been a philosopher, Nikos," I replied laughingly. But I knew that his question was really a difficult one which I had not myself answered. Sometimes it was best not to disturb matters; 'let sleeping dogs lie'; but there must also be times when there was justification for unearthing the curious past, to ensure justice was done. To me Stephen had vindicated himself, but there was no purpose now in broadcasting his story to the world. Certainly in the eyes of many Greeks he had become a national hero, a modern Byronic soldier and a healer of medical casualties.

We crossed once more the Plain of Thessaly. The Pindus Mountains were still snow-clad.

The road improved somewhat as we skirted Mount Olympus, and Nikos and I fell into a silence as the car engine remorselessly chugged along.

As before, we had the usual lunch break at Larissa, and then we motored on steadily into the afternoon. Our speed increased on the main Athens to Salonika road. It was as though our 'black beetle' sensed the approach of our destination and gathered speed to reach it.

I looked forward to seeing the Sophoulis family again, but regretted to think that my time with Nikos and his reliable small car was coming to an end.

We had left Kalambaka as the sun rose in the east, and as we entered Salonika the westerly sun was sinking at the watery horizon.

★ ★ ★

Marina Sophoulis had prepared another appetizing meal, and once more Costos had plied us with wine.

"You remember that before you left we drank a toast for your successful journey? Was it successful?" Costos asked.

"Yes," I answered. "At least it was successful in the sense that I found Stephanos and Anna, but of course the future is bleak and sad for them." I had already told them all that there was to know; after all they were far from England, and I knew that I could rely on their promised discretion. To change the subject I added, "I remember that we also drank a toast to the future happiness of Bill and Zoe. It won't be long before your wedding day now Zoe," I smiled and raised my glass to her.

"Only another month." She seemed quietly composed, and I thought back to our happy day together on Thasos. Inwardly I prayed that life would be kind to Bill and Zoe. How different their lives would be from those of Stephen and Anna. I could only be envious of Bill and Zoe's promised future together.

Even if Zoe had her worries concerning her ageing parents when they were without her, she seemed so well matched with Bill. Some good things had come out of the War, I mused to myself. At this point in time Lydia was non-available and Zoe was unobtainable.

The following morning it was time to thank Nikos before he left for Florina.

"Without all your help nothing would have been possible. Thank you a million times."

"Your Greek is improving, David. Perhaps you should stay in Greece a little longer and then you can become an interpreter," Nikos laughed at me as he squeezed the air out of my body in a bear-like embrace.

I watched and waved until I lost sight of the little 'black beetle'.

Later that morning there were more farewells as I said goodbye to Costos and Marina Sophoulis. It was Zoe who accompanied me to the Salonika Airfield.

Before I boarded the light plane that was to take me to Athens I kissed her on both cheeks as she whispered to me:

"I will always remember our day together on Thasos."

"So shall I. A happy Easter and a happy wedding, Zoe." I kissed her again.

The noise of the engine precluded any further conversation, and soon I was airborne and looking down at the small specks of civilization.

The plane banked over the water and then it headed south towards Athens, the capital, and the last stage of my return journey to England.

★ ★ ★

Ken and Sofia Dacre were at the airport at Athens to greet me. They had brought Athena to welcome me as well.

Ken's owlish bespectacled face lit up when he saw me emerging from the throng with my battered suitcase, and he hastened forward to take the suitcase. There were enthusiastic kisses on both cheeks from Sofia and Athena, and I had a feeling of being glad to be with them again and back in the civilized, material world.

Soon we had returned to their comfortable apartment in Kolonaki within the shadows of Mount Hymettus. It seemed to me that Athena had grown even during my comparatively short time away in the north.

It was pleasant to hear Ken's lazy American drawl again as we enjoyed a drink together. It was like my previous visit, with Sofia preparing an appetizing meal in the kitchen, and as before, I had this feeling of envy—not for any material possessions they had, but for the comforting natural bonhomie of their family life.

It was with regret, therefore, that when Sofia asked if I could stay a while to rest before returning to England, I had to decline.

"Tom Preston, our Senior Partner, is no doubt at this moment rubbing his hands, and awaiting my return. The documents and files with pink tape will have begun to amass on my desk," I laughed. More sombrely I added, "Tom has been very patient, but I was owed some back leave, and I'll soon make up for lost time."

Ken looked knowingly at Sofia: "I expect he has a girlfriend or two in London that he is anxious to see again. Is that right, David?"

"Well, there is one especially. She comes from South

Africa, and she has worked in our law firm for a while. Her name is Lydia, Lydia Maidment." I don't know why I was telling them about my private life, but it seemed to be a natural consequence of my thoughts on their harmonious domestic scene.

"Perhaps you will only fall in love in Greece," Sofia smiled as she led us towards the food-laden table.

"Do stay, Uncle David. Later on I can show you the roses and the jasmine and honeysuckle," Athena looked appealingly at me.

"You see David, you already have a young conquest here," Ken quipped as he recharged my glass of wine. "You can only fall in love in Greece you know."

Presently I thanked them for the research they had carried out which had enabled me to trace Stephen and Anna to the Meteora. I told them what I had learnt up at St Nicholas, and about all the kind people I had met in this Grecian tragedy. I stressed to them that Stephen and Anna's actual whereabouts and their secret life was not to be divulged to anyone except to Anna's sister, Elena. I explained that it was unlikely that the two sisters would meet again as Anna would remain in the Meteora even after Stephen's demise whenever that came.

I thought that it would be pleasant if Ken and Sofia and Athena could get to know Bill and Zoe. Although Zoe was at that time in Salonika and would not be able to be with us, I managed to contact Bill by telephone, and it was agreed that we would have a farewell get together on the following evening, before the day of my departure for England.

And so it was on the next evening that Bill called on us in the Kolonaki district. He promised the Dacres that he would bring Zoe to meet them after the early Spring wedding.

In Grecian style, after Sofia had provided us with a more than satisfactory meal and we had said our good-nights to her and Athena, the three males, that was Ken, Bill and I, descended quickly onto the centre of the city.

I think it was Bill who led us to the cellar cafe. As we went down the steps into the cellar I could hear the canned bouzouki music and the waves of sound of a woman singing.

Some people in the cafe were eating at the small tables; the chairs were hard. They were ordinary Athenian people. There was a couple at the next table; the girl, who was overweight, was forking some food into the man's mouth.

As we sipped our ouzo we watched the machinations between the sexes. Clearly here there were girls of easy virtue with their cork shoes, plastic handbags and short skirts.

The vibrant bouzouki music mingled with the smells of food being cooked in the adjacent kitchen.

A few men were dancing on their own in Greek fashion. As the night wore on the noise became fiercer, the music and the singing became louder and the drink flowed more freely.

We raised our voices to overcome the clamour. I could see that Ken and Bill were on the same wavelength and hopefully a permanent friendship would be forged between them. This would also be helpful to Zoe when she came to Athens to live there permanently.

I looked around at the young women; some of them in the artificial neon light seemed like painted dolls; some of the men seemed to be drowning their sorrows with drink and with chain smoking. I thought of Stephen and Anna in their mountain haven. Perhaps they were to be envied, away from these sordid material outlooks of the big city.

Eventually we settled up our bill, and stood outside the

cellar cafe. The night sky was brilliant. We walked along the street, past girls standing in doorways waiting for the usual male clients.

We arrived back at the apartment, and I thanked Bill for all his help. I seemed to be indebted to so many people. We shook hands, and jokingly I apologised for having to miss his pre-wedding stag party.

"Good luck to you and Zoe," I called out after his retreating figure.

"Thank you. David. Don't forget your friends out here, will you?" His voice carried through the night air.

"No. I never will."

I knew I would never forget the details of all my travels of the recent months—and yet when I went to bed that night my thoughts were all of Lydia. Surely I would soon be seeing her again now, holding her in my arms, our bodies intermingled as they had been in the Autumn.

★ ★ ★

I was back at the airport again, and Ken, Sofia and Athena had come to see me off on the last leg of my journey back to England.

It was a somewhat sad farewell. Would we ever meet again? I sincerely hoped that we would. I hoped that we would meet again when I was married, when I had a settled life—similar to theirs. I needed no more adventures.

I was about to leave them to board the plane when Athena said:

"Uncle David, when I am older I want to marry an Englishman, don't you think that would be nice?"

I looked at Ken and Sofia and we laughed joyfully. Athena had sent away the sadness of our parting.

★ ★ ★

Now the plane was circling over Piraeus. Strangely it was up in the plane that I could see how the Spring was coming rapidly to Greece.

The sky was more blue, the clouds more fleecy, the sea flecked with glints from the sun, the very air was festive.

Spring would advance from the sea, travelling ashore and up the hills of the villages, through the olive groves and vineyards, along the fields covered with the flame of poppies and blue trumpet flowers. Spring would leave its imprint along the Aegean, in Athens and up in the Meteora.

There would be a bustle in the harbours as the caiques would be made ready for the seas; boats would be caulked and painted; there would be the smell of sea air and boiling tar.

I looked down at the rocky outline to the waters; the crevices in the cliffs would soon be awash with the clumps of broom, yellow and golden against the cornflower blue of the sea.

I felt strangely sad to be leaving Greece at such a time of year, yet when I thought of the cold granite rocks of the Meteora, instinctively I shuddered. There was a bleakness there that I was glad to leave behind, and friends were there whom I knew that I would never see again.

★ ★ ★

By today's standards the buildings at Heathrow Airport were primitive, and after the plane had landed without incident I struggled through the customs and passport control.

There was a sharp easterly wind to greet the arrivals, and after some difficulty I managed to call up a taxi. At last I was on my way home to South Kensington.

I had sent telegrams both to Tom Preston and to Lydia telling them of the date and approximate time of my return home. I did not expect to see either of them at the airport, but I was looking forward with keen anticipation to seeing Lydia at the Little Boltons in South Kensington.

It was dusk as my cab turned off Old Brompton Road into the old familiar street. Another couple of weeks and the clocks would be altered, and the promise of another Summer would be at hand. The daffodils were nodding their heads in welcome as I found my key for the flat.

There was quite a pile of mail scattered on the hall floor inside the front door and as I moved into the remainder of the flat it had an air of unoccupancy as though no one had entered the flat since Lydia and I had left together in the Autumn.

Of course I had been engaged in anticipatory and joyful expectation of receiving a loving welcome from Lydia; I had missed her very much, and I had assumed that she had missed me too, that we had experienced a mutual deep love.

My enthusiasm gradually gave way to disappointment. There was no food in the flat. I had thought that Lydia would at least have seen to that for me; I could perhaps explain her absence—maybe she had been kept late at work or the trains perhaps were causing delays.

There was nothing for it but to walk down into the Old Brompton Road and seek out a restaurant—perhaps the one that Lydia and I had gone to before we had travelled to Italy together.

I must admit that I was not really sorry to be having English food again; the novelty of moussaka and the various cheeses had now worn off, although as I ravenously devoured a sirloin steak I thought with nostalgic mouth-watering affection of the roast lamb at our little party on the Meteora.

Eventually, somewhat tired after the air travel, and somewhat disconsolate that Lydia would not be with me on my first night back in England, I retired to the comfort of my old bed. Before doing so I phoned the number of Lydia's digs in Earls Court but there was no reply.

My return to London seemed to be an anti-climax to all that had gone before, and I felt a sense of unease until eventually sleep overcame any nagging doubts that lingered in my mind.

★ ★ ★

"I hope that you enjoyed your holiday. I was getting a little anxious as you extended your stay in Greece."

Tom Preston removed his noisy pipe from his mouth.

"Why were you anxious?" I asked.

Tom shifted his large frame in his swivel-back chair, and looked out through the window across the London skyline. I suppose Tom was no more than fifty years old, but to those of us who had not so very long ago fought in the War, someone of Tom's age seemed quite ancient. His hair was greying prematurely so I suppose this added to his air of seniority and learning. He was still a good-looking man, and had a somewhat rugged facial expression, thin tight lips and defiant chin. His grey eyes seemed to match the greyness of his hair.

He knocked out the ash from his pipe into a glass ashtray.

"Well, I had the impression that something was attracting your attention in Greece, especially as Lydia had returned to London. Some Athenian Goddess maybe?"

"That's not funny Tom. I had to follow through some unfinished business," I countered.

"And did you conclude your business?" he asked.

"Yes; at least as far as it can ever be concluded. Where is Lydia, why isn't she here in the office? I had visualized that you had been keeping her nose to the typewriter in my absence."

There was a pause as Tom shuffled through some papers on his desk.

"After she came back from Italy she only stayed on working here for a few weeks, and then she left."

"Why did she leave? I thought she was happy working here?" My questions tumbled out one after the other.

There was another pause. I sensed that Tom was giving some thought to his answer, although when it came it seemed natural enough.

Shrugging his shoulders he said: "I've no doubt it wouldn't be difficult to find legal employment elsewhere for more than we were paying her."

"Wait a minute. She came to work for us because you knew a friend of hers in Durban in South Africa. Why would she take off like that?" I asked.

"How should I know? Perhaps she had other fish to fry." It

was clear that he wanted to get on with his work without further interruption, so I returned to my office and started on picking up the tabs again on the various clients with whom I would be dealing.

As I went out to lunch, a pleasant looking girl with dark brown eyes behind her spectacles and with short and black hair, introduced herself to me as Kathy Morse. She was not unattractive with a warm smile and striking figure. Apparently she had replaced Lydia in the office, and I suppose looking back over the years it was on this day that my search for Lydia began. First of all I had searched for Stephen, now I had to search for Lydia.

★ ★ ★

After finishing work for the day I did not go straight home, but called at the address near Earls Court Road where Lydia had been in digs before we went abroad together.

Tentatively I pressed the bell of the grey stone house, looking up at the several storeys above the stone steps. After a long wait an elderly square, stocky woman with wisps of white hair stroking her face came to the door. She stood there like a captain on his bridge, prepared to repel all raiders, her fat arms akimbo across her heaving breasts.

I asked her if Lydia Maidment still had a bed sitting-room at this address, and if so was the lady concerned presently at home.

"She left here about five weeks ago. Took all her things with her. At least she paid up her rent that was due before she left—not like some of them."

"Didn't she leave a forwarding address?" I asked hopefully.

"No. Often they don't bother you know. Here today and gone tomorrow. I remember she left in style in a taxi."

"If you hear from Miss Maidment at all, will you please let me know?" I handed her my card with my name and telephone number. "Perhaps she has taken a holiday and will return here."

"Perhaps, but we're full up now anyway."

The door was then shut in my face, and disconsolately I descended the steps, and made for the exit from the Square.

In the cool evening air, activity in the Square was increasing as city workers returned to their domestic quarters. There was the usual mix of young men and women, and some older, but mostly with that extra optimistic and upbeat walk as they headed for their homes after a day's work in the heart of the Capital.

A few more elderly men and women were sitting on benches in the gardens in the centre of the Square; contentedly they watched the waving daffodils and the emerging tulips.

Why couldn't she have left a forwarding address? Why had she left the firm? Perhaps she had never received some of my letters and postcards.

I returned to the Little Boltons. My flat had been cleaned by the daily help who came in regularly, but I realised that I had no food and would have to go out for another solo meal in a restaurant.

Wistfully I thought back to the times when Lydia would unostentatiously prepare an appetizing meal after our day at the office.

There was still some drink in the flat, and I poured myself a large whisky and water.

I decided that on the following day I would telephone Bob Chester. Perhaps he would be forthcoming with news of Lydia.

Later on that evening I sat down in my favourite armchair in the flat. I was feeling tired. It had been a hard day in the office, and then the visit to Lydia's old digs, and then going out for a meal.

The night sky seemed black and starless as I gazed up through the window.

I could not see any signs in the flat that Lydia had been there since we went to Italy together, no friendly trace of her or her perfume.

The silence was overwhelming. My tongue seemed to wither drily in my throat, and like an Autumn bird I felt a foreboding in the night-time air.

★ ★ ★

It seemed like old times to be fighting my way to the bar of the familiar hostelry in Fleet Street.

The beery, smoky and crowded atmosphere was another home to many of the City customers as they jostled and tried to make themselves heard by shouting.

Presently I returned with the two beers to a quieter corner of the saloon bar where Bob Chester had managed to commandeer a small area in which we could stand and talk without too much pushing and shoving.

"So how did you get on after Lydia left you in Italy and she returned to London?" Bob asked as he drank swiftly at the beer glass.

Strangely, although I had previously thought out how

much of my travels I would tell people like Margaret Hardinge and Tom Preston, I had not premeditated about the information I would give to Bob Chester. On the one hand he was a newspaper journalist whose main object would be to disseminate any interesting news; on the other hand it was only because his newspaper had published the photograph of Stephen that I had embarked on my journeyings.

At first I turned the question back at him:

"So you did meet Lydia in London after she returned from Italy?" I asked animatedly.

"Yes, I had a telegram asking me to meet her at the airport when she returned from Italy. Naturally I was a bit puzzled as I thought she would be returning with you," he paused. "But you never could keep a lady friend for long, could you?" That long-remembered smirk enveloped his face. The sardonic humour was more rasping and seemingly more unkind than Stephen's had ever been.

"Never mind about that, what happened to Lydia?" I drained my glass and put it down on the small, crowded table.

"We met a few times, but to be honest, David, I cannot admit to Lydia being one of my conquests. I remember after the last time we met I phoned her at your office, and at her digs. At first she put me off, saying she hoped to see me soon. Then after a few more days I phoned your office again, and it seemed that she had left your firm; my phone calls to her digs were equally non-productive. I think it must have been the landlady there who said that Lydia had left her digs. Apparently she left no forwarding address, no phone number either." He shrugged his shoulders. "Anyway, plenty of fish in the sea, as they say."

"But some are rare," I added.

"I'll get two more beers and then you can tell me of your adventures after Lydia returned to London."

The short break whilst he manoeuvred through the throng to the bar would at least give me time to compose my account of the last weeks, and tell him only as much as seemed pertinent in the circumstances. Certainly Bob Chester had been instrumental in my tracing the Manzonis to Urbino in Italy, and I told him all the information I had obtained there.

I also told him about the contacts I had traced in Greece from wartime days. I did not go into any details, but explained to him that eventually I had found Stephen, but that he hadn't long to live now.

Although there was no reason why he should do so, I asked Bob not to divulge this piece of information, and indeed he kept his promise although I imagine his newspaper would have liked to have published a follow-up story to the earlier photograph printed by them.

"So now you are busy with your law work again?" Bob quaffed his beer steadily.

"That's right. Making up for lost time. I wish to God, however, that I knew where Lydia was, what she was doing and why she seems to have disappeared." I was putting on my raincoat preparatory to facing the Spring rains outside.

"You'd be better off forgetting about Lydia. It's all too enigmatic, David."

I could do without Bob's philosophising on the nature of women and their relationships with the opposite sex.

As I said goodbye to Bob I added, "If you hear any news of Lydia, will you let me have it?"

"Yes, of course, David. You know me," he replied.

"That's the trouble; I do know you." My laugh was slightly forced as I struggled to the exit of the crowded bar.

London optimistically began to embrace the Spring, and the parks and flower beds were green in their growth; at the same time my life seemed to go into an uneventful decline of solitude so easily experienced in the Capital city.

In such circumstances I worked late in the office most evenings, and I remember that one weekend I motored to Dorset to see my parents.

My father had now retired from his teaching, but he had not entirely left behind at the school his historical wealth of information. Most days in the Spring and Summer he acted as a guide at the famous castle nearby. His tall frame with gingery hair and clipped moustache over a gaunt face made quite a striking silhouette on the castle battlements.

I still had little in common with my father, not even physically. I had persuaded him to indulge in a beer at the local public house whilst mother prepared the Sunday lunch.

"Why don't you set up in practice here, in this town?" he asked. "Your mother would like that."

I didn't think that my mother really wanted that. She enjoyed her charity work and bridge sessions. Physically I suppose I took after her, for my mother was plumpish with her grey hair wisping over brown eyes in a round face.

"I'm afraid it all seems too provincial for me now. One has to be working in London to get on these days." My answer seemed glib and patronising, and I wondered to myself whether the real reason for my working in London was so that I could continue with my independence, my own life.

I left them after tea on the Sunday, and it seemed to me

that they were as content as ever in each other's company. They didn't really need me back at home in Dorset. Even my brief visit seemed to intrude on my mother's good works at the church, and my father's regular walks with Bosun, his springer spaniel.

Of course there was one further main reason for my being in London. I felt sure that by being in London I had my best chance of finding Lydia again, of regaining my lost love and obtaining enduring happiness.

The search for Stephen had tired me, and now I was engaged in a further search—for the elusive, willowy Lydia.

Was it a poison in my blood, spreading dangerously through all my body? Certainly as the days and weeks went by my anguish became more acute.

So often one read in novels or watched on films how characters who had been long apart would suddenly meet again. Coincidence, however far-fetched, was allowed to explain so much.

Alas! This rarely if ever happened in real life in a large city like London.

Time and again I would be following a throng of people on the city streets or climbing the steps at Earls Court Underground Station; I would catch a glimpse of long titian hair, a slender back, a walk of feminine allure. Dodging and pressing my way through the hurrying people I would catch up with my quarry, only to find that when I was alongside I realised that I was gazing at a stranger.

I remember one Sunday morning when overnight rain had given way to Spring sunshine. I walked to the Round Pond in Kensington Gardens, a walk I had enjoyed several times in the past when Lydia had been with me. I was looking at the water and a graceful model yacht; the waters rippled; I thought I saw a reflection of Lydia in the sunlit water. Quickly I turned around, but it wasn't her. The long hair belonged to a nursemaid anxiously watching the model yacht, and more keenly overseeing her young charge close at hand to whom she spoke in pidgin English.

I had become quite adept in the confines of my Kensington kitchen, and my cooking produced quite palatable meals. Yet sitting in my flat as the evening daylight lengthened, I realised that my life had become stationary, the hours had become elongated.

When I finally retired each evening to bed, I remembered how we had lain close together. Irresistible currents had driven us together. Surely we had been meant for each other, surely the passion had been mutual.

Every morning as I prepared my breakfast I listened out for the postman, to hear the rustle through the letterbox of a letter of reprieve.

Such a letter did not come—but another letter did come. It was from my friend Nikos in Florina. Stephen had died peacefully in his sleep one night up in the Meteora. Anna had decided, as I knew she would, to remain up in the craggy deserted monastery heights, and the faithful Georgios and Marika would be there to look after her.

Although I had been expecting this information at any time, it was still a heavy blow. It did, however, galvanise me into action as far as Stephen's affairs were concerned.

Perhaps this was as well, and hopefully in doing what I could for Stephen, I would not think so much about Lydia and the happiness she had once brought me.

I would have to fight against the ever-growing weed of despair, the anguish sharper than a serpent's tooth.

★ ★ ★

I was mindful of the fact that Stephen had specifically asked me to endeavour to ensure that the previous account of his death in action in Italy should not be undermined as far as Justin and the Regiment were concerned, and he, Stephen, had made the same request as regards his sister, Margaret. He had also asked me to keep a watching brief on the welfare of his son, Eric.

I decided, therefore, that there was no further point in seeing Justin again. Someone in authority had taken a vital piece out of the War Diary at the Records Office. I doubted if it had been Justin himself, but he may have arranged for that piece of dirty work to be done by someone else, possibly his one-time Adjutant. My reasoning was that the War Diary might have contained a suspicious reference regarding Stephen and his subsequent disappearance, and that there had consequently been an inference of possible discredit on the Battalion which those in authority had thought best to eradicate. Certainly I had no desire to pursue this matter further. My searching days were over. I would act in accordance with Stephen and Anna's wishes.

I realised, however, that I would have to visit Margaret again. Stephen had warned me more than once to watch my step with her, but I had to ensure that she had received the portrait of Stephen from Italy, and my legal mind was turning over certain aspects of Stephen's estate and the welfare of Eric for the future.

Before I made contact with Margaret, however, I knew that I would have to write a letter to Maria in Urbino. God knows it would be a difficult enough letter to write. Maria had known that Stephen had gone to Greece all those years ago. She didn't know that he was no longer alive.

I suppose I drafted my letter several times before I was finally able to send what was inevitably a sad note to her.

As I recall, my letter was not long. I told her that after much difficulty in wintry weather I had located Stephen in the Meteora in Greece. I did not tell her anything about the serious burns, nor about Anna; I told her that he had recently died since my return to England after a long illness affecting his lungs.

I knew that whatever I wrote would sound prosaic; I knew also that Maria would never forget Stephen. His shadow would always hover over her life. Maybe she would settle down and marry one day, but it would not be with me. I had to try and forget her love, her sadness, her spasms of Italian joy. Certainly I myself would never be able to vie with Stephen, dead or alive, as far as Maria was concerned.

I posted the letter in Fleet Street, and walked on to the office. Before the arrival of the first client of the day, I resolved to make an appointment to see Margaret again. It was because of this that I refreshed my mind on the legal texts of Law of Succession. I was primarily concerned regarding types of wills, also the law regarding illegitimacy as it then stood.

It had been quite an arduous day at the office with difficult clients, and I was not sorry to shake the City dust from my feet and walk along the riverside to Chelsea.

It was a cool Spring evening, and it was enjoyable to have daylight again after office hours.

I hadn't been in this particular neighbourhood since the previous Autumn. Although that was really not all that long ago it seemed like a different age to me, as though in the interim I had travelled back in time, and was now transported back to the present.

As I pressed the front doorbell I could hear the strains of a Beethoven piano sonata. There was a sudden breaking off of the playing, and then Margaret opened the main door to beckon me into the house. Our mutual greeting could scarcely be described as over-enthusiastic.

Once more I found myself in her well-furnished sitting-room. Little seemed to have changed since my last visit, except that I noticed that the portrait of Stephen painted by Arturo Manzoni was now hanging in one of the alcoves by the fireplace.

As Margaret poured me a whisky and water she saw my eyes focus on the portrait. "Thank you for arranging for it to come here," her words of appreciation were somewhat grudgingly made. "Do you think I have hung it in a satisfactory position?" she asked.

"Yes," I answered. "It seems quite satisfactory. Has Eric seen the portrait of his father yet?"

"He is at home here for a few days. It is half-term; so he has seen it, and he seems proud of it."

"Good. I hope he will always think of his father as a brave soldier."

"So you met the artist in Italy, arranged for the portrait to be dispatched to England, and then what? Did you do anything else?" Her stare was piercing.

I looked at her grey-green eyes, the nose and high forehead, the fair hair. Again, and not unnaturally I was reminded of Stephen, except that Margaret had that tightening of the features, especially around the mouth.

I phrased my answer carefully: "I'm sure that Stephen is dead, but we must now consider the boy's future."

"You mean Eric? He's perfectly happy at his preparatory boarding school, there's nothing further to consider." She spoke sharply, and rose to pace up and down in front of the fireplace.

"I'm sure Stephen must have made financial provision for him. You received a letter from Stephen before he died."

"Yes, I've already told you that on your last visit. He told me in his letter that Joy had died giving birth to Eric."

"That's not all that was stated in the letter, was it? The letter gave instructions to settle Stephen's estate on Eric if he, Stephen, died abroad. Is that not so?"

"Stephen's proper will already left everything to me." She looked at me defiantly.

"If such a letter as I described was written on actual military service it is known as a privileged will, and overrides a previous formal will—Re Wingham, 1949."

"You don't need to spout your law at me." She was becoming angry now.

In some ways I was playing a kind of double game. I knew that I had rattled her with my talk of Privileged Wills—and the fact that such wills didn't need witnessing—but had Stephen been on actual military service when he made the privileged will? Legal arguments could no doubt be far-reaching as to whether Stephen had been engaged in actual military operations. He had, in effect, deserted from the British Forces, but had then been embroiled in further conflict on behalf of the Allies. Certainly a privileged will stood until it was superseded by a later formal will. A privileged will didn't need the formalities, such as witnesses.

I was also worried about the fact that Eric was illegitimate. It was long before the days of the Family Reform Acts of 1969 and 1987 and there was a Common Law construction in force. Normally a gift by will was construed as being to legitimate persons, but the presumption could be rebutted by evidence of a contrary intent. Clearly here there had been a contrary intent.

As all these different legal aspects coursed through my mind, Margaret suddenly stopped her pacing up and down. She smiled down at me as I sat ensconced in a comfortable leather armchair and then she poured another whisky into my glass.

Quietly she broke the silence: "I'm sure something satisfactory to all can be worked out."

"I know your parents lost everything in the blitz, but that didn't affect the capital in trust for Stephen, did it?" As I asked the question for which I already knew the answer, I heard the tread of a youngster running up the stairs after slamming the front door.

She didn't answer my question, so I continued: "It seems to me, as I look around, that you have been using the money to give yourself a lifestyle of luxury when the money was really intended for Eric's future. Perhaps I had better speak to your solicitors about it."

"Part of what you see here is due to my own work, my musical work," she snapped back at me.

"You must at least get your solicitor to set up a trust for Eric—to ensure his future. That is what Stephen would want."

"How do you know what Stephen would want? After all he has been dead a long time."

I was about to contradict her and say that Stephen had

only just died, until I remembered that I had promised Stephen that I would not divulge to Margaret the details of his Greek tragedy.

Eventually, after persistent pressure, she agreed to see her solicitors and have an appropriate trust set up for Eric. I could, of course, legally have insisted that all Stephen's capital was made over to Eric, but I saw no reason to be vindictive, and the more I insisted on such a course the more Margaret would become suspicious as to how I knew the contents of that letter that Stephen had written to her.

I felt we had come to an amicable arrangement which, although perhaps not entirely in conformity with Stephen's wishes for the future of Eric, certainly went a long way towards it.

I was about to take my leave, and had risen from the plush armchair, when a youth of about ten years burst open the sitting-room door; he was starting to ask his Aunt about the supper meal when his Aunt cut in:

"Eric, this is an old friend of your father's. They were together in the War."

Momentarily I was startled; it wasn't only that I had noticed the resemblance to Stephen, particularly the nose, but a memory of Rome came flooding back to me; of Joy with the fair hair, the deep blue eyes. Yes, he would take after both his parents with his luminous features.

We shook hands politely. Looking at the portrait of his father he asked:

"Is it a good likeness of my father?"

"Yes," I answered. "Very good."

"I'm glad of that. He looks so brave, such brave eyes."

"He was very brave, Eric." Turning to Margaret I said, "I must go now."

The boy surprisingly hoped that I would call again soon, but I was even more surprised when Margaret added:

"I'm taking Eric to a concert at the Festival Hall before he goes back to school next week. Would you like to come with us? I'm sure I can get an extra ticket." She hesitated. "Perhaps you are not a music lover."

"Yes, I like music, but I do not have your knowledge and appreciation of it." Now it was my turn to hesitate. I glanced at Eric. "All right, yes, thank you, I'd love to come."

I walked under the street lights towards Sloane Square Tube Station. It had been a strange evening.

I had started out in a pugnacious mood, determined to press home Eric's legal rights. The battle hadn't been easy, but essentially won.

And yet I hadn't fallen out with Margaret as I had anticipated. We had argued, of course, and there had been a coolness for a time, but the evening had ended on a pleasant note. At the same time I could not forget Stephen's warnings about his sister. Somehow the evening had gone too well.

By the time I had reached my flat the church clock was chiming eleven o'clock; I felt tired. Somehow although I had achieved the plus of some success regarding Eric's future, there were still too many minuses.

The biggest minus was that there was still no news of Lydia. It seemed a Spring without hope.

★ ★ ★

The following morning, however, I received a postcard from Kavalla in Greece.

It was from Bill and Zoe; they were on their honeymoon

after their early Spring wedding in Salonika. They had obtained an apartment in Athens where Bill was still based. Apparently they would be living not far from Ken and Sofia, and I could foresee an enjoyable social life together for them all—with Athena adding her cheerful youthful presence as well.

No doubt Zoe's parents would get used to Zoe's absence in due course.

As I breakfasted and sorely tested my teeth on some burnt toast I thought again of that happy, peaceful day I had spent with Zoe on the island of Thasos. I envied Bill and Zoe their happiness together; I envied them their Aegean Spring with the sky and sea more blue as the season advanced, the shimmering water once more flecked with glints of a warm sun, the coloured sails of the craft drying on the harbour front. The sea would bring the Spring to them, like Aphrodite emerging from the foamy waters, but unlike Aphrodite I knew that Zoe would always be faithful to her husband; also she would always be Greek at heart—the roots of an olive tree go deep.

Such news made me feel more benevolent towards the world, but that did not stop me looking up and down the Earls Court platform, the crowded train and jostling crowds as I went to work. My search for Lydia was a search so painful and seemingly never-ending.

Sometimes I could picture her smile, but the smile of joy would turn to a smile through tears. If only I could reach out to touch her—but my daily journey to the office seemed pathless, just as the evenings seemed starless.

I resolved that I would make time that morning to contact other large legal firms and agencies to see if they knew of

Lydia and her movements, but inwardly I knew that there would be no laughing magic at the day's end.

And so it proved.

Before I went home I had arranged to have a game of squash with Tom Preston at Chelsea Cloisters. It would be more correct to say that Tom dragooned me into playing. I think he liked to show that he still had the physical prowess of a younger man in spite of his age, and he won our battle on the court. It must be said, however, that I was not truly concentrating on the game, and after a shower and a solitary beer I bade goodnight to my legal senior.

I had a fairly ordinary meal in a Kings Road restaurant, and soon I was back at home.

Several files were near at hand as I sat in my favourite armchair, but I couldn't concentrate on the legal niceties dallied before me.

From my armchair I could look out at the clear sky with the moon rising over the Capital. The early days of Summer were at hand. Lights blinked on and off in the countless homes across the gardened area.

I poured myself a large whisky and then sat and stared at the telephone willing it to ring, willing it to produce the cadences of that South African voice of Lydia's.

By the time that I had nearly finished the third whisky the night silence was creeping over the capital. As I looked at the amber liquid in my glass I had a Graham-Greene-ish vision that it would not be difficult to enter 'Greeneland' wherein I would be reduced to aching loneliness and furtive nips at the bottle, a world of decay and seediness.

I knew I had to fight against this at all costs, but as it seemed that I could only be with Lydia in my dreams—so let me dream.

* * *

My evening at the Festival Hall with Margaret and the youthful Eric passed off without any undue waves to ruffle our meeting.

I quite enjoyed the concert, but from our conversation I sensed that Eric had been persuaded to attend and that his recreational interests were directed more to sport than music.

I escorted them back to their Chelsea home after the concert, and the proffered coffee and sandwiches were welcome. I would not be seeing Eric again for a few months as he would be returning the next day to his boarding school.

As he retired for the night I gave him a handsome tip to fortify him for the new term, and I was left with Margaret in her sitting-room, the room now embellished with the portrait of Stephen.

Suddenly I turned to her and asked her if she would like to come out to dinner one evening during the following week. She agreed, and we fixed an evening when she did not have to give any piano lessons. If I was to analyse why I asked her out like that on the spur of the moment I suppose I would have come up with different answers. Certainly Margaret was an attractive woman—in the same way that Stephen had been attractive to women, so I had no doubt that she would be attractive to men. Like Stephen also, she carried herself with a certain style and class, she was intelligent and her conversation was never dull.

However, Stephen had several times not only told me of the lack of harmony that existed between him and Margaret, but he had also warned me to be cautious when dealing with her. Certainly I had found her less than honest on the question of wills and the legal provisions for Eric, and yet she had not objected too strongly when I asserted the boy's legal rights.

I realised that my fixing of the forthcoming dinner date with Margaret was more than a quid pro quo for the concert invitation. I think probably that I wanted to remain in touch with her so that I could monitor Eric's future.

Perhaps most important was an inner wish to withstand a Lydia-less 'Greeneland', and to avoid the loneliness of despair in the big city.

★ ★ ★

It was an early Summer evening the following week when I called at the Chelsea home again.

The windows of the house were slightly opened, and I could hear Margaret's light fingers on the piano as I approached the front door.

I knew that she had been practising for a forthcoming concert, and the music, not unpleasantly, seemed to fill the street with its sound.

The piano playing stopped when I pressed the front door bell, and Margaret seemed smilingly content as she ushered me into the sitting-room, and poured a gin and tonic for me.

It was pleasant to relax in this ambience after a day's work; the house seemed strangely quiet now that Eric was back at boarding school.

I looked up at Stephen's portrait, and wondered what interpretation he would have put on this evening's meeting. Would he have disapproved of my taking Margaret out to dinner, or would he have shrugged his shoulders with indifference? He would scarcely have approved, knowing his opinion of his sister. Margaret was swathed in a long blue silky dress which suited her colouring and coolness. It was a dress which seemed to cling seductively to her body, although discreetly screening her slender legs.

I remember that we went to a small restaurant near to Sloane Square; it was a restaurant hidden away down a side street, and known to Margaret.

I was glad that we weren't going to my familiar restaurant off the Old Brompton Road. That would only have reminded me of nostalgic happy days with Lydia, with the candlelight causing her long auburn hair to glow so warmly.

The Chelsea restaurant was not very full, and there was an air of subdued respect and bonhomie from the waiters. London was still struggling through the Fifties before the advent of the Swinging Sixties with its marked differences in dress, music and sexual freedom. It seemed that we Londoners were still walking tentatively after the last World War, and we were still some years before the first walk in space. Anyway, both of us only pecked at our food that evening. I suppose we were sparring with one another. Over coffee at the end of the meal I asked:

"Margaret, does Eric really need to be at boarding school at such an early age?"

"It is the best plan. It is difficult to give him much attention; music has a monopoly of my time. It seems to work out," she smiled defensively.

"If he was at a local school perhaps I could help, taking him out, looking after him, keeping an eye on him." I threw the words out casually.

"You wouldn't be able to keep an eye on him with your work occupying most of your time. Besides, he likes it down on the Sussex coast. Now that he has become used to the rigours of a boarding school he has made quite a few friends."

I didn't pursue the subject any further at that time. I settled the bill and escorted Margaret back to her home.

The street lamps shimmered through the plane trees, and a lone aircraft pierced the night sky with its lights.

Soon we were indoors again, and Margaret handed me a nightcap of my usual whisky and water.

It had been quite a pleasant evening, and at least for a few hours I had managed to lay aside my obsession with Lydia.

Quietly Margaret had gone to the piano. She was playing some Debussy this time.

"Do you know what this is?" she asked.

"I know it is Debussy, but I am not very good at names, titles," I replied.

"La Fille Aux Cheveux De Lin."

"I like it. It has an underlying haunting melody, I think. But you know that I am not very musical."

I smiled across at her upright, statuesque figure, her attractive features, the fair hair and blue eyes, the Roman nose and thrusting chin of Stephen—yes, all the reminders of Stephen.

She had finished playing.

I put down my empty glass on a small table and walked across to the piano. Then I put my arms around her, turned her face to mine, and as I felt her breasts straining through the blue silk, I kissed her sensuous lips. She seemed to welcome this with responsive kisses.

I suppose that if we had been in the Swinging Sixties I

would have shared a bed with Margaret that night, but the Capital still observed the proprieties in those days, at least publicly it did so. Yet Lydia and I had acknowledged sex with abandon.

After our embrace I left the house and returned to my lonely flat. Perhaps I ought to leave this flat, I thought; it would always remind me of Lydia, but then a great part of me always wanted to be reminded of Lydia.

As I went to sleep it seemed to me that the old saying was correct—lust makes everything simple—it is only love that complicates the act.

There were so many paradoxes and anomalies in life—someone whom I once thought of as a sinner such as Stephen—in his way he became a Saint, whereas I had always thought of myself as somewhat philanthropic—until it seemed that I might become a destroyer, a destroyer of other peoples' happiness.

★ ★ ★

I met Margaret several times in that early Summer, but our lovemaking was always of the more formal kind; we observed the niceties of life.

There was no denying her attractions, but I am sure my feelings were more lustful than love-inducing. She was a lively companion, and we had many shared interests.

We had now become joint guardians for Eric, and this arrangement seemed to suit us both well. Primarily, we hoped that Eric would be pleased.

Then I remember our first row. Eric was going to be allowed to spend the Whitsun holiday at home. Margaret was scheduled to be out of London at the Whit weekend; she was giving some piano recitals in concerts in the Midlands. Her instinctive reaction was that she intended to ensure that Eric stayed at his school over the holiday period; in her view there was no question of any other arrangement.

"That is absurd, Margaret," I argued heatedly as we walked along the Chelsea Embankment one dusky evening. "The boy might find himself alone in those school buildings, all the others having drifted off, except for some master left on duty."

"Well, why don't you have him to stay at your flat, then, if you're so keen that he should have a holiday?" A somewhat triumphant smile spread across her face. She knew too well how I valued my independent self-inflicted lonely home, but it was a challenge that I had to accept. Besides I was now partly responsible legally for the boy—all the parental rights and duties, as the law says.

"All right, I will. Perhaps it's time Eric and I became better acquainted."

And that is how on the Whit Monday I took Eric to see Middlesex play Sussex at Lords. Always at this time of year I travelled to Lords to watch the cricket, the exciting batting of Edrich and Compton, the ceaseless, unflagging Sussex bowling, and the Langridges.

Often Tom Preston had come with me, but now that I had returned to the office following my peripatetic voyaging, he was able to take his wife and two children on holiday to the West Country. He intended to be away for three weeks, but I had considered the extra workload would be a salve for my fantasies of Lydia.

I think that Eric enjoyed his long weekend with me. We had eaten out mostly, and as I sat beside him at Lords I could see that he was immersed in the cricket and the thrill of the shots, the loose-limbed fielders and the milling crowds.

It had been a warm day, but I had struggled to keep my young companion plied with soft drinks and ice-cream.

It was during the tea interval that Eric suddenly turned to me and asked, "Was my father good at cricket?"

The question somewhat jolted me. I answered somewhat enigmatically: "There wasn't much time for cricket, or other sports at the time I knew your father, Eric. I expect he was good, though," I added.

"Why do you think that?"

I looked into his deep, round eyes: "Because your father was good at everything—everything he turned his hand to."

He turned away to watch the cricketers emerging from the main pavilion after the tea-break. I suppose I was watching them as well, but briefly my thoughts went back to the Meteora, and my last days with Stephen and Anna.

★ ★ ★

It was only to be expected, perhaps, that later on that evening, after we had fed well on cold chicken and salad, and fresh fruit and cream, a further questioning would ensue. He was standing by the window in my sitting-room, and wistfully looking out across the chimneyed rooftops of Kensington.

"Did you know my mother?" he asked quietly.

I looked up from my newspaper. "Yes, I knew your mother. It is quite a long time ago now. Your father and I had a few days leave in Rome. The weather was very hot," I added as a non sequitur.

"What was she like? My mother, I mean."

"She was tall and fair—just like your father in that respect. She was very attractive."

Don't look back, it's all in the past now, I kept saying to myself. Besides, the mutual magnetism between Stephen and Joy, leaving me on the sidelines, had turned to tragedy; the only joyful outcome had been Eric of course. And here he was with the same features and deep blue eyes to remind me of both Joy and Stephen all over again.

"If only my mother or father was alive it wouldn't be so bad. But I've lost both of them. Aunt Margaret is all right, but mostly I'm packed off to school. She doesn't really seem to want me around too much." Bravely he was fighting back the tears.

I put my hand on his shoulder. "Is boarding school all that bad? Perhaps as you grow older you will find that you have advantages over others who do not start boarding until say they are 13 years old?"

He nodded his head in assent, albeit a reluctant agreement.

"Will you come and visit me sometimes at school?" he asked.

I paused whilst I thought of the implications. "Yes, of course I will. Besides, Sussex is not far. It's not as though you are hundreds of miles away."

Looking back I recall that I kept my promise over those visits to Eric's boarding school. I could scarcely have done otherwise; he was clearly so pleased to see me every time I visited the stately portals and cloistered quadrangles of his school; I remember the lunches at the local hotel and the brisk countryside walks. One thing I knew for sure. He had the mould of someone who would never contemplate running away from school whatever his inner feelings were about the place.

At first, of course, the outings which I arranged for Eric were intended to ease my conscience as far as Stephen and Joy were concerned. But gradually a mutual trust and respect—and indeed a form of love—built up between the boy and myself. It was as if his character incorporated the best of Stephen's traits without some of his overbearing mannerisms and yet at the same time there were the softening features of Joy's make-up both physically and in his generous outlook to life.

Sadly the day after that visit to Lords Cricket Ground I had to drive Eric back to school, but he brightened up when just before leaving him to re-join his fellow pupils I promised that I would visit him again before the Summer term had finished.

With Tom Preston away on holiday with his family, my workload at the office was quite heavy, and London was warming up with the June sun. Added to this were my frequent visits to Margaret in Chelsea and the spasmodic visits to Eric's boarding school.

The trouble was that even with all this activity my mind was always directing itself back to Lydia and her disappearance. When she had walked away from me in Italy I had seen it as only a temporary disassociation, and I had always visualized then when we were both back in London together our rediscovery of each other would be complete.

But it hadn't worked out like that. Instead I kept searching for a shadow that eluded me every time I thought I could sense it nearing me.

I was inoculated with a love that could withstand all other attachments, and yet it was a love that was denied fulfilment.

By mid-summer I had taken Margaret to several functions, and occasionally we went to the theatre together. I had also gone to concerts at Wigmore Hall when she was playing there.

I managed to get some tickets for the tennis at Wimbledon, and although she accompanied me there it was really not her scene. However, clearly she enjoyed our visit to the Tate Gallery, and that evening after our visit to the art world, she cooked me an appetizing meal at her home.

Like the sitting-room, the dining-room exuded an air of opulence with its heavy mahogany table and Regency chairs. Sporting prints were spaced along the pale grey striped wallpaper, and the sideboard displayed many pieces of silver and silver trays.

I had made appreciative noises about the veal dish which we had just consumed, but she must have read my inner thoughts as she said, "A few of these items were kept in the bank by my parents; they lost most things, but not quite all, in the air raids."

"And the rest?" I asked.

"Now that we have set up that trust for Eric, he will get his fair share of everything as you know. I'm sure, David, you will see to that," she smiled challengingly at me, and cleared away the dishes.

I sipped my cool white wine. The strawberries and cream were very palatable to my sweet tooth. Presently, as I sat once more in the comfortable armchair in the sitting-room, Margaret brought me some coffee and a brandy.

As she sat opposite me I was reminded of her attractive features, her slender legs, the colour of her eyes and her nose.

Usually the physical features that reminded me of Stephen were a bar to our sexual involvement, but that evening all I could see was a fair-headed elegant beauty whose grey-green eyes sent out tantalizing and alluring signals.

I took her hand, and willingly she joined me on the settee. I kissed those provocative red lips that sometimes tightened in defiance. Through her flowered cotton dress I felt the bold outline of her breasts against my chest.

She seemed to respond to all my advances, and for once with her our relationship had become quite physical. Our differences, such as they were, had been put aside. Stephen's warnings stayed unheeded as she switched off the lights and guided me upstairs.

A distant church clock struck the midnight hour as we undressed in her comfortably chintzy bedroom.

It is difficult to describe that night of love. Sometimes I could feel her warmth which brought out an equal response from me; at other times she seemed cool, almost distant, always the dominant force.

★ ★ ★

The next morning I had breakfast with her before leaving for the office. There seemed no point in going home to collect my personal mail before travelling to the city.

Margaret had proffered some shaving kit without comment as she left me in her bedroom. I heard her moving about below, preparing a breakfast of cereal and toast as I shaved in the comfort of her carpeted bathroom. The appetizing aroma of coffee drifted up through the house.

It is easy to philosophise to oneself when shaving, being

alone and uninterrupted; to survey the paradoxes and anomalies. Was my previous philanthropy now turning to cause destruction? A sinner often became a Saint, but it was more difficult surely for a Saint to become a sinner?

Certainly I was no Saint, but I had tried to help— particularly Stephen and his family.

There could be no objection to my having sex with Stephen's sister, yet he had warned me about her, and strangely I had felt no elation following my night with Margaret.

Certainly when I joined her for breakfast she behaved simply as though I was a house guest, a mere friend staying a night or two.

She didn't try to persuade me to return the following evening for a second night together. Her whole attitude was matter-of-fact, and she gave the impression that our behaviour of the previous night was nothing out of the ordinary.

It was later on in my relationship with her that I discovered that men came and went in her life, that she viewed them as necessary—but only when it suited her—she had in fact a disdainful view of the opposite sex. I had temporarily become caught up in her web, but fortunately the wounds were not deep. No real harm had been done.

I suppose it was as we were finishing our breakfast that particular morning that she opened a letter, read it and turning towards me said:

"I've had a wonderful opportunity to go on a concert tour at the end of the month, to the Midlands again. You can come with me if you like. I'll cancel Eric's half-term. He can stay in the school for half-term this time."

I stopped chewing the sappy toast in my mouth and gulped

some tepid coffee. The coffee cup nearly smashed as I slammed it onto the saucer.

"No!" My shout was defiant. "You can't just have him when it suits you, and then make him stay in school if it doesn't suit your purpose."

"I thought that you enjoyed last night. You couldn't wait to get me upstairs. I've made my mind up. I'm going on this concert tour to the Midlands. We could have a good time together."

"Damm it, no! You go on your tour. I'll look after Eric. He can stay with me again at the Little Boltons." I rose from the breakfast table and prepared to take my leave.

As I left the room her words cut across the silence: "You're so ordinary looking, dark and inconsequential. A pity you don't have the physical attributes of Stephen."

Momentarily I felt jealous of Stephen again, but quietly I buried such thoughts. I remembered his burnt and devastated body, his lungs fighting against time.

It was certainly time to go, time to reflect on my life on my way to work. I anticipated that in time Margaret and I would find a modus vivandi so that we could at least remain sufficiently friendly to ensure a smooth guardianship over Eric, but I determined that I would never be overcome by her sexual allure again; I would leave that for other and more compliant men.

It was a bright, sunny morning, and the London Squares were silvery green and fresh after overnight rain.

Tom Preston had returned from his holiday, and so I was able to ease up on the work. We resumed our weekly squash sessions at Chelsea Cloisters. Afterwards we would have a welcome beer before making our separate ways homeward. It seemed to me that Tom was looking older now. I could not see that he would be able to keep up the squash much longer. That would be a blow to his ego if he had to live more sedately as far as physical exercise was concerned.

That evening, when I returned to my flat, I took from my writing bureau the coral bracelet, the one I had bought for Lydia when I was in Kavalla. It had been some time since I had set eyes on it. It seemed to glisten, even in the dusky light. Would to God that I could give it to her in London, here in South Kensington where she had brightened up my life so much.

★ ★ ★

The Summer days were lengthening, and often I would make my way to a riverside pub after the day's work.

One evening I sat overlooking the Thames at the back of a popular hostelry. In the crowd I did not seem to mind being alone. It was only when I returned to the Little Boltons that solitude seemed an unwelcome intruder.

The only provisional late and unadventurous holiday which I had planned was to take Eric down to Dorset after the school term had finished. We would stay with my parents. Already both Margaret and my parents had agreed to this, and for my parents it would be a pleasant diversion from their daily routine. It would also salve my conscience in that I saw my parents so rarely now.

As I sipped the cool beer, I took from my pocket several letters which had remained unopened after their delivery to my flat that morning. I had rushed off early after breakfast to see a client just outside London, taking my unopened personal mail with me. Most of this personal mail usually consisted of unexciting bills or receipts, and it was only now as dusk was falling that I brought the crumpled letters out of my pocket.

Then I noticed that one of the letters had a Greek stamp on it, and hurriedly I tore open the envelope.

It was a letter from Zoe. I suppose that because I was not expecting a letter from her that I was apprehensive of what I might read and my foreboding was correct.

Bill had died. Apparently almost immediately after their early Spring wedding Bill had been assigned as a war correspondent to work in French Indo-China. The French had been in deep trouble in their beleaguered garrisons fighting off the Vietminh in the north of the country. The details were sketchy, but Zoe had been informed that Bill had lost his life at Dienbienphu when the Vietminh shelled an airstrip. The French had been hopelessly outnumbered, but nevertheless their top General Staff living in comparative luxury in Saigon had woefully miscalculated the intentions and capabilities of the Red enemy.

It was on the morning of May 7th, 1954 that Bill had been killed—before that particular day was over the Vietminh's red flag had flown over the French command bunker at Dienbienphu. The following morning various delegations met in Geneva to discuss the Indo-China problem—this was some time before the deepening American commitment in Vietnam and the escalation of the war in that troubled region. Unfortunately there had been delay before Zoe had been advised of her husband's death, and it was only now in late Summer that she had finally steeled herself to write to me and his other friends in England.

I suppose that up until that moment I had assumed that those of us who had survived the World War would have a fair span of years of peace, but no doubt war correspondents would always be from time to time either at risk or on the fringe of dangers.

As young pub habitués jostled to obtain their last orders before the pub closed, a wave of sadness enveloped me under the starry night sky. Was I never to find peace and happiness? But quickly I realised that I was being selfish, and my thoughts and sympathy were all for Zoe. The memory of that day we had together on the island of Thasos came flooding back yet once more. How envious then I had been of Bill and Zoe, their deep love for one another. I remembered how Zoe had touched the statue of the satyr at the Silene Gate on the island of Thasos, giving the legendary hope for having children; her touch may now have been in vain. That day had ended silently yet perfectly as our caique had headed back to Kavalla. Zoe's hair had flown across her face in the Aegean breeze; the image of her peaceful and expectant smile still remained with me.

Then there was Bill who had survived all the horrors of the last War only to meet his end in some foreign and strange hinterland.

They had both cheered me up in Kavalla when I was feeling low at Christmas; they had led me to Nikos and my adventures in the search for Stephen.

Poor Zoe. I imagined she would now return to Salonika and look after her parents after all. My envy of their joint happiness was turned to sadness.

Deep in thought, I hadn't noticed the pub crowd thinning out. A barge loaded with rolls of paper glided smoothly on the river; the tide was full.

The car lights cast shadows along the riverside backwater; the rumble of tube trains, occasional buses and taxis completed the late night London scene.

I would write to Zoe of course—but no letter could convey the sorrow I felt. It was a sorrow compounded of the time when Bill and I had been together in the liberation of Greece, and the time when both Bill and Zoe had taken me in as a friend in that war-torn country. Sorrow caused so many wounds, no one profited by it.

I supposed that Ken and Sofia would already be aware of what had happened, and it was comforting to know that Zoe had friends and family not only in Salonika but in Athens as well.

★ ★ ★

Over the next few weeks I began to wonder whether any further bad news was on its way.

If there was a Damoclean Sword hanging over me then I wanted to know the worst, let it happen so that I could then start to pick up the pieces again.

I tried to tell Tom Preston about Zoe's tragedy, and what Bill's friendship had meant to me, but it was difficult. After all, Tom had never met them, and was never likely to meet Zoe.

As we were talking, Kathy Morse, who had replaced Lydia in the office, came in with some letters for me to sign.

I thought I detected a knowing look between Tom and Kathy, but perhaps I was imagining things, especially with relationships these days. After all, Tom was a happily married man with children, a 'pillar of society'—to use a hackneyed expression—but I had seen him lunching once or twice with

Kathy. I had assumed that they were talking business over lunch. Kathy was such a quiet young girl, I could not think what else their lunchtime conversation would consist of. But then I was naive in those days.

I suppose I would have thought no more about it, except that Tom began to cancel our weekly game of squash. His cancellations were not regular, but sometimes he would excuse himself because of the warm weather, or family commitments or working late.

Even then I did not give much thought to these last-minute inconveniences. Some evenings and weekends I played tennis at a popular club in South-West London, but our fickle weather at that time of year controlled my leisure activities.

A letter arrived from my parents, and it was clear that they were looking forward to seeing Eric and myself. I hoped that my father would not take too much of a schoolmasterly attitude towards Eric. After all, school holidays were meant to be holidays.

I think that it was about this time that I made some tentative plans in my mind for holidays for Eric for the future. For instance, I visualized in years to come a holiday in Greece for him—not a holiday in the Meteora, but one where he could share some happiness and love of the country with people like Ken and Sofia and Athena—not forgetting Zoe— and where he could enjoy the Greek hospitality, the country and understand the meaning of philotimos.

★ ★ ★

The August sun was pleasantly warm as Eric and I drove down to Dorset to stay for a week with my parents.

Whether it was the benign weather or the presence of youth in the house I do not know, but this time my parents seemed genuinely pleased to see me.

My father had taken a week off from his work as a castle guide to be with us, although he promised to take an enthusiastic Eric around all the battlements. My mother had also surprisingly arranged to have a week away from all her charity work. Even the springer spaniel, Bosun, sensed that life would be varied and exciting, at least for a little while.

I think, to be truthful, that it was Eric's presence that had brought about this change, that had caused a reawakening of the long dormant affection between my parents and myself.

Some mornings my father took Eric and I for long walks in the countryside, with Bosun panting on ahead of us. On these days my mother would greet our return to the mellow stone house with long drinks and appetizing lunches. On other days we drove down to the coast, and whilst my mother and father set up a picnic lunch, Eric and I would brave the cool water for a swim, with Bosun reluctantly following us.

The day we went to Lyme Regis brought the shadow of a cloud to my contentment; it was here during the War that I had tried with other umpires to sort out the chaos of the practice landings of the Canadians before their grim reality at Dieppe. Some memories never fade.

It was the Saturday, the day before leaving my parents, that my father took Eric around the castle. My mother was busying herself with preparing the lunch as usual, so I strolled around the town of my youth.

The weather continued fine, and the sun was already warming the pavements and solid stone buildings.

Perhaps I should have gone with Eric and my father, but

the castle always brought back memories of the War to me. I suppose I had been lucky to have been billeted in the castle before going abroad, but it had meant that my parents expected me to go home on every leave.

Some of the officers had been billeted in the town, and I remembered going to a party at one of the houses. I became friendly with one of the daughters of the house, the young and petite brunette Valerie—dear Val—what with her parents being over protective, and my parents forever encouraging us, we never had a chance. But I suppose it was not meant to be, and Val became part of the VAD establishment at the military hospital some distance away.

Later I learnt that she had married some brilliant surgeon. I remember being happy for her, as though this was another reason to sever my roots from this historic town. What had become of Val I wondered?

The ghosts of my youth seemed everywhere here as I passed through the Abbey precincts, yet I seemed not to know anyone. It was as though I had now cut myself off from my roots.

I climbed up to the hillside park overlooking the town now bathed in strong sunlight.

The abbey bells were chiming the hour—for an instant I recalled the monastery bells in the Meteora, but it was only for a moment.

The town was soaking up the heat of the August day against the backdrop of the park greenery. All was peaceful and still. To me it represented everything that we had fought for. Yet I knew I couldn't live here now, not at this juncture of my life. Perhaps there were too many memories, but the overriding thought, as always, was that I would never find Lydia here.

★ ★ ★

On the Sunday afternoon we watched some local cricket, and then as the evening shadows fell on the grass we waved goodbye to my parents from our London-bound car.

Clearly Eric had enjoyed his week's holiday, and I felt a strange gratitude towards my parents. I suppose it had also been a refreshing therapy for my mother and father, and it bode well for any future holidays in Dorset.

As Eric and I drove back to London the warm weather became thundery, and by the time we reached the outskirts of the Capital there was a faint murmur of rain on the windscreen.

Usually I returned from visiting my parents in Dorset with a sense of relief, of a sense of a duty accomplished, but this time it had been different. The boy's presence had brought a fusion of parental regard and happiness.

Yet there was an underlying reluctance to return to my flat this time. The recent mail had brought the tragic news about Bill, and I wanted no such further mail at present. Sometimes my thoughts and sympathy went out to Zoe, and at other times I dreaded that the mail would bring me news of Lydia, unwelcome news that I wanted to shut out of my thoughts.

I bade goodnight to Eric and the threat of heavy rain became a reality; this depressed my earlier good cheer. It was as though my temper and emotions were directly affected by the weather patterns, as though my history here and now was written in the image of rain. Perhaps I had to abandon myself to the flood, to the flood of events over which I had no control any more.

Yet there was still a pain every time I thought of Lydia. It was like a thorn buried so deep that no questing needle could recover it. Perhaps one day the thorn would be absorbed altogether and I would feel nothing, but I doubted it.

Eventually a heavy sleep possessed me, and for once I was late in arriving at the office the next morning.

Tom was sharing some joke with Kathy in the outer office when I arrived, and they seemed too absorbed in themselves to notice my late arrival.

During the course of the morning I received a telephone call from Margaret—she had just returned to London from a concert tour, and wanted to discuss some matters relating to Eric's future.

The mail and telephone calls and client meetings had become fairly light. It was August and many Londoners were away on their annual holidays either by the sea or in the country or on the Continent. The workload having lightened it seemed opportune to visit Margaret to discuss these matters concerning Eric, and accordingly to have lunch with her in Chelsea. Certainly I didn't want a repetition of my last embarrassing night-time visit. We had to establish a modus vivandi which was practical, and in the daytime she was hardly likely to endeavour to entice me into her net again. Besides the truth had slowly dawned on me that if I had allowed myself to succumb to her charms I would only have been one on her list of conquests. Somehow I could not imagine Margaret having deep emotional feelings over anyone. Just as Stephen had possessed physical qualities that attracted female companions, so his sister Margaret had the same such qualities that caused men to pursue her—but somehow her attractions seemed artificial and hollow, and I could never forget Stephen's warnings about her.

His warnings had been justified, but now I felt that a reasonably friendly platonic relationship could continue between Margaret and I. As I travelled to Gloucester Road Underground I resolved that I must think of Eric's future above any personal animosity between Margaret and myself.

She had agreed to meet me in Kensington for once.

The little restaurant was crowded with a lunchtime throng, but I felt that it was better for us to meet this way than in her Chelsea sanctum. Eventually we found a free table, and after consuming some veal dish accompanied by the house wine, I think we both felt more equable.

"Have you thought about Eric's future education after he has finished at his preparatory school?" Margaret shot this question at me as though she was a school matriarch herself.

"No. I assume that he will still be at his present school for another couple of years, won't he?" I hedged.

"Yes, but we have to plan his future. He has become used to boarding now. I suppose it is a question of deciding on a suitable public school." She poured the remains of the carafe of wine into our respective glasses, and then lit the inevitable cigarette.

"You know my opinion over sending him to board at a prep school at such an early age. I've no doubt also that you want to feel that the future years will not impose any further burden on you. However…"

"We don't need to argue all the time, David," she cut in.

"I was going to say, however, a public school seems a good idea to me for Eric when he reaches, say, his thirteenth birthday. The school fees can be paid for out of trust funds."

"What public school, David?"

I couldn't claim to have thought about it much before, but

suddenly I remembered the happy week that Eric and I had shared in Dorset with my parents. Eric could go to the school where my father had once taught. I felt that both Eric and my father would like that, and my parents would enjoy having Eric to stay for weekend holidays.

I gave to Margaret the name of the public school and my reasons for choosing it, and she agreed. We would put the proposal to Eric, and then all being well, we could make the necessary arrangements in advance.

We emerged from the restaurant and said our adieus in a friendly spirit, having proved that we could at least solve domestic problems in a practical way.

The earlier morning cloud had given way to a sunny, blue sky. I looked at my watch, and decided that with the office work being light at present I could afford to spend another hour out in the sun and fresh air.

Fortified by the lunchtime wine I strode out at a brisk pace. My thoughts were still on our lunchtime conversation. It had been further proof that as long as my relationship with Margaret remained on a business footing the future relationship could be a relatively smooth one. I would not become entangled in any more intimate schemes that she might have in mind. Anyway, I felt sure that she simply moved from one sexual encounter to another without any deep emotion being involved. I had been neither the first nor the last of her dalliances. Perhaps her continental musical tours did not make for stability in relationships with men.

So ran my thoughts as my steps seemed to guide me, as though by ingrained custom, to the Round Pond once more in Kensington Gardens.

The gardens were quiet at this time of a weekday apart

from the usual pram-pushed babies safely shepherded by their nursemaids, several of whom quite naturally knew one another.

I looked out over the Round Pond as the warm sun shimmered across the still waters. The London traffic was not far away, yet it seemed blissfully idyllic, a dreamy English Summer scene.

A reflection suddenly appeared in the water, a girl with an arabesque of long flowing hair was plainly discernable. I didn't turn round excitedly as I had in those early months after my return from Greece; I wanted no more elation followed by acute disappointment.

But then the air seemed to take on a musky perfume that I remembered so well, and just as I was beginning to think that my fantasies had now even started to give an aura of her scent, her dusky voice broke the silence of my thoughts:

"Hallo, David. I thought I might find you here, but not in working hours." Her sapphire blue eyes laughed at me as I turned to face her.

"Lydia. Oh! Lydia my dear."

Instinctively I hugged her. I kissed her and held on to her as though she might disappear if I did not do so. She returned my emotional embrace and I realised how much I had missed that face, those eyes, the sensual lips, the long titian hair speckled with the afternoon sun. My display of affection was very public, but only it seemed to the peripheral nursemaids who were clearly more concerned with their charges than they were over Lydia and I.

She was wearing a cool summery cotton lilac frock with her firm breasts straining at the material; her walk was as provocative as ever. I guided her by her slim waist and we went back home to the Little Boltons together.

Needless to say I had given up any thought of going back to the office that afternoon. Later on it seemed like old times when at sundown I sipped a gin and tonic as Lydia prepared the evening meal.

★ ★ ★

During the course of the meal I noticed that she seemed well, her face tanned as though she had been abroad rather than relying on our British climate.

Her neck usually so snowy was bronze below her almond shaped face, but her blue eyes shone and smiled at me.

"So where have you been?" I asked. My words sounded so ordinary, as though she had only been missing for a few hours.

Her long eyelashes fluttered and her eyes searched mine:

"I had fallen in love with you, David," she whispered gently.

I looked at her, trying to puzzle out her answer. "That's a non sequitur if ever I heard one," I answered quietly. "If you had been in love with me, why did you disappear like that?"

She paused a moment and sipped her glass of chilled white wine. "Reasons, David—you want reasons?"

I nodded emphatically as she continued:

"You were too involved with your search for Stephen. It was like an obsession with you. Then in Italy your dalliance with Maria cast a further shadow over our personal relationship. In Urbino I decided it had all gone far enough; I would return to England, and hoped that you would re-join me soon, but…"

"But what?" I interjected.

"You went to Greece, you extended your leave, and then there was Bob Chester and Tom Preston."

"What do you mean, Bob Chester and Tom Preston?"

"First of all Bob Chester started making a nuisance of himself until I made it clear that I would not go to bed with him."

"I can understand that, knowing Bob Chester. But Tom Preston?"

"When Tom realised that you were not coming back, at least for a time, he also started pestering me. His approaches in the office became embarrassing; he wanted to take me away for a weekend, with one thing in mind of course. I refused him several times."

"My God, I never thought, I never knew…" I was at a loss for words.

"You never thought that a married man with a family, and your partner, would try to pursue his own sexual desires? David, you are naive."

As she spoke I thought of Tom and his recent familiar attitude with Kathy in the office, and then I remembered his uneasy attitude when I had questioned him about Lydia's disappearance on my return from Greece. Naturally he hadn't mentioned any of this to me even when we had played squash after office hours.

"But you then disappeared. Why?" I asked.

"Both Bob and Tom wanted the same thing of course. I was contemplating a move to another legal firm when I had news from Durban."

"From Richard Prentice, that purser chap?" I could scarcely utter the name.

"No, from my sister. You see, my mother was seriously ill. So what with the awkwardness of my situation in the office, and my mother's health causing anxiety I decided to go to

Durban, and see how things were for myself. At that stage I didn't know when you were coming back either. But you see, you came back and now I've come back." Her sensuous rowanberry lips smiled across the table at me.

I took her bronzed hand in mine. "But why didn't you tell me all this earlier, leave me a message or write to me?"

"I had to sort things out, stand aside from it all. Probably if I had written to you to say that I was in Durban, you would have suspected that I had gone back to Richard Prentice."

"Did you see him, did you want to go back to him, I mean?"

"Yes, I did see him, but only a few times whilst his ship was in Durban. The old magic had gone, and I realised that it was only a shipboard romance compared with my love for you. Then I was busy helping my sister to nurse Mother after her discharge from hospital. They managed to arrest the spread of cancer in time."

"That is good news." I was beginning to have an upsurge of a myriad of emotions, and uppermost was a feeling that I had been thinking too much of myself over the past few months. I hadn't given a thought to any possible harassment that Lydia had endured from other males, nor indeed that she had her own family to worry about. Perhaps I had been too selfish.

She broke into my reverie. "I had time to think it all through in South Africa, time to realise how much you really meant to me. I knew that I was taking a chance on coming back here. For all I knew you might still have had a complex over Stephen, you might have returned to Italy and Maria or found someone else. Physical looks aren't everything."

The Little Boltons had become strangely silent in the

dusky evening. The only sounds were the plane trees rustling, and the distant barking of a dog.

"Do you want to give it a chance again?" I felt I had to be sure.

"I still have the spare key of this flat, haven't I? I'm not giving it up to anyone else." She laughed joyfully as I took her in my arms and held her closely. I knew I would never let her go again.

There had already been a plotful of life between us.

Later on we made love as a full moon shone through the thin curtains. Whilst she slept I stroked her beautiful long strands of golden, auburn hair. Now at last I had so much to be thankful for.

I had always understood that writers were told never to write a book at the scene of the event, that you can't write about passion whilst making love. But then I wasn't a writer—until now.

I have set out the facts as I remember them, but then one must always use one's imagination as well to arrive at the truth.

It seemed that I had searched so long, firstly for Stephen and then for Lydia. My searches had covered a full year of Autumn, Winter, Spring and Summer; it had been a search for all seasons.

As dawn approached, the London sky was streaked with a pale red glow; it was a warm glow, a fitting backdrop for the glow of my love for Lydia.

EPILOGUE

As the jet streaked through the cloudless blue sky I thought of Athena's wish in the early Spring of 1954—when I had left Greece after that strange search for Stephen in his mountain eyrie.

Athena's wish was now being realised. She was going to marry an Englishman as she had wanted when she was a child, and a smile played on my lips as I looked at Eric across the aisle in the plane. Yes, he was the prospective bridegroom.

I suppose that I had been instrumental in bringing Athena and Eric together. Being one of his guardians I had encouraged him to travel on the Continent as he matured into manhood, and it had been only natural that I had given him Ken and Sofia's address in Athens.

Then there became a pattern to Eric's holidays abroad, always in Greece, always with Athena. I had never told him of Stephen's last days in the Meteora. For Eric I wanted Greece to be the cradle of civilization, the home of friendly people where he could find happiness. And now we were going to Athens, to attend his marriage with Athena.

I looked alongside me at Lydia's almond shaped face, with her snowy neck. Her sapphire blue eyes seemed to match the sky. A wisp of her long titian hair strayed towards my face. Smiling at her I allowed her strand of hair to touch my cheek.

We had been married just over twelve years now. It was the Swinging Sixties, the era of Beetlemania, the mini-skirt, Carnaby Street and British success in the Football World Cup.

Our two sons were growing fast, but Lydia and I had decided that they were best left at home to continue with school rather than attend the celebratory visit to Athens. They would have plenty of time for visiting Greece and Italy later on as their lives stretched out before them.

Then there was Zoe. It would be just wonderful to see her again, to identify some part of the past I had shared with her and Bill. She had never re-married, but as each book of life unfolds her memories were surely treasured ones. I pictured her travelling south from Salonika to be with us all in Athens in the Spring.

So often I had reminded myself of the special pink light in Greece, of the sea sparkling in the sunlight and caressed by the moon at night, of the pepper trees and the cyclamen and the anemones, of the olive trees and the red earth. No wonder that Eric and Athena had fallen in love in Greece.

The plane was now beginning its descent and I could discern once more the shining blue waters of the sea. I remembered yet once more how Spring comes to Greece from the sea; the waters become brisker in their rhythm, there is a freshness in the glistening sea, an iridescence like a peacock's feathers. The sky is a silken blue flecked with lambswool clouds. The footprints of Spring advance from the shore to the villages, to the olive groves and to the restless cities. The air intoxicates both humans and beasts—and if Anna was still alive she would be welcoming the Spring on the Meteora.

Maria in Italy, too, I hoped, would be happy once again—as long as she could stop the past from intruding.

As we fastened our seatbelts for the landing I took Lydia's hand in mine. She smiled at me and whispered:

"You always seem to make contact when I want you to." With a sigh she continued: "I suppose there are times when we all need reassurance—I'll always be here with you, David, I'll never leave you again."

The plane had now landed. Were Lydia and I too romantically old-fashioned, I wondered? Established ideas of sexual morality and passion were changing, yet hadn't Rousseau himself tried to elevate romantic love?

The difference was, of course, that Rousseau's heroine had attained virtue by her refusal to marry a bourgeois she loved and had slept with. Instead she became the faithful and dedicated wife of a nobleman she did not love.

Well, Lydia and I had loved one another and slept together, and she had become my faithful wife, but then we were hardly bourgeois and certainly not noble.

A long time ago I had searched for Stephen, and then searched for Lydia. I think that my searches had been virtuous, even if I hadn't searched for virtue.

Travellers continue to search for their Xanadu, but Lydia and I have now bridged the savage romantic chasm.

---

[1] United Nations Relief and Rehabilitation Agency
[2] My golden one—commonly used as a form of endearment in Greece .